DANGER IN THE DEEP

Prior to the dive, Brimley had supplied each of us with a camera. I took mine out and began shooting pictures of the depression. I still had a couple of angles to go when we all heard Kit scream.

The shrill, piercing sound was bouncing around inside my comsys when I heard Brimley's voice asking, "Kit, where the hell are you?"

Brimley's senior diver had lost it. For the next several seconds, there was nothing but confusion. The audio-detection unit indicated Bench's transmissions were coming from a northwesterly direction, which wasn't a hell of a lot of help considering the fact that, because of the anomaly, the compass was spinning like a cheap top. I activated the NV unit to see if I could pick up any kind of infrared image on my lens mask. When I did, I had two hot spots, both converging on the northwesterly fix where the transmissions had originated.

"He's in five-K-d," Brimley said. In five-K-d the darkness was blacker than any I had experienced. There was no sign of Brimley, but I shoved the beam of my halogen around until I picked up Packy; she was hovering over Bench. In the sand before them was an object that, from where I was standing, I couldn't quite make out.

By the time I did, I wished I hadn't. It was Gabe Lord or, maybe I should say, what was left of him. The top half of him was there, but the bottom half was missing.

THE SEA

R. KARL LARGENT

LEISURE BOOKS   NEW YORK CITY

A LEISURE BOOK®

March 1999

Published by

Dorchester Publishing Co., Inc.
276 Fifth Avenue
New York, NY 10001

ISBN 0-8439-4495-1

The name "Leisure Books" and the stylized "L" with design are trademarks of Dorchester Publishing Co., Inc.

Printed in the United States of America.

SEA

Incident:

On balance, things had been going rather well for several months. I had used my last royalty check, which wasn't all that large to begin with, to make a down payment on a Morgan Out Island forty-one-foot ketch that an old poker buddy had located for me in a marina on Long Key.

The yacht's owner, a greasy little man with a marathon-mouth wife, seemed just a tad too eager to accept my less-than-asking-price offer. In the final analysis, his acceptance fostered a condition that caused me to spend literally weeks suspecting I would find terminal dry rot or dreading the arrival of the Coast Guard. The latter, of course, to inform me that my new investment and my bill of sale were blatantly bogus.

Fortunately, neither turned out to be the case. The *Perpetual Motion* was as sound as she was trim, and to my astonishment, Ferguson Harrison Lloyd of Naples, Florida, had actually been the legitimate owner.

Lloyd, who insisted that no amount of money could make him spend another night aboard his toy with his wife, proved his point by snatching up my initial offer and heading north on Highway One, top down on his powder-blue BMW, sun gleaming off his bald dome, and Motor Mouth nowhere in sight.

Why am I telling you all of this? For two reasons: It sets the stage for what happened next, and it explains why I happened to be where I was at that time.

This story really begins two weeks later. I was still discovering the joys of *Perpetual Motion* ownership when Packy Darnell showed up. She was thinner than I remembered her, her mascara was streaked, and her eyes were swollen. Packy Darnell clearly did not look as good as the last time I had seen her, shortly before she got married.

The day she arrived, the *Motion* was still tied up at the Sunset Point Marina. I had been spending the better part of my nights putting the finishing touches on a manuscript that was already three weeks overdue, and most of the daylight hours trimming out some of the ship's neglected teak appointments.

Between chores, I was mentally preparing to test my seamanship by sailing down to Snipe Key, where I was being led to believe my friend Cosmo and I were going to do a little yellowtail and Beatrice fishing.

The moment I saw Packy Darnell's condition, I deduced that she was in dire need of some of Elliott Grant Wages's special brand of TLC. So after the obligatory barrage of small talk, I fixed her a Scotch and water, assured her that she was more than welcome, and showed her around the *Motion*.

"Make yourself at home," I told her. "This just may be the port in the storm you've been looking for."

Packy cried, protested that she couldn't impose on me, and finally disappeared into the aft cabin. I didn't see her again for twelve hours. When she finally reappeared, after sleeping and showering, she didn't look much better.

She fixed herself a Scotch. She rummaged around in her purse until she found a cigarette. Then she sat down on one of the bar stools in front of the *Motion*'s cozy wet bar and studied her reflection in the mirror. "Elliott," she said, "you will be happy to know that I dumped the son of a bitch."

"Any son of a bitch I know?"

She shook her head; a lot of her apparent calm was bravado. It wasn't long before she was shaking like a sick puppy. She put out the first cigarette and lit another. "It took me a while to work up the courage, Elliott, but I left him. It's been a week now. I've been on the road ever since."

Packy Darnell was an old friend. She was, on her better days, an auburn-haired stunner. She was also one of the few woman for whom I had actually considered forfeiting my long-guarded and cherished bachelorhood. As fortune would have it, however, before I got around to making up my mind, she had made up hers. She discovered a Navy fly guy by the name of Ensign Randolph Holloway Mays, fell madly in love with him, and departed for romantic Pensacola. If Packy had been living a fairy tale, the story would have ended right there. But she wasn't, and it didn't.

An old girlfriend of mine loved to say, "Life is never easy, not even for the beautiful people." She was right. A year or so after Ensign Randy Mays married Packy, he unceremoniously buried his low-altitude attack Grumman A-6 Intruder in the tidewaters near Gulf Shores, Alabama. End of fairy tale. Since I heard about Packy's misfortune after the fact, I didn't attend the funeral. Then I lost track of her.

Lest you think I'm a cad, let me clarify. Under normal circumstances, Packy Darnell was not the sort of girl a guy thought about in a protective sense. So I didn't worry about her. Because she was young and beautiful, I naturally assumed that she had lots of friends. It was equally easy to assume that, after the appropriate period of grieving and adjustment, Packy Darnell would get on with her life.

Why? you ask. Everyone knew that when she wasn't playing wife, Packy was a pretty fair country diver, and rumor had it that not long after young Mays bought the farm, she caught on with a professional salvage diver by the name of Peter Cannon. Rumor further had it that Packy and her new live-in lover had opened a small dive shop somewhere north of Vero Beach.

Oh, yeah. Just for the record. Peter Cannon is the one who turned out to be the aforementioned son of a bitch.

At any rate, after the initial vindictive venom was spent, Packy fixed herself another drink and lapsed into a benign line of chatter until she concluded by saying, "It was sweet of you to offer me a place to bunk, Elliott."

I think she was sincere, but I had the feeling she would have been equally grateful if she had been offered a flop on an old army cot at the local soup kitchen. Even though she gave one hell of an effort, she couldn't make her voice ring with the same old magic. Her voice was as weary, empty, and washed-out as the expression on her face. The sad part of all of this was she knew I noticed it.

Eventually, Packy got tired of forcing idle chatter, slipped into a reflective mood, and turned silent. After studying her for a while, I decided she had come to the best place. I didn't know what Packy was all about anymore, but I figured a good dose of the old E. G. Wages healing elixir couldn't hurt her. Despite the hour, I rustled up some scrambled eggs with crabmeat and sour cream, fixed lots of hot coffee and toast lathered with honey, and insisted that she eat. Next, I started the therapy. I massaged her shoulders first, worked on her neck for a while, then headed down to the small of her back. It took some time, but she finally started to relax. When she did, the tears erupted again.

"So what happened?" I asked.

Packy tilted her head to one side. "Competition. You've heard it all before: younger, prettier, a little trimmer. There's no honor among sluts. Peter's glands got in the way and he told me to hit the bricks."

"And you said?"

"Pay me what you owe me."

"Which means?"

"I told him he could have it any way he wanted it, as long as he bought out my half of the business."

"Half of the business?"

Packy looked a little sheepish. "That's the part I didn't tell you. I used most of Randy's insurance settlement to help Peter buy the dive shop. He was a better lover than businessman. We lost a lot of money. Since he wanted out and couldn't buy me out, he started punching me out. That went on for a couple of months until I couldn't take it any longer and jumped ship."

The confession brought on more tears, more sheepish looks, and the desire—on her part and mine—for another drink.

"Look," I said. "It's none of my business. Friends are friends without qualification. And I make the offer without qualification: You can bunk down here as long as you like."

"You're sweet, Elliott," she said. "But I think you should know I don't have a cent to my name. Everything I own is in the back room of that damn dive shop in Vero. I can repay you, but it's going to be a few months before I get back on my feet."

As I indicated earlier, things went along rather smoothly for the first couple of weeks. Packy was little more than a blip on the screen; she didn't change my life much. If anything, the *Perpetual Motion* was the better for her presence. Slowly, and without much help from me, she was starting to put her life back together. She spent several bikini-clad hours each day adorning the foredeck of the *Motion,* slowing traffic on the footbridge to the shops along the pier, and picking up some color. When she wasn't worshiping the sun, she occupied herself and amused both of us by scheming and discussing ways to get her money back.

It was early evening, a Friday, some two weeks after Packy showed up, when I went up on deck and held a package over my head. "A little fanfare please."

"You're done?" she asked.

I held the package out for her approval. She understood. She had been around on other occasions to celebrate the firing off of a manuscript. She knew the routine. Packy had been a part of my life during a couple of my earlier efforts when I was just getting started. That fact alone enabled her to demonstrate appropriate recognition for the accomplishment.

"Four hundred and forty pages. We eat," I announced, and Packy applauded. "I'll drive into town and drop this little gem in the mail at the Southtown Station. In the meantime, you put on your party clothes. When I get back, we'll celebrate."

"Celebrate? How?"

"We'll swing over to Shanty Morgan's for some of his famous bisque, have a few pops, come home early, and prepare to leave." I was surprised that when I said leave, Packy seemed to expect the word.

"Where?" she said.

"Snipe Key."

Up until then, I hadn't mentioned my impending rendezvous with Cosmo for a couple of reasons. One, despite my repeated assurances to the contrary, Packy Darnell was nervous about wearing out her welcome; two, I didn't want her being worried about being stuck aboard the *Motion* if that wasn't where she wanted to be.

And there was another reason: The *Motion* was forty-one feet long and had double cabins. Despite the size of the ketch, we had gotten overly cozy on a couple of occasions—a situation I did not want Packy Darnell to regret. She was at a point in her recovery process where I didn't think her psyche needed the hassle.

"Suppose I said I didn't want to go?" Packy asked.

"You're more than welcome."

"Maybe it's time I got myself a job," she said. "By now I probably owe you a fortune."

"Look. Cosmo and I are going to do a little fishing. You can soak up some more sun and do a little diving. Besides, you know Cosmo. He'll love having a beautiful woman around."

"If I went with you, Elliott, I'd just be putting off the inevitable. The sooner I go back and face Peter, the sooner I can put the whole affair behind me. The way I've been mooching off you for the past couple weeks, no one would ever believe I'm eager to get my money and my dignity back."

"Think you're ready to face him?"

Packy hesitated. When she answered, she was tentative. "If you're asking me if I'm still afraid of him, the answer is yes. This time I'll be smart enough to make certain there are witnesses. Maybe it will slow him down."

"Why don't you wait until you come back

from Snipe Key? You'll be stronger with another couple weeks under your belt."

"Let me think about it," she said. She smiled, stood on her tiptoes, and kissed me on the cheek. The gesture could have been read two ways. One, there was a trace of invitation in her body language, or two, she appreciated the fact that I had given her an option. I decided to forgo the male ego trip and chalk it off as the latter.

"Go mail your manuscript," she said. "I'll take a shower and pretty up. By the time you get back, it'll be soup time."

"Which is another way of saying don't push, correct?"

"We'll talk about it." She laughed, then kissed me again a little more earnestly.

As Packy Darnell headed down the companionway toward her cabin, I decided that she had made significant progress along the road to recovery. I was even more convinced when I heard her whistling.

I dropped off the overdue manuscript at the Southtown Street Station post office just as they were making the last pickup of the day. That done, I stopped at the Village Wine Merchant in the Ballard Square Shopping Mall to pick up a bottle of cabernet sauvignon before heading back to the Sunset Point Marina.

As I pulled into the parking lot near slip 55, I saw an oversize, muscle-bound blond with a crew cut emerge from below deck on the *Motion*, walk down the ramp, and start up the pier.

When he saw me, he broke into a dead run. He was headed for the marina parking lot. By the time I managed to get out of the car, he had a good twenty-yard lead on me.

As it turned out, the intruder not only looked athletic; he was. He scaled his way over two Ford utility vans and used the roof of the second to vault over an eight-foot security fence. But he lost what advantage he had when he ran headlong into a kid on a skateboard.

Just as Crew Cut was scrambling to his feet, I decided I was close enough to take a chance and leapt for him. Actually, I was surprised at the outcome. When I launched, I caught him with a belt-high shoulder block in the midsection. The move would have made my old college coach proud. Crew Cut hurtled backward, landed on his back, and let out a yelp. For a moment or two, he was actually too stunned to do anything but lay there and moan.

That was when I made my first mistake. Instead of following my instincts and burying my size-twelve Reebok in his groin, I tried leaping on top of him. That was when my small problem suddenly became a big problem. He managed to get his equally imposing size-twelve knee up in time to catch me in the same vulnerable area.

When someone hits you there, all reactions are instantaneous. First my stomach rolled over. Then it tried to hide. Pain shot down my legs and the taste of bile backed up in my mouth. I was, as the kids like to say, dead meat. I toppled to one side and Crew Cut was all over me like a homely hooker. He was definitely one of those guys my daddy would have described as a big son of a bitch.

Before I could work up any kind of defense, he started tattooing my face with his fist. Then he brought his knee into the fray again, battering it against my face. Big surprise: His knee won. What I had once referred to as my nose was plastered to the left side of my face and the score was two to nothing, knee over crotch and knee over nose.

My second mistake was starting to get up. I didn't even see Crew Cut produce a piece of steel pipe and swing from the heels. The blow caught me on the side of the neck. The next thing I knew, my world was full of miniature fireworks that looked like hiccuping butterflies. His aim and his timing were dead on. I went down like a cheap date, and I was too dazed to retaliate.

Like Custer, I had a brilliant battle plan but my ground forces took the ten count. All I could do was look up at him. He was bigger than life, but all fuzzy and blurry-looking. It occurred to me that he might be getting ready to send me to wherever we all go when we take leave of our senses, but instead, he got up and stepped back, ready to declare himself the winner.

I blinked several times and tried to regulate my breathing. A discordant symphony of

groans, footsteps, distant noises like dogs bark-
ing, doors closing, and the sounds of the marina
was clawing its way back into my awareness.

I was struggling to regain my equilibrium,
and by the time I was able to get to my hands
and knees, Crew Cut was crawling into a dark-
colored Plymouth sedan. He started the engine,
squealed the tires, and headed straight for me.
Suddenly I had that oh-shit feeling.

At the last minute, he threw the car into an abbreviated four-wheel drift and skillfully wheeled
around both me and the confused-looking kid
with the skateboard who was supposed to be
manning the marina's security gate. Seconds
later, Crew Cut had wheeled on to Sunset Point
Drive and disappeared into the flow of traffic
heading over the bridge toward the mainland.

I stood, yelled out a couple of unprintable but
appropriate epithets, checked to see if the kid
at the security gate was all in one piece, and
went back to pick up my bottle of wine. I could
have saved myself the trouble. The marina
parking lot was awash in some of our domestic
finest.

For whatever reason, Crew Cut's purpose for
being where he was still hadn't hit me. I looked
around, took inventory, cursed my luck,
scanned the row of ships tied up at the marina
dock, and conducted a cursory assessment of
my own bumps and bruises. I started calling
Packy's name as I boarded the *Motion*. The
problem was, she wasn't answering.

I started my search in the galley. Then I checked out the forward cabin. Finally, I heard water running and went aft. I knocked on the door to the head, and when Packy didn't answer, I opened it.

Only then did I understand why Crew Cut was so damned eager to get out of there. Packy Darnell was doubled over the rim of the tub and her face looked like a Florida road map. At first glance, I couldn't tell where one bruise ended and the next one started.

Blood trickled from both nostrils and her lower lip was split open. Her head lolled back, and between sobs she tried to spit out her assailant's identity. I listened hard. Packy had some trouble, but finally the name tumbled out. Peter Cannon. Daddy Wages was right. Son of a bitch was the appropriate name for him.

For the next thirty minutes, I tended to Packy's sobs and injuries. Then I tried to figure out what had happened. I started by tracing back over the past couple of weeks. Just exactly how long had Cannon been waiting? How had he timed it? With the exception of a couple of trips to the marina office, Packy and I hadn't been apart for more than ten minutes since she had come aboard. I could only chastise myself for leaving her alone, because one time was all Cannon needed.

I plucked Packy out of the tub, dried her off, carried her into the aft cabin, and laid her across the bed. She had never looked smaller nor more vulnerable. I pulled a sheet over her and left her alone just long enough to get ice from the galley and some fresh towels from the locker in the head.

On the plus side, most of the bleeding had stopped and she was breathing regularly. On the negative side, she had a lump under one eye about the size of a glassy shooter, an obvious contusion to the right temple, and a nasty horseshoe-shaped cut on the side of her jaw, where Cannon's ring had gouged out a chunk of flesh.

She drifted in and out of reality a couple of times before she finally got herself collected to the point where she could ask, "Is he gone? Did you see him?"

I indicated that I knew what she was trying to say. I did not tell her how stupid I felt for not anticipating such an attack. All the warning signs were there. The problem was, I had been just a little too involved in my own world, a little too careless, a little too casual, and a damn sight too preoccupied to notice what I should have.

All Peter Cannon had to do to find out where his former lady love was hiding out was put the word out to his diving buddies that he was look-ing for his squeeze. The diving fraternity took care of the rest. Locating Packy was a piece of cake, especially with the lady adorning the sun deck of the *Perpetual Motion* in her string bikini every afternoon. Who says Floridians don't take time to appreciate their surroundings?

21

It took a little doing, but gradually Packy began to regain her equilibrium and composure. By the time I got around to checking her pulse the third and fourth time, she was starting to get things under control. At five feet eight and tipping the scales at around 140 pounds, she was no pushover when it came to getting her ready for bed. I gave her a couple of ibuprofen tablets, waited until her breathing reflected the depth of her sleep, and went topside.

There was still a faint hint of daylight in the west, but the clouds had moved in and the sky was beginning to look a bit ominous. In the distance I could see sporadic flashes of cloud-to-cloud lightning. The pyrotechnics were accompanied by repeated peals of throaty thunder. I had seen these summer storms move in over the Keys before; this one had all the earmarks of an all-nighter.

When the first few drops of rain spattered the deck of the *Perpetual Motion*, I went below, fixed myself a stiff drink, and decided to batten down for the night.

Even though I was hungry and had my own bumps and bruises to contend with, I was distracted—and that distraction wasn't the approaching storm and the sense of urgency it created. My thoughts kept tilting back to Packy. The question of whether the lady would be aboard when we sailed out of the Sunset Point Marina in the morning was no longer up for debate. Cannon knew where she was, and unless he got what he wanted, she was in for a second dose of thumps. It was my job to prevent that from happening.

Hey, I'll be the first to admit that I'm no expert in the field of domestic relations. But I was certain Peter Cannon had the word *dangerous* written all over him. From the way Cannon had roughed Packy up, I surmised he was not the kind who listened to reason. At the moment, it didn't seem particularly prudent for Packy Darnell to try to reason with her muscle-bound former boyfriend—without, that is, a like amount of muscle for backup.

I was still mulling over my next move when I went topside again, grabbed a deck chair, and rewarded myself with a front-row seat to watch the clouds gather. The peals of thunder were long enough, loud enough, and frequent enough that I almost didn't hear the phone ring. When I answered it, I realized that Packy's former paramour was not your ordinary son of a bitch. He was a very nervy son of a bitch.

He had a raspy, mutton-mouthed voice, and a style that didn't mince words. "Wages," he growled. "Put my wife on the phone."

"Sorry. She's incapacitated. Leave your name, number, and kennel address, and I'll tell her you called."

There was a momentary pause while the hissing snake summoned up more poison. Finally he managed to say, "Butt out of this, Wages.

You're screwin' around in a private matter. This is between Packy and me."

"From the looks of things, Cannon, the lady needs a little more moral support and a little less of the bush-league crap you hand out. And since I don't have anything better to do, I think I'll hang around and lend that support."

"Know somethin'? You're bitin' off more than you can chew, writer boy," Cannon said. "If you had any fuckin' sense, Wages, you'd stay out of this."

The caller was still huffing and puffing a string of threats and obscenities when I hung up. Since I couldn't be certain where Packy's former playmate was calling from—or how much time I would have if he decided to do something stupid—I went below, dug out the old E. G. Wages survival kit, and took inventory.

The survival kit was a gift from the stunning Honey Bear Leach when she married my former mentor and chased all of his freeloading male cronies out of her new husband's seaside digs on Key Largo. As one of the more entrenched cronies, I received one of the more thoughtful kits.

"Cosmo tells me you have a penchant for getting yourself in hot water, Elliott," Honey Bear said.

"It does seem to find me."

"Then maybe this will help you survive."

She handed over a carefully wrapped package. It was full of goodies, but the crown jewel of the packet was a vintage genuine broom-handle C96 Mauser. It was a 712 Scnellfeuer model that had been manufactured somewhere back in the thirties. Honey Bear had discovered and purchased the collector's persuader in a seedy little pawnshop in South Miami.

"So what am I supposed to do with this?" I asked.

"Get yourself out of trouble. From here on out, no more phone calls in the middle of the night. No more telling Cosmo you want him to bail you out of one of your typically insensitive and brutish male situations."

I winced. But at the same time I knew she was right. Needless to say, I didn't like Honey Bear much in those days. Her mandate had put a serious crimp in my lifestyle. But to the amazement of all Cosmo's old drinking buddies, she took better care of the old boy than we did, and in the process, the seventh Mrs. Cosmo Leach won our grudging admiration.

Eight years later, I was taking out the Mauser, admiring it, wiping it off, and slapping home a ten-round clip. The broom-handle added a little muscle and a whole lot of reassurance to the home team's side of the ledger. If Mr. Peter Cannon wanted to make a second attempt at getting in touch with Packy Darnell, I had a clip full of 9mm surprises for him.

Incident:

If Peter Cannon was entertaining visions of a return engagement on the *Motion*, he was doomed to disappointment. While the Saturday night storm did a lot of huffing and puffing, it ended up actually skirting the Sunset Point Marina. In the meantime, I caught a couple of hours of nervous sleep and awoke surprisingly refreshed. After I had Mel Cookerly, our Sunset Point host, cut the phone and other marina services, I weighed anchor.

My original plan had been to hang close to land, working my way south past Conch Key into the Marathon area. After Cannon's attack on Packy, it seemed prudent to alter those plans. If Cannon wanted to play tagalong, the *Motion* would be a shade too easy to track. So south of Marathon and Sombrero Beach, I kept the *Motion* far enough from the shoreline that Cannon would have a difficult time keeping an eye on us.

Through it all, a plan was beginning to develop—one that saw me swing a shade north around the lower Keys, pass to the west, loop back, and approach Snipe from the south. Following that course would take a little longer, but doing so was safer than heading straight to our destination. And I knew that if the situation dictated, we could put in at Hurst Baylor's place on Cudjoe Key to stock up on water, diesel fuel, and the latest news. Baylor's place would provide a welcome sanctuary.

As it was, Packy refused to come out of the shadows until late in the afternoon of the fourth day. When she finally relented and let me assess the damage, she had to fight to hold back the tears. Even though I think she was aware that there was no way Cannon could get to her, she was still nervous and jumpy. Any time she was on deck, she kept an uneasy surveillance on the shoreline.

On the fifth day, I asked, "Don't you think you and I should have a little talk?"

Packy gave me that age-old expression that all women practice from the day they first learn there is such a thing as a man. That expression is designed to make men think that women don't have the foggiest notion what they're talking about.

"You didn't tell me that you told that trained ape of yours where you were heading when you left Vero," I said anyway.

She gave me that look again, and I said, "How the hell else would he have known where you were hiding?"

This time there was no fast answer and no casual shrug. She gave me what sounded like an honest answer for a change. "I guess I didn't want you to think that I was that stupid."

"You have to admit it puts a different slant on things."

"Why does it?" she demanded.

"Come on, Packy. We go back a long way."

"All right, Elliott, so I wasn't using good judgment. I thought maybe—"

"You could make him a little jealous?"

"Nothing gives him the right to treat me like a punching bag," she protested. "All I need is thirty minutes with a goddamn lawyer to start the paperwork. If I had known then what I know now—" Her voice trailed off and she had to dig deep to catch her breath.

"Did you marry the creep, Packy?" When she hesitated, I repeated my question. Then Packy nodded and started to cry. I felt like a heel.

"He was gone so much," she said. "He would be home for a couple of days, then off at some salvage site for two or three weeks. When he finally finished that big diving contract and

29

came home to help me run the dive shop, we started bickering."

I let Packy ramble on with her story, and it wasn't long until she was struggling with every word. Finally she gave up the ghost and had a good cry, the soul-purging kind. When she was finished, she collected herself and ask where we were.

"Does it matter?"

"I suppose not." she said with a shrug.

But the more I watched her, the more I realized. The more I realized, the more I listened. The more I listened, the more I was convinced the chemistry between Packy Darnell and Elliott Wages was changing. Even then, I couldn't put my finger on it.

That night and most of the next day, Packy kept to herself again. Conversation was at a bare minimum. While I stayed at the wheel in the center cockpit, Packy kept forward, staring straight ahead. It wasn't until we began to tack north toward Snipe Key and our rendezvous with Cosmo that Packy confronted me again.

"I think you'd better put me ashore," she said, her words somewhere between a plea and a demand.

"Too much of a good thing?"

"I need a drink," she shot back at me.

"In the galley. Some of the finest Scotch money can buy."

"I don't want any of your goddamn Scotch," she snarled. "I'm tired of Scotch. I'm tired of this damn boat. I'm tired of you. I'm tired of your Mr. Always-in-Control attitude and your Mr. Always-in-Control fucking logic. I've had enough of you and this damned boat. I want to see people and—"

Before she could finish, the crying jag was on again. Wherever she was going with it, Packy Darnell Cannon lost her way. There were epithets, then tears, then frustration, then anger, and finally hysteria. When she could stand her situation no longer, she leaned into me, slamming her fists against my chest. She clawed, scratched, held on, and ultimately buried her face in my shoulder. Whatever it was, whatever kind of clinical name you give it, it had passed.

The Snipes are nothing more than a series of tiny, mango-infested tangles of sometimes rocky outcroppings of real estate south and west of Sugarloaf Key. Rumor claimed that Cosmo had won the title to a couple of these hardened parcels in a poker game years earlier.

Whether or not the story had any validity is immaterial. Traditionally Cosmo and his friends set up their week-long floating poker game offshore on the smallest of these outcroppings, Maco Key.

Packy and I had inadvertently timed our arrival just as the game was breaking up. I anchored the *Perpetual Motion* in a small lagoon some five hundred yards or so from our host's floating palace, donned some semicivil attire, and assisted Packy into the runabout. Moments later, we pulled alongside Cosmo's rented *Reef Runner*. It was the same opulent floating casino Cosmo and his friends had hired for previous week-long gambling forays.

We were piped aboard by a young crewman, who had difficulty taking his eyes off Packy's tanned and well-contoured legs. The lad couldn't have been more than twenty. Nevertheless, his attention did the lady's ego a world of good.

"We're looking for Cosmo," I said. "This is Ms. Darnell, and my name is Wages."

I have the feeling I could have told him my name was Michael Jordan and I still wouldn't have gotten his attention. He was completely captivated by Packy Darnell.

We took the scenic route. Along the way, I counted eight cabins, two gaming rooms, a sizable and well-appointed dining room, and the captain's quarters before we got to where Cosmo was situated in the lounge. It came as a bit of a surprise when I discovered that the old boy was not alone.

"Elliott," he said, rising to his feet. I could read him like a book. He was happy to see me all right, but he was downright thrilled to see Packy.

I introduced my old buddy to my traveling companion, and stood back while he did his Cosmo thing. He didn't disappoint me, nor did he disappoint Packy. He systematically extolled her every virtue. And he did it with such caressing detail that, by the time he had finished, a gushing Packy Darnell was ready to declare him a national treasure.

"You didn't tell me that Dr. Leach was so charming, Elliott," she cooed.

It did not seem to be the right time to try to explain to Ms. Packy that my smooth-talking former mentor, Dr. Cosmo Lorimar Leach, a highly regarded and world-famous anthropologist and psychologist, treated every woman as though she had just emerged from the pages of *Vogue*.

Packy was delighted by Cosmo's opening volley. She was no different from the rest. She was doing what I had seen every woman do upon meeting the old boy. She was ignoring the fact that he looked every bit like a skirt-chasing reprobate in his early seventies, choosing instead to savor every word he said.

I had the distinct feeling that Packy intuitively knew what it had taken me a little longer to figure out. Only a person bordering on sheer lunacy would take on Cosmo Leach—either verbally, mentally, or maybe even physically.

"Well, Ambrose, this is the man I was telling you about." Cosmo was addressing the only other person in the room, a man who resembled what I'd always imagined Ichabod Crane must have looked like. Only this man was thinner.

I felt Packy move in a little closer to me. When she did, I understood why. Cosmo's

R. Karl Largent

friend looked like the personification of death-warmed-over.

"Elliott," Cosmo said, "I would like you to meet Ambrose Thurston Vance."

While he introduced Vance to Packy, I reached out to shake hands with the man. What I grabbed hold of felt more like a bundle of kindling twigs than flesh and bone. As Daddy Wages would have said, the bloom of youth had wilted when it came to Ambrose Vance. The man's skin was blue-white and textured like parchment. Prominent veins made his face resemble a Braille reader. The really curious thing was, through much of the conversation, Ambrose Vance didn't talk to me. He didn't even look at me. Instead, he talked to Cosmo Leach about me.

"This is the man you are suggesting for the job?" Vance asked.

"What job?" I snapped.

Cosmo held his index finger up to his lips. "Come, come, Elliott, where are your manners?"

Ambrose Thurston Vance cleared his throat. "Can I assume, Mr. Wages, that since you have seen fit to have this lady accompany you to this meeting, you are not averse to having her hear the details of our little business venture?"

"What business venture? What details? I don't know anything about any—Cosmo and I are planning to do a little fishing."

Cosmo's eyes had narrowed, and he was holding his finger to his mouth again. I wasn't about to say it out loud, but I was beginning to smell another one of Cosmo's setups.

Vance seemed oblivious to the byplay. "Please make yourself comfortable, Mr. Wages. What I'm about to tell you may take a while."

We all waited while a white-coated member of the *Reef Runner*'s crew discreetly circulated with coffee, filled our cups, then left the room. I took a seat next to Packy, who had suddenly forgotten how unhappy she was with yours truly. She was sitting closer than usual—and closer than necessary. Either Packy Darnell was one hell of an actress, or despite Cosmo's reassurances otherwise, she was already feeling vulnerable and out of her element again.

She made a shivering gesture. "I don't know about you, Elliott," she said, "but all this intrigue sounds exciting. I'm eager to hear his story." She gave the word *story* a decidedly feminine twist. Even Vance, with his near-death appearance, caught her innuendo.

The old man doctored his coffee, took a sip, and said, "Project yourself back in time, Mr. Wages. It is the night of August 6, 1944. You are standing on the wharf in Bremerhaven as a ship is being loaded. A rather clandestine event is taking place. In the number-three hold of a German freighter by the name of *Wilhelm Leichter* is a closely guarded secret cargo—a cargo that supposedly only four men in the entire

Third Reich know about. One of those men is the Führer himself, Adolf Hitler."

"Am I supposed to ask what is in that shipment, Mr. Vance?"

"Gold bullion," Vance replied. There was a catch in his voice when he said the word *gold*.

"How much gold?"

Ambrose Vance shrugged. "I imagine, Mr. Wages, that the only men who could have answered your question exactly are all very much dead." He paused long enough to take another sip of his coffee, light a panatella cigar, savor the first draw, and slowly exhale. For a moment, I thought he might have trouble remembering where he was in his story.

Cosmo, like Packy, was completely engrossed. That was when I realized that if Cosmo was willing to put up with the old man's fancies, the least I could do was hear him out. That way I would know what I was saying no to when I declined the aforementioned job.

"Okay," I said, "I'll play your game. In round numbers, how much gold bullion and from where? According to everything I've read, the Krauts had gold stashed everywhere at the end of the war, and all of it belonged to someone else."

Vance gave Cosmo a look that seemed to say I had just passed some sort of a test, a test that began by asking the right question.

"Estimates run as high as three hundred million or so in 1944 dollars, Mr. Wages. The question is, how many ounces are there? No one can say for certain just exactly how much was loaded aboard that ship that night. Men don't count quite as carefully in times of war, Mr. Wages."

"What about the cargo manifests?" I asked.

"During the dying days of the war, Mr. Wages, the German high command was trying to salvage what it could. We are told that the bullion being put aboard the *Leichter* that night had been stolen from the Spanish National Treasury of Francisco Franco. Whether all or part of that bullion was loaded aboard the *Leichter* or some other ship will probably never be known."

"What do you mean by some other ship?" Packy asked.

"It only stands to reason that the Germans would try to cut any possible losses by splitting up the shipment. That way if one of the ships ran into trouble, the other—"

When Packy leaned forward in her chair, Ambrose Vance smiled strangely. On Ambrose Vance, the expression came off as a gesture of inner satisfaction that had nothing to do with overt pleasure. I suddenly had the feeling that having the gold wasn't what was most important to Vance—finding it was the game.

"That shipment aboard the *Leichter* was destined for a little-known German stronghold, a harbor near the village of Infante Dom Henrique on the island of Principe in the Gulf of Guinea."

"And?" I said.

Vance smiled again, this time quickly and uneasily. There was something disturbing about the reaction, perhaps because it was never quite completed. It was as if he was holding some of the smile back.

"This is where the story gets interesting, Mr. Wages. According to one version of this saga, there was a German submarine waiting in the harbor at Infante Dom Henrique when the *Leichter* arrived. And I have it on very good authority that the captain of the U-boat ordered his crew to open fire on the *Leichter*."

"The U-boat opened fire on a German freighter?" Packy asked incredulously.

"Indeed," Vance said. "According to the journal of one Captain Albrecht Hess of the U-564, a Type VII-C U-boat, the *Leichter* was engaged at 1442 hours on 12 August. After the freighter was disabled, Captain Hess ordered a squad of his men to board the *Leichter* and dispose of the crew."

Vance took a sip of his coffee. "Captain Hess was your typical German officer, Mr. Wages: very thorough, and very methodical in his methodology. According to one version of the story, Hess loaded as much of the gold as possible aboard the U-564 and then sank the *Wilhelm Leichter*."

I leaned back in my chair. "I have to ask why."

"Both a reasonable and prudent question, Mr. Wages. However, it seems quite obvious that

Captain Hess had been instructed to deliver the gold aboard the U-564 to some undisclosed hiding place. Then, no doubt, he was scheduled to return to the wreck of the *Leichter* to relieve the sunken freighter of the balance of its cargo."

"Quite a story," I said. "But I'm curious. Did anyone ever stop to think that maybe this guy Hess was stealing the gold for his own use?"

"In all probability, that is exactly what happened," Vance replied.

"Four years ago," Cosmo said, "Ambrose's divers were able to retrieve over one hundred and thirty million in gold bullion from the *Leichter*, Elliott. Hess got away with the rest."

Using three hundred million in bullion as a benchmark, I didn't need the brains of a mental giant to figure out that more than half of the bullion was still waiting to be retrieved. Was Vance being cagey, or did he really know where the rest of it was? "Hell of a haul," I finally admitted.

Ambrose Vance's eyes, or at least what I could see of them in the shadows, appeared to harden. "A noteworthy sum, Mr. Wages, but as you can see, the job is only half done. I will consider it a hell of a haul, as you put it, when I also retrieve the bullion stolen by Captain Hess."

"So where is this guy Hess supposed to have stashed his ill-gotten booty?"

Vance reached down, and when he did, I realized for the first time why, even with a cool 130 million in his pocket, he needed guys like me. There was an ivory-colored blanket with the initials ATV draped across his lap. From the contours beneath the blanket, I could see that was where Ambrose Thurston Vance ended.

His hand emerged with a well-worn black journal. He laid it in his lap, extracted a single sheet of paper, and handed it to me. It was a cutaway, detailed drawing of a Type VII-C U-boat.

"You will notice," Vance said, "that aft of the main diesels in section B and below the torpedo loading hatch, there is an area marked Reserve Torpedo Storage."

As I scanned the drawing and located the section, Vance held up the black book. "According to this journal, Mr. Wages, the aft firing tube and the emergency steering section were removed and only the essential aft controls were left in place. In essence, the good Captain Hess was providing a place for a pound of gold every time he removed a pound of equipment from his U-564."

"You can appreciate the irony of it," Cosmo said. "The ultimate eye for an eye."

"All of this is in that journal there?" I asked.

Vance nodded. When he did, I noticed that Packy's breathing was shallow and her eyes appeared to be slightly glazed. Ambrose Vance had found her on button.

"So what's the problem? Sounds to me as if all that's left now is thumbing through Hess's journal until you discover where he stashed the rest of the gold. Correct?"

"If it were that simple, Mr. Wages, I would not have gone to all the trouble of having my friend Dr. Leach arrange this meeting. Instead, I would have concluded our little game of cards and departed this floating pleasure palace along with the rest of the good doctor's guests."

Cosmo was smiling as I asked, "Then you've told me everything but the last chapter, right?"

"Even that is there," Vance said and sighed. "But I am afraid that it does us very little good."

I had to give the old boy credit. Ambrose Vance had a flair for the dramatic.

"What Ambrose is telling you, Elliott," Cosmo said, "is that even though we think the whole story is all there in the journal, we still haven't been able to decipher it."

"What do you mean you can't decipher it?"

"According to Hess's journal, he sailed the U-564 out of the harbor at Infante Dom Henrique, heading west. Some folks think that his journey, had he completed it, would have eventually taken him to South America. He marked his coordinates along the way and on the twenty-fifth of August, after nearly two weeks of playing hide-and-seek with the Allied forces in the Atlantic, he describes seeking sanctuary in the infamous Sargasso Sea."

Packy started to laugh. "Come on now. Are you telling me this is going to turn out to be one of those Bermuda Triangle stories?"

"I see you've heard of that mysterious region," Vance said.

"It's not exactly a closely guarded secret," Packy said. "Half of the people think you're a fool if you put any stock in what people say about the Triangle. The other half think you're a fool if you don't."

"And which half do you fall into, Ms. Darnell?" Vance asked. From the tone of his voice I gathered that Ambrose Vance was genuinely interested in her answer.

Packy's voice was a bit strained. "Look, Mr. Vance. I'm just along for the ride, so it doesn't matter what I think. But I am a professional diver and I'll say I have enough to worry about when I'm down there. I don't need to conjure up all kinds of mystical and supernatural elements to confuse the situation."

"What happened after Hess got into the Sargasso?" I asked, hoping to get back to the matter at hand.

Vance sighed. "You can read the journal for yourself, Mr. Wages. But I am afraid that what you find will not be very lucid. In his journal, Captain Hess describes a series of misfortunes that befall the U-564, and finally his journal entries give evidence of a totally different type of a problem."

"A nervous breakdown," Cosmo said solemnly.

Vance cleared his throat. "You'll see what we mean when you read Captain Hess's account of his final days aboard the U-564. There is a rather disturbing account of the netted seaweed, of the stench of the sargassum, of soaring temperatures, and depleted water supplies, and finally of his crew's mysterious disappearance."

"Disappearance?" I said.

"To use Captain Hess's words, Mr. Wages, as if some terrible creature was plucking them from the very deck of the U-564 as they stood watch."

With Cosmo and Ambrose Vance looking on, and Packy Darnell straining to read over my shoulder, I rifled through the last few pages of the journal, scanning what appeared to be little more than a desperate scrawl. In the end, the entries were too chaotic, and my German was too rusty. I closed the journal and looked at Vance. I was about to tell him that I couldn't help him.

It was Packy who saved the day by giving me a subtle wink—just enough of a sign to make me think she was getting more out of what was going on than I was.

I took her lead. "Maybe," I said, not at all sure why I was saying it, "I'd like the opportunity to study the journal a little closer."

Ambrose Vance had appeared old, tired, and worn out when we'd boarded. But he gave every indication of still having enough resiliency to overcome those burdens when I indicated I was willing to take another look at the journal. He leaned forward, pressed a button on his control panel, and propelled his wheelchair into the middle of the room. He was staring hard at me.

"May I assume a modicum of interest, Mr. Wages?"

"In Hess's journal maybe. Anything more than that, not likely."

"How do you know you would not be interested in becoming a partner in this potentially lucrative business venture until you have heard my offer?"

"Define *lucrative business* and *partner*," I said.

Vance's face lit up. "One percent of everything we recover."

Let's face it. Mama Wages didn't raise a fool. If Ambrose Vance was convinced that Albrecht Hess had managed to depart Infante Dom Henrique with something close to one 170 million dollars in gold bullion, and was likewise willing to spend major-league bucks searching for it, I would have been a fool not to listen.

Vance repeated his offer. "One percent of what some people believe could total more than one hundred and seventy million in gold bullion, Mr. Wages."

"So what do I have to do? Find Hess's U-boat?"

"That part of it should not be difficult. We believe we are reasonably close to discovering the U-564's location. The problem comes after we locate it, Mr. Wages."

I was waiting for Vance to elaborate. In the meantime, Packy was grinning like a woman with a fistful of charge cards.

"Sounds to me as if they've done the hard

part, Elliott—especially when you stop to consider that the Sargasso covers about two million square miles of ocean," she said.

"What's the catch, Ambrose? You'll have to forgive me, but where I grew up, people didn't just up and offer a stranger a slice of that kind of action without wanting something slightly crooked in return."

Vance sighed. He reached under the ivory-colored blanket again and produced a cigarette holder. He inserted a long, oval-shaped cigarette, lit it, and inhaled. It was a long time before he allowed the smoke to curl from his nostrils.

"Quite right, Mr. Wages. There is a catch, as you put it. Suffice to say that not long ago one of our support vessels—a supply barge containing some of our most sophisticated electronic equipment, a dear friend and colleague, and two of his technicians—literally disappeared from the face of the Earth."

I held up my hand. "Interesting choice of words. You said the supply barge disappeared."

"I use the word *disappeared* because that's how it was described to me. According to the report, a heavy fog developed concurrent with WMO reports of unusual seismic activity in the area. When I first heard about the seismic activity, I had no idea what to think, so I called our friend Cosmo. He informed me that the technical term for the phenomenon is *swarm quakes*. They're clusters of small but frequent, low-magnitude earthquakes. I have since learned that no single quake of this magnitude causes much damage, but occurring in clusters as they do, they are often devastating, particularly those that occur underwater."

"I still don't understand what happened to your equipment barge," Packy said.

Ambrose Vance hesitated, "When the crew of the *Barbella* received warning of seismic activity in the area, Lucas Brimley, the salvage-site dive master, canceled operations for the day. But Dr. Cameron of the Lancer Down Oceanographic Institute and two of his technicians decided to stay aboard the *Hedgehog*, the mission's salvage barge."

"I've seen these swarm quakes, Elliott," Packy said, "and I've never seen them strong enough to curtail operations."

"Dr. Cameron felt that the *Hedgehog* would be more stable and ride out the quakes better if it wasn't tethered to the *Barbella*. But he reported that he thought he had hit something while maneuvering away from the *Barbella* to ride out the swarm quakes. Dive Master Brimley and another one of the divers investigated, found some minor hull damage, and repaired it."

"Then what happened?"

"The following morning, the *Hedgehog* disappeared."

"You mean, it went down?"

"Disappeared," Vance repeated adamantly.

Vance was a little wart of a man with no real

knowledge of the sea. I couldn't help but regard the whole story as being a bit far-fetched. Nor would I have been at all surprised if he had tried to offer me a Rod Serling–style explanation for the barge's disappearance. But neither Cosmo nor Packy was laughing; they weren't even smiling.

Outside was a beautiful day, and I was wasting it, not to mention the fact that I was getting that old storm-warning sensation. I get that feeling when I'm about to get tangled up in something I don't belong in. When that happens, I've learned to ask some very direct questions. As far as I was concerned, it was time to ignore the fact that Ambrose Vance was Cosmo's friend and business associate.

"Let's cut to the chase, Vance," I said. "If you think you know where the U-564 is located, why don't you send your cast of thousands down after it? Secondly, if you think there's something strange going on out there, why don't you spell it out?"

"Reasonable questions, Mr. Wages. When I explained what was happening to Dr. Leach, he thought about the situation and then suggested that I contact you. When I heard that you and Dr. Leach would be joining up for a few days of fishing, I decided to delay my departure for a couple of days to see if I could interest you in my proposal. If you decide to become involved, Mr. Wages, I believe the venture could prove quite profitable for you."

"Let me think about it," I said. "I'd like the opportunity to get a better look at Hess's journal."

"Fair enough, Mr. Wages. Take as long as you like. But I would like to have your answer no later than tomorrow morning."

Back aboard the *Motion*, Packy and I went to work on Hess's journal. She did the translating and I did the note-taking. Ambrose Thurston Vance was right; Albrecht Hess's final journal entries were chaotic. In many cases, we couldn't determine where reality ended and fantasy took over.

It took a while, but we were able to work our way through the last two weeks of the journal. After we had gone back and checked a second time, Packy closed the battered diary. She went to the galley, fixed us each a drink, and sat down in the vee berth with her long legs curled under her.

"So what do you think?" she said.

I shrugged. "As far as I'm concerned, that journal raises more questions than it answers."

Packy tilted her pretty head to one side. "Let's hear 'em."

"Start with the man who supposedly wrote the entries in the journal, Albrecht Hess. Despite Hess's obvious confusion toward the end, Vance seems rather confident about the whereabouts of the U-564."

Packy nodded.

"And while Vance didn't exactly say so, I get the distinct impression that he thinks something is amiss out there in salvage land."

"I agree," Packy said. "Hess's journal entry for August thirtieth is the last one that records the coordinates. And at that point, Hess is already focusing on the strange occurrences aboard his submarine."

"The question is, was he already addled at that point? Or were these so-called strange occurrences really happening?"

"We'll never know for sure—at least not until we find that submarine." She took a sip of her drink. "Okay, next question."

"It goes something like this: How did the journal of the captain of the U-564, supposedly lost in the middle of the Sargasso, get to wherever it was that it was found?"

"You're questioning whether or not the journal is legitimate?"

When I nodded, Packy leaned back against the bulkhead and said, "I guess it's confession time, Elliott. Right now the only thing that really surprises me is that you haven't heard about Hess and the infamous lost U-564 long before this."

"So sue me. What about it?"

Packy had an almost dreamy look in her eyes. "Every diver from Key West to Saint Augustine has probably heard the story of the lost German sub with the Franco bullion. My father used to say that before they died, half the divers in

Florida had made some kind of half-assed attempt to locate it."

"Lay it on me."

"The way I heard the story, Elliott, a young German submariner was found floating in a raft. Significant details like time and location have long since been lost. The survivor had three companions in the raft with him, all dead. Supposedly, one of the bodies was that of Captain Albrecht Hess. The way my father heard it, Hess was carrying only two items on his person: a picture of a young woman and a journal."

"And the survivor?"

"Nothing more than a combination cook and cabin boy who knew absolutely nothing about where they were or why they were there."

"What happened to him?" I asked, but Packy only shrugged. "What about Hess's journal?"

"The most often repeated version is that a Miami pawnshop owner ended up with it."

"And that's where Vance or one of his people found it?"

Packy nodded. "Every salvage diver worth his salt has heard of Ambrose Vance. He goes after the big ones, and if his people find them, he rewards them with the big bucks."

"Then he's legit?"

"Legit, but weird. I guess you can afford to be weird when you have as much money as he does."

"Define weird."

"Well, for one thing, he believes in all this

Bermuda Triangle stuff. One diver I know told me that he worked on a Ambrose Vance salvage job off the coast of Bermuda. He said that Vance hired a resident psychic to interpret the signs."

I started to laugh, but Packy cut me off. "Hey, you may think he's loony, Elliott. But keep this in mind: Ambrose Vance has already recovered one hundred and thirty million in bullion using Hess's journal as his guide. That's the kind of mazuma girls like me only dream about."

I stared out the cabin port for several minutes before I finally picked up a pencil and began to doodle. Seeing my perplexity, Packy said, "Penny for your thoughts."

"I was wondering," I said, "just how much is one percent of a whole bunch of millions?"

Packy closed her eyes, then started to laugh. "It's a lot, Elliott. It's a whole, big bunch."

Incident:

The early morning Florida sun was just beginning to sort its way through a nearby tangle of cypress and mango trees when I stepped out on the deck of the *Motion*. The heat was already evident.

Packy was soaking up the sun. She was sprawled out on the foredeck, poring over Hess's journal. When she heard me, she said, "Good morning."

I didn't sound cheery. I grunted. Grunts are as good as I can do before I have coffee.

"How about Vance's offer, Elliott? Now that you've had a chance to sleep on it, what do you think?"

53

I sat down, poured a cup of coffee, and took a sip before saying, "Well, for one thing, I think it's a hell of a lot of money."

"Then you're going to do it?"

"Don't know. My head says no, my wallet says yes. I keep coming back to the same old question: If I were Ambrose Vance and my people had already isolated the damn object of the search, why would I want or need a guy like me?"

When Packy frowned, I said, "Seriously. Consider what he's getting for his money. Although I do a little diving, I'm sure as hell not a professional diver. I don't know that much about the Sargasso. And as much as I wish I did, I don't know anything about gold either. I'm a writer who investigates things. I'm a loner."

"Maybe he's after that old Wages integrity," Packy said, and I grunted again.

"Or maybe Cosmo oversold you." Packy laughed as she sat up and wrapped her arms around her knees. "Come on, Elliott. Lighten up. What's wrong? What brings on this un-Elliott-like wave of humility and inadequacy?"

I wanted to tell Packy that it wasn't the things that people told me that bothered me. It was the things they didn't tell me or forgot to tell me. From such omissions came problems.

"Salvage barges don't just disappear," I said. "Something very real happens to them."

"Meaning what?"

"For starters, let's take Vance's salvage-site

manager, the one they call China Porter. Why would he tell Vance that the equipment barge disappeared? Why wouldn't Porter just tell Vance the damn thing sank?"

Packy frowned. "Maybe the guy doesn't know the difference. Maybe lots of things. How would I know why he used the word disappeared?"

"Try this one on for size," I said. "Suppose this guy Porter, the salvage-site manager, is trying to capitalize on Vance's preoccupation with the more mystical or supernatural dimensions of that salvage operation."

"You're reading things into this situation that aren't there, Elliott. What would anyone have to gain by doing that?"

"You can start with something called one hundred and seventy big ones in gold bullion. Maybe it's as simple as this guy Porter is trying to figure out how to cut himself in for a bigger slice of bullion pie."

Packy stood up and disappeared down into the galley. She emerged moments later with more coffee and listened to more of my pondering.

"What about Vance's crew? Are they on the up and up? Is this guy China Porter legitimate? How did Vance pick his crew—on the basis of low bidder?"

Packy laughed. "God, you're a skeptic."

"It's my job," I said. "Besides, five will get you ten that Ambrose Vance didn't give us the whole story yesterday."

"Which means you're going to turn him down?"

I slumped back against the spar, took a long sip of coffee, and stared out at the blue-green water. The difference between the day before and today was that I knew the whole affair was no coincidence. It smacked of Cosmo's duplicity. Right out of the box, Ambrose Vance had hit me where I was most vulnerable—not once, but twice. It would be a long time before any more royalty checks came floating in, and money has always been my number-one weakness.

"You still haven't answered my question," Packy said a few moments later.

"That's because I don't know the answer."

I walked to the prow of the *Motion* and stared down into the water at the reef creatures. If Packy had been listening, she more than likely would have heard me muttering under my breath. What was wrong with spending the summer doing exactly what I was doing? Where was it written that I had to go sailing off to some forgotten corner of the world to satisfy my damned curiosity or make enough money to pay Uncle Sam more taxes?

Besides, didn't I already have my problem figured out? If I cut a corner here and there, I could make it through the summer on what was left in the old bank account. With a little luck, I might even be able to stretch my savings into the fall.

When I finally stopped deluding myself, I said, "Suppose I did take Ambrose Vance up on his offer. Who'd be around to look after you? Surely you haven't forgotten about Mr. Peter Cannon."

"I could go with you." Packy was doing her best to sound as if the idea had just occurred to her.

I shook my head. "No way."

"Why not? You know I'd be safe if I was with you."

Finally I heard myself saying, "I don't even know if I'm going to accept Vance's offer."

What I wasn't saying was that Packy's proposal had its merits. Even though she had been away from the salvage scene for a couple of years, she still enjoyed a reputation as a first-rate commercial diver, one of the best in the Keys. And if I did accept Vance's offer, having Packy to back me up and cover my backside wasn't all that bad an idea.

"At least consider my offer," Packy said.

I put my arm around her shoulder and gave her a hug. "Why not? Maybe, just maybe, we'll be able to figure out what happened to Vance's supply barge and, in the process, grab us a piece of the action."

Packy threw her arms around my neck and hugged me. "Elliott Grant Wages," she said, "I can smell money. And, oh, how I love that smell."

* * *

We had our second session with Ambrose Thurston Vance later that day. While the old boy never did answer all of my questions, I was able to get the cast of characters somewhat straight. I even garnered enough satisfactory answers for us to shake hands on a thirty-day trial run.

Cosmo was the catalyst. I think Ambrose bought the concept of Elliott Wages because Cosmo recommended me. I in turn bought Vance's story because Cosmo was willing to go to bat for him.

Vance's salvage effort in the Sargasso was in chaos. The mission had originally consisted of twenty-two people. Some of the crew members, as Vance described them, sounded essential; others did not. The situation had been further complicated when the mission lost Dr. Joffre Cameron of the Lancer-Down Oceanographic Institute. Cameron was the mission's heart and soul, a world-famous authority on the Sargasso. Cameron and two of his technicians had been aboard the *Hedgehog* the night it disappeared. Vance considered their deaths unfortunate but routine.

Then there was the mission's captain, a man even I had heard of: China Porter. Porter, like Cameron, was considered to be an authority on the Sargasso. I was vaguely familiar with China Porter for an entirely different reason. The captain had been involved in a seven-year-old drug-trafficking affair in Miami in which two top IRS officials had been found guilty of laundering Cuban drug funds. One of the two officials had ended up floating in the Miami River.

Porter and Cameron, along with Professor Eberhard Kritzmer, from the university in Leipzig, appeared to be the key figures. Kritzmer was there as part of the salvage agreement. The U-564 was a German submarine, and even though the money had been stolen from Franco, the Germans were still claiming a portion of whatever Vance's people recovered.

There were others: a fellow by the name of Luke Brimley, the dive master; Kritzmer's assistant, Dr. Marion Fredrich, who had spent his time studying Sargasso marine life forms; and a woman by the name of Jewel Simon. Ms. Simon was there, I was told, because of Vance's firm belief in the supernatural. Ms. Simon's job was to make certain the Bermuda Triangle's possible effect on the mission was taken into consideration.

In essence, my job was to get the salvage effort back on track after the loss of both personnel and equipment in the disappearance of the *Hedgehog*. To seal the deal, Vance gave me an out: After thirty days, I had the option of packing my bags and heading back to the Keys with ten thousand dollars in my pocket for any trouble or inconvenience. It was a deal that, at the time, I thought I couldn't refuse.

Two days after reaching an agreement with Ambrose Vance at Snipe Key, Packy and I hus-

tled the *Motion* down to Boog Masters's marina
in Key West. We picked up a few personal effects courtesy of Vance's advance, and char-
tered a Brazilian-built turboprop Bandeirante
for a Sunday-night flight to Bermuda. So well
prepared were we that by the time we actually
got around to boarding the island-hopper, I had
even remembered to bring my trusty survival
kit.

In Bermuda, we hooked up with the captain
of a timeworn commercial transfer vessel. The
mariner made his living transporting supplies
and replacement equipment to a number of is-
lands and salvage operations throughout the
area. He said he had not heard about the loss
of the *Hedgehog* at Vance's salvage site.

"Them folks out on the *Barbella* are a secre-
tive bunch. They ain't tellin' a soul what they're
after."

And so it was that, amid a heavy, hanging
haze, we boarded the *Barbella*. An emaciated
deckhand with the unusual name of Mookie
Boots showed us to our cabins and offered to
take us to the captain when we were ready. After Packy freshened up, we were ushered into
Porter's cabin. He may have been knowledgeable about the Sargasso, but I had the distinct
feeling that he was ignorant of any social skills.

For the most part, Porter's appearance hadn't
changed much since the trial in Miami. He was
older, and he had put on more weight. If anything, he was even more surly than I remem-

bered him. He stood around six feet three inches, and weighed in somewhere around the 275-pound mark. His enormous head was almost bald. To round out the picture, he had hedge-thick eyebrows, microdot eyes with a bourbon glaze, and the skin of a bronc saddle.

At the same time that we were appraising China Porter, he was giving us the once-over. On the surface at least, he appeared to be mildly pleased that Packy had joined the expedition. My presence, on the other hand, appeared not to give him much pleasure.

All in all, Porter scowled a lot. His greeting was little more than a series of semiaudible grunts, and his demeanor brightened only after he learned that Packy was an experienced salvage diver. At that point, he actually manufactured an insincere half smile.

When Porter saw Packy, he made one concession to propriety. He spat out his tobacco, opened a porthole, and threw it overboard before he shook hands. Then he motioned for us to sit down and lit a cigarette. As if to bless our journey, he pulled the cork from a bottle of cheap bourbon and splashed the contents into three paper cups.

"Well, here's to keepin' your fuckin' sanity." Porter bolted his drink. Then he said, "Old Man Vance says he sent you out here to whip us into shape, Wages, Do you think we need to be whipped into shape, Wages?"

"When you have a chance, I want to sit down and go over some things," I said.

Porter took the packet of papers Vance had ask me to deliver, wadded them up, and threw them in a nearby wastebasket. Then he filled his paper cup with more bourbon. In the process, he offered Packy a refill and ignored me. For a moment or so there was a strained silence. Then the captain sighed and started for the door of his cabin, saying, "Ain't no secrets on the *Barbella*, Wages. If I know it, the crew knows it, and vice versa. Got it?"

"Well, Mr. Wages, who won that round?" Packy giggled when Porter left without waiting for a reply.

I ignored the lady's question and took China Porter at his word. There was no better time to start snooping around and asking questions. The *Barbella* was as good a place to my investigation as any.

Ambrose Vance wasn't exactly cutting corners on his expedition. From the bow to stern the *Barbella* was eighty-seven feet long, and if a person had to spend a long, sultry summer in the Sargasso, the *Barbella* appeared to have enough amenities to make the stay semitolerable.

The bridge towered over a top deck that contained the radio, radar, communications, and electronic gear. In addition, there were two staterooms and the control room. Neither of the staterooms appeared to be occupied; I won-

dered why. On most ships, the topside staterooms were the choice quarters. The *Barbella*
did not appear to be an exception. If the crew
was keeping one ready for Ambrose Vance, I
couldn't understand why. The Sargasso was
clearly not Vance's kind of playground.

The A deck had several rooms: six more staterooms, a complete laboratory with all of the
necessary scientific gear, the captain's quarters,
a huge galley, two wardrooms, and the top diving locker. On the lower deck, the aft hold contained a veritable fleet of sea sleds and a K-55
recovery-and-salvage vehicle. The sleds and the
K-55 could be winched out of the aft hold by
the hydraulic crane on the stern.

The engine room housed twin 75T40 diesels,
and was just fore of the aft hold. The balance of
the trim deck was occupied by a photo lab, a
machine shop, more crew quarters, and a forward hold—which, according to one of the
crewmen, was always kept locked. I made a
mental note to find out why.

Finally, there was a curious little observation
chamber fore of the lower-deck stateroom. It
too was locked. If everyone knew everything, as
Porter had indicated, why was it locked? I made
a second mental note.

I ended my abbreviated tour of the ship in the
chart room. At that point, I realized just how
close Ambrose Vance's crew was playing its
cards. The charts were complete except for one
vital component: the coordinates.

Score one for Vance and Porter. I had neglected to ask where the hell I was going, and I couldn't find out without coordinates. "Somewhere in the Sargasso" wasn't enough to satisfy my curiosity. Nonetheless, I had a strong hunch it was the only answer I was going to get.

After the chart room, I drifted topside and stepped out of the air-conditioning into the oppressive Sargasso night air. Thirty seconds later, I could feel myself start to sweat.

"You must be that new guy Wages," a man said. His words were accompanied by the slightly pungent aroma of pipe tobacco.

"And you would be?"

"Maydee Hew." He stepped out from the shadows into the pale illumination of the instrument lights on the bridge. Even in the poor lighting, I could tell that there wasn't much to Mr. Hew. "If there was to be a second mate aboard this here floating nightmare, I reckon I'd be it," he said.

Maydee Hew could have passed for an over-the-hill jockey. He was short, skinny, and ugly. His head was shaved, but his chin sported a neatly trimmed, salt-and-pepper Vandyke. Hew was a gabber, and when he talked, he belched dirty little puffs of gray smoke that seemed to hang in the saturated Sargasso air.

"Know how I know'd you was Wages?"

"Maybe you're psychic."

"Naw," Hew said. "I heard 'em talkin' about you down in the galley. Scuttlebutt, ya know.

Most of us figured Old Man Vance would have to do somethin' purty soon. It don't take no college type to figure out it's been all downhill since the *Hedgehog* disappeared."

"Downhill?"

Hew spat over the railing. "Yeah, downhill. Between Brimley tryin' to take over the whole damn thing and Porter and Kritzmer bickerin' all the time, they ain't much gettin' done."

Hew talked like Vance—with one big difference. I had the feeling Maydee Hew would not know how to mask the obvious. Sensing a chance to rip into the mystery of the *Hedgehog*, I asked him about the sinking of the vessel.

Maydee shook his bald head at my suggestion that the *Hedgehog* had sunk. "You ever been around when a ship goes down, mate? 'Cause if you have, you know there ain't no mistakin' what's a-happenin'. They hiss and choke like they're gaspin' for every last breath of air—even foul air like we got here. It's a sound no man ever forgets."

"Are you saying that didn't happen?"

Hew stoked his pipe, lit it, and spewed smoke into the darkness. "If you're askin' me straight out do I think that barge sank, I'd have ta say no. I'd have ta say she disappeared. When a ship sinks there's an explosion—because she hit somethin' or because somethin's gone bad wrong. There wasn't nothin'. She was there. Then she wasn't."

"Who was on watch that night?"

"I was," Hew said. "I was standin' right here on the bridge. Heard every word that passed between Cameron and Kritzmer and Brimley."

"So Cameron was talking to Brimley. Where was the skipper?"

"Porter was below," Hew said.

"Would Professor Kritzmer describe what happened to the *Hedgehog* that night as a disappearance?"

Hew's laugh was riddled with disdain. "Who cares how that bastard Kraut would answer the question? He don't know shit about ships."

I had the distinct feeling Maydee Hew was just getting warmed up, but he clammed up the minute he saw Packy step out on deck. This time the fair Ms. Darnell had done more than freshen up; she had spruced up as well. She was wearing an enticing little off-white ensemble that accentuated her tan. Her shoulder-length hair was tied in a tidy little arrangement that complimented her symmetrical face and long, slender neck. I offered her a couple of appropriate compliments to let her know I appreciated the show.

In response, the lady made a playful pirouette and tilted her head to one side. *"Gracias."*

"What's the occasion?"

"Dinner," she said. "I was in my cabin when Captain Porter came by. He suggested that you and I join him and Professor Kritzmer for dinner at 20:00 hours."

"Message acknowledged," I said.

Packy laughed. "Good. I'm hungry. I could eat a whale."

The ingredients for what turned out to be a superb meal had probably arrived on the same provisions ship that delivered Packy and yours truly. The dinner part of the evening was excellent. The best that could be said for the rest of it was that it was informative and, frankly, a bit unnerving.

As for any personal assessment, it may have been way too early in the game, but I was already convinced that someone needed to tell Ambrose Vance that his so-called salvage team looked less like a team and a whole lot more like a collection of self-serving egomaniacs. So far, everyone I had met had a decidedly suspect agenda. And recovering the U-564 and its bullion for Ambrose Vance didn't particularly seem to be a priority item on any of those agendas.

Professor G. Eberhard Kritzmer turned out to be a jut-jawed tyrant with no innate charm. He spent most of the dinner glaring at Packy and me through a pair of half-glasses perched on the end of a supercilious, if slightly bulbous, nose.

"Tell me, Mr. Wages," he said as Mookie cleared away the dishes, "how is it that you and Ambrose Vance became acquainted?"

"Introduced by a mutual friend," I replied. I saw no reason to introduce Cosmo's name into the scenario. At that point, I was still wondering if there was any way to avoid all further contact

R. Karl Largent

with Kritzmer for the next four weeks. Try as I might, I couldn't picture myself having more conversations with the man.

"So tell us, how did you connect with Vance?" Packy said to Kritzmer.

The professor leaned forward and contemplated his cigar. He had a habit of not looking at people when he was talking to them. He had avoided eye contact with me most of the evening.

"I am here because of Albrecht Hess's journal," he said. "Like so many of my countrymen, Ms. Darnell, I have devoted a great deal of my time to trying to help my country recover the documents, papers, artifacts, and icons that were plundered by the Allied forces at the end of the war."

Porter leaned back in his chair and laughed. "What Kritzmer keeps forgetting to mention is that he and his Nazi buddies were the ones who stole the damn stuff in the first place."

Kritzmer ignored the captain. "As I was saying, Mr. Wages, we all have our agendas. Mr. Vance and Captain Porter here are interested in the recovery of the bullion for purely mercenary reasons. Quite obviously, Dr. Fredrich and I have other interests."

Kritzmer was the kind who kept trying to manufacture a smile and never succeeded. "When we recover the bullion from the U-564, I will have reclaimed a part of the Fatherland's heritage."

68

"And a hell of a lot of money," Porter added.

"True. Herr Vance has promised a rather attractive sum of money to our national archives," Kritzmer said. "As you can tell from Captain Porter's contributions, not everyone associated with this effort is so patriotic in his thinking."

At that point, Packy turned her charm on Porter. "How about you, Captain? How did you get wired into Vance's operation?"

Porter ran his index finger around the rim of his glass and shrugged his shoulders before he began to speak. "Take a look around you," he said. "What do ya see? In case you hadn't noticed, Old Man Vance didn't send you on no luxury cruise. He plunked your ass down smack dab in the middle of one of the biggest bodies of stinkin' stagnant water on the face of the Earth. And for what purpose?"

"The answer seems fairly obvious to me," Packy said. "If we find the sunken vessel, there's more than enough money to justify a little discomfort."

"Let me tell ya somethin', little lady," Porter said with a grunt. "Ambrose Vance don't care shit about that money. He's got more now than any man could spend in six lifetim s. His thing is his damn ego. Ask any schoolboy who the greatest maritime salvage expert in the nineties is and he'll tell you Mel Fisher. Hellfire, Mel Fisher is ten leagues ahead of Vance."

Porter paused just long enough to mop the

sweat off of his brow with his handkerchief. "Hey, I'm tellin' ya this ain't no Holy Grail like Kritzmer here is tryin' to make it sound. We're lookin' for a goddamn German submarine—a submarine that scuttled one of its own, killed off its crew, and skipped off with part of the Spanish treasury. Now tell me just how lofty a goddamn goal that can be. I got news for ya. There's more to this Sargasso thing than findin' a bunch of damn gold bars. Vance wants a bigger place in the history books than Mel Fisher."

Porter took a drink, then wiped his mouth with the back of his hand and laughed. "Wages, you don't know the half of it."

"Meaning?" I wondered whether China Porter could give me any specifics or whether he just wanted to hear himself talk.

"You'll see," he said cryptically. "You'll see."

The big man poured himself another bourbon. His focus switched from the conversation to the glass in hand. From that point on, the conversation hit a lull. Finally Porter and Kritzmer announced that they were calling it a evening.

As Porter stood up, he returned to the subject of the downed *Hedgehog*. "We're goin' down to take another look for her in the mornin'. When we lost that barge, we not only lost some damn good men, but we also lost some damned important equipment."

"Who's going down?" I asked.

"Brimley and Lord."

"Got room for one more?"

"Why not? Might as well get your feet wet," Porter said. "We'll see how good you are. How about *her*? I hear she's done some diving."

I had no intention of volunteering Packy for any of the underwater expeditions until I knew more about what was afoot. At that particular moment, I was focusing on something else altogether.

"What about Brimley?" I said. "Is there some reason why he wasn't here tonight?"

Before Porter could answer that question, Kritzmer interrupted with his own observation. "It might be well, Herr Wages, if you would inquire about a number of things aboard this ship. In my opinion, our esteemed employer's objectives are not being served."

"Before we can continue our search for that damn U-boat, we'll have to recover some equipment from that barge," Porter said.

The two men glared at each other until Kritzmer excused himself. Porter waited, then announced his own departure. Again he stopped just as he was about to leave. "We're plannin' to put the divers over the side at 09:30, Wages."

When Packy was certain both men were gone, she polished off the last of her wine and started to laugh. "What the hell have we gotten ourselves into, Elliott?"

I shook my head. "Ninety minutes with those two and I've got more questions than when we started."

"Like?"

"What about this guy Brimley?"

"He's got a good reputation," Packy said. "He's been the lead on several big salvage dives. From everything I hear, he knows his business."

Vance had prepared a roster of the *Barbella*'s personnel for us, and while I listened to Packy's assessment, I dug it out. Brimley's profile was brief.

Lucas Brimley, (Luke), 46, Boston, single, Lauderdale Salvage, 11 years, certified, D.I.D., Op Lic. 45987, contract date 2/25/94, Blanchard ver.

"That's curious," I muttered.

Packy tilted her head to one side. "What's curious?"

"Behind most of the names on the personnel roster there's a notation: 'Blanchard ver.' Got any idea what that means?"

"Maybe Vance had some agency verify employment and credentials. Or maybe that's where they were bonded. I do recognize the names of the divers. They're all pros."

On the whole, Packy's guess made sense. So I checked the names of China Porter and Maydee Hew. There was no "Blanchard ver." notation next to the name of either man. Maybe my observation was important, maybe it wasn't. I folded up the piece of paper and stuffed it back in my shirt pocket.

When I stood up, Packy asked, "What now?"

"We get some sleep and tomorrow we look for the world's only disappearing salvage barge."

"I notice you didn't invite me," she said.

Anything I would have said would have smacked of male chauvinism. So I said what was on my mind. "I'm not buying everything I'm hearing."

"You know I can outdive you," Packy said.

"Try it my way."

Packy did one of her tiptoe routines. Stretching, she kissed me full on the lips. Everything was there but the invitation. "Thanks for caring," she said.

I've heard it said that the Sargasso does strange things to people. I could think of no other explanation when, moments after leaving Packy, I found the only other woman aboard the *Barbella* sprawled across my bunk examining the contents of my survival kit. She had the Mauser in one hand and my miniature voice recorder in the other.

The lady took a long look at me before she spoke. "You know, when I heard that Ambrose was sending us another so-called salvage expert, I figured it would be another sorry excuse for a human being. But from the looks of things, you may not be so bad."

"By whose standards?" I laughed.

The woman eyed me from head to foot. "I like

your credentials. But I do have to ask if you are a cop."

"Why? Don't you like cops?"

"Policemen are our friends," she said, "but that doesn't mean I want to sleep with one. Anyway, if you're not a cop, are you an insurance investigator?"

"Wrong again."

She fell into a mock pout. "Okay, you win. It's your turn. Now you guess who I am."

"Jewel Simon," I said.

"I'm impressed. Ambrose finally sent us someone who's clever enough to do his homework."

"I hate to burst your bubble, but Vance gave me a duty roster. There was only one woman on board." I showed her the piece of paper. "See? Right here. Jewel Simon. It tells me everything I need to know: height, weight, date of birth, and duty on board."

"Well," she said, casually dropping the Mauser on the bed, "I guess there's no need for me to try to construct some elaborate story about my life prior to Ambrose Vance, is there. You probably already know all about me."

Jewel Simon had mastered the decidedly feminine trick of appearing both delighted and disappointed at the same time—delighted that Ambrose had remembered, disappointed that there was no opportunity to be mysterious.

I did not tell her that Ambrose Vance's personnel roster did not reveal nearly as much as

I was letting on, but the information it did contain was clearly working in my behalf.

Jewel Simon was either thirty-five or 105 years old. She had the taut, clear skin and incandescent eyes of youth, but she wore her savvy mask like a medal of honor. Her dark brown hair was drawn up in a tight little bun, and her mouth alternated between asexuality and smoldering sensuality.

"Well, then," I said, "since there are no big revelations to sort through, let's have a drink." I dug around in my luggage until I found the jug of Scotch. "You can tell me what a project coordinator does on a salvage ship."

The lady scowled and perched on the edge of the bunk. "Never mind all of that. Why are you here?" When I hesitated, she said, "Ambrose is pissed, isn't he."

I held up my hand. "I think he has the right to be. For starters, three men have been lost. Then there is a nasty rumor going around that a very large barge has come up missing. And there is the rather disturbing matter of no progress being made on locating the U-564."

"No one actually saw the *Hedgehog* disappear."

"Then you heard it sink?"

"I didn't say that."

Some women can look a man right in the eye without so much as a hint of what they're really thinking. Jewel Simon had that feminine trick down to perfection. I had the feeling she would have happily let me hang myself.

I sagged back against the bulkhead. "You too, huh? Look, Ms. Simon. I've been aboard this floating den of intrigue for just over six hours now, and I've yet to get a straight answer from anyone. If you want to know why Ambrose Vance's sent me out here, consider what I just said."

Jewel Simon shrugged. "Any other observations?"

"One or two. It didn't take long to learn that Porter and Kritzmer are singing from different sheet music. Does Vance know that?"

"Ambrose knows everything—or least he should—and we know who and what we are. What we don't know is which side you are going to come down on."

"Neither do I yet."

Jewel pushed herself to her feet. "You realize, of course, that you walked in before I had the opportunity to go through your luggage. The others are going to be very disappointed when I tell them that the only thing I learned about you is that you are not a cop, an insurance investigator, or a professional diver. But the fact that you carry a Mauser will put their nervous little minds at ease."

"You probably could get by without telling them anything."

"But that's my job, Mr. Wages. I'm in charge of gossip as well."

"Then go do your thing."

Jewel Simon brushed past me. "Oh, I almost forgot. There's another reason I came to see you." She reached in her pocket and her hand emerged with a fist-size object wrapped in a piece of cotton. "Unless I miss my guess, Mr. Wages, I have a hunch this will change the way you sleep tonight."

After she was gone I closed the cabin door and examined Jewel's little gift. At first, I wasn't certain what it was. It was too big for a shark's tooth—at least it was too big for any shark's tooth I was familiar with.

I laid the object on the desk, opened my survival kit, and took out the tape measure. The mysterious gift measured 5.13 inches by 5.21 inches. Triangular in shape, the strange object had serrated edges on two sides. It was slightly over an inch thick, if I considered the edge without the serrations as the base. Across that base, there was a slight pinkish discoloration, probably where it had been connected to the tissue in some creature's skull.

I picked my gift up and slumped down in the chair. I had seen some big shark's teeth before, but none of them had been more than one quarter the size of the one I was holding in my hand.

I studied the peculiar object until my eyes started getting heavy. Then I poured myself another drink and leaned my head back. Some time during the night, I must have undressed and crawled into bed. But Jewel Simon was right: That was one night I didn't sleep all that well.

Incident:

Monday, July 11—06:13L

The first feeble rays of Bermuda sun began probing the long shadows in my cabin a good hour before I finally rolled out of my berth and faced reality. Some sadistic soul had left one of those indoor-outdoor thermometers with a wire probe running through the casing of the portholes. It was eighty-six degrees.

I stretched and tried to record the thoughts I'd had since Jewel Simon had departed my little corner of the world. Sometime during the course of the night, perhaps even twice, I had experienced the slight undulating action associated with the ongoing swarm quakes in the area. And while I was aware that such quakes often go unnoticed on a boat the size of the *Barbella*, these particular quakes had been plenty noticeable because of the otherwise torpid surface of the Sargasso.

At the same time, I had been aware of what sounded like an argument conducted in whispers. I screened the voices I had mentally recorded in the last few hours and decided who it wasn't. Neither voice belonged to China Porter; the *Barbella*'s captain didn't strike me as the kind of man who even knew how to whisper. Nor did either voice belong to Kritzmer; Kritzmer's accent would have been too evident. I didn't think either voice was Hew's, and certainly not Jewel Simon's.

I had heard a man's voice: authoritarian, angry, threatening, a voice I had heard before somewhere, sometime. At the moment, though, I didn't have a clue as to where.

I was still trying to put the pieces together when there was a knock at the door. Thinking it would be Packy, I pulled on a pair of boxer shorts and muttered something semicivil. When the door opened, I felt a little foolish. It wasn't Packy. In fact, it wasn't anyone I had even met on the ship. The newcomer stood about six feet tall. He had unruly blue-black hair, deep-set hazel eyes, balanced features, and a nonchalant smile.

"Sorry I couldn't make it down to your briefing session last night," he said, holding out his hand. "That supply boat you came in on had some equipment on board that we had to install so we could get back to work today."

"Then you must be Luke Brimley," I said.

"Guilty." He perched himself on the corner of the writing desk and folded his arms. "Gotta admit, I half expected you to be wearing a halo or walking on water, Wages. When I told her you were joining Vance's expedition, she talked like you can do all of the above and then some."

"Her, who?"

"Dr. Hannah Holbrook. She said the two of you spent a couple of harrowing weeks together a few years ago down in the Caribbean."

That was all it took for me to drop my guard. No further credentials were required. Brimley and I spent the next several minutes discussing Hannah and his diving assignments for one of Hannah's research expeditions.

"How is she?" I finally asked.

"Still lovely, still charming, if that's what you mean." That was what I meant.

While Brimley recited a litany of equipment repairs that had been necessary before divers could return to the search for the U-564, my thoughts hovered around those weeks with Hannah.

"Look," Brimley said. "We're having our pre-dive session at 08:30 hours. We'll be going over some of the new computer charts and some of the data we accumulated prior to losing the *Hedgehog*. I understand both you and the Dar-

81

nell woman have done some diving. We're counting on your help."

"First observation: I was looking at your charts last night. None of them had coordinates."

"Ambrose's idea. Can't say that I blame him. Divers come and divers go. Ambrose says once they go, he doesn't want them returning—at least not with some other salvage crew. When they leave the project, we pay them off. They forfeit any claim to anything we uncover later."

So far I liked what Brimley was saying. There was the little matter of clearing up the extent of my actual diving experience, but I could do that later.

"Were you anywhere near deck the night the *Hedgehog* went down?"

Brimley sobered for a minute before the boyish grin crept back over his face. "I see you've been talking to Maydee Hew."

"Put it this way: He talked to me. All I did was listen."

"And he told you that it was like some ghost just slipped in through the fog and spirited away an oversized utility barge weighing several hundred tons."

"In so many words."

"I'm afraid Jewel's been pumping him and the rest of the crew full of that Bermuda Triangle stuff. No doubt you were warned about Jewel Simon."

"Nary a word."

Brimley laughed. "On paper, at least, Jewel is our so-called project coordinator. And I have to admit, she does a pretty good job. She seems to know a good bit about almost every aspect of the operation. On the other hand, she can be a little unnerving when she claims to be psychic. Some of the yarns she spins get pretty wild. Lately she's been warning us—are you ready for this—that we're beginning to irritate some damned giant sea creature."

I reached into my valise, pulled out the cloth-wrapped packet Jewel had left behind the previous evening, and pitched it on the bunk. "Is this what she's talking about?"

Brimley unwrapped my mysterious present and examined it. His brow furrowed as he rolled it over in his hand. "What the hell is it? It looks like a shark's tooth but it's too damn big for that."

"Don't know. Jewel stopped by last night to introduce herself. She left it with me."

"Does she know what it is?"

"She implied that she did."

"There's a way to find out for sure," Brimley said. "Kritzmer has a computer setup and reference library down in his lab that would make your mouth water. It's run by his associate, a man by the name of Marion Fredrich. He's not much on small talk, but he seems to be the resident authority on the Sargasso. Maybe he could give you some clues."

As Luke Brimley prepared to leave, he repeated the time of the predive meeting. I was still juggling the pieces of my little mystery and evaluating Brimley's suggestion on Kritzmer's assistant. At that particular moment, I wasn't certain how many people I wanted to know about Jewel's little jewel.

I glanced at my watch and realized I still had a half hour before Brimley's meeting. That moment seemed like as good a time as any to introduce myself to Marion Fredrich. I headed for the lab.

Dr. Marion Wilhelm Fredrich was a moon-faced little man with wire-rimmed glasses and a sparse head of hair. He was the prototypical lab rat. He wore a white lab coat and carried a clipboard, and he was the only one I had met thus far on the *Barbella* who looked as though he had not been hung out to dry in the Bermuda sun. His complexion was sickly white and pasty. When I knocked and walked into the lab, he was too engrossed in his work to respond.

"Dr. Fredrich?" I asked.

He appeared to be slightly annoyed that I had interrupted his train of thought, and finally acknowledged me. He wasn't the homeliest person I had ever met, but he wasn't far from it.

"Yes," he said. "Do you want something or do you practice being rude?"

"Rude?" At eight o'clock in the morning, I wasn't expecting a frontal assault.

"You are interrupting my work."

"Sorry," I muttered, and dropped Jewel's little

package on the table in front of him. When he saw me waiting, he sighed, unwrapped the object, and held it up to the light. Only then did he look at me; his expression had changed.

"Where did you get this?" His accent was as thick as Kritzmer's and about as friendly.

"Luke Brimley thought you might be able to identify it for me."

Fredrich laid the object on the table and went back to what he had been doing. But he gave himself away by stealing furtive glances at Jewel's gem. Finally he said, "There is no mystery. You have a shark's tooth. That should be fairly obvious."

"What kind of a shark?"

There have been occasions when I've been told my unflagging persistence tends to get under people's skin, but this was a record. I had been in Fredrich's lab less than five minutes and already his patience was gone. He picked up the tooth, sized me up, determined that my proportions were at least twice his, and decided there was merit in civility.

Fredrich waddled over to his reference library and searched around until he found the volume he was looking for. He rifled through the pages and finally stabbed his finger at the section he wanted me to read. There was a picture of a drawing that compared a tooth similar to the one I had given Marion Fredrich with one very much like the one that Lucas Brimley wore on a gold chain around his neck.

"The size and configuration of the tooth you are showing me," Fredrich wheezed, "is not unlike that of a *Carcharodon megalodon*."

"A what?"

"In other words, that tooth came from a creature that was probably at least five times larger than a *Carcharodon carcharias*," Fredrich said.

I moved in a little closer to him. "Try plain, old-fashioned English." I was trying to intimidate the good doctor without actually rapping him on the head.

"Five times larger than that of a Great White." When I let out an involuntary whistle, the little man knew he had me. He decided it was time to heap on a little dazzle. "All things being equal, the mouth of the creature that tooth came from could very likely swallow what you Americans call a pickup truck."

When I countered by asking what kind of a pickup truck, Fredrich graced me with the same expression of total disdain that China Porter had worn earlier.

"I don't suppose that computer of yours can tell you when's the last time anyone around these parts saw one of these so-called *megalodons*?"

"The *Carcharodon megalodon* has been extinct for millions of years," Fredrich said, bristling. "Therefore it is highly unlikely that anyone around these parts, as you so quaintly put it, has seen one of these creatures."

The time to back off had come. I had accomplished my goal. Marion Fredrich had, in fact, confirmed my suspicions about the *megalodon* tooth, and I was now reasonably confident he would tell Kritzmer that the new guy was too dumb to be a threat.

"May I inquire where you obtained that specimen?" Fredrich asked.

"It was a gift from Jacques Cousteau," I said.

For a fleeting moment, Marion Fredrich looked impressed. Then he realized I was jerking his chain, and his dour little scowl returned.

Before Fredrich became completely annoyed, I muttered a semicivil thank-you, made certain I retrieved the *megalodon* tooth, and headed for Brimley's meeting.

By the time I got there, everyone on Vance's A list was accounted for. Packy had introduced herself around the room. She was sitting with the two remaining divers, Gabe Lord and Kit Bench, both of whom she later informed me she had worked with on other projects.

China Porter, Eberhard Kritzmer, Maydee Hew, and Jewel Simon were also sitting around the table. Jewel moved over and made room for me. Luke Brimley was standing at the head of the table, where he could operate the slide projector and refer to his wall charts.

"If I repeat something that most of you regard as common knowledge, be aware that I'm doing it for the benefit of our newcomers, E. G. Wages and Packy Darnell," Brimley said. "But for everyone's information, a little before midnight last night, Gabe, Kit, and I finished replacing and installing most of the monitoring equipment we lost on the *Hedgehog*. As a result, I think we're just about ready to make a couple of test dives. If everything comes off without a hitch and the equipment tests out, we should be ready to make another exploratory dive early tomorrow morning. Then, if we can locate the barge, we'll see what else we can recover. With any luck at all, we should be able to get this project back on track by the end of the week."

Out of the corner of my eye, I caught Kritzmer nodding his approval. He was still nodding when Marion Fredrich entered the room and took a seat next to him.

"Good, Marion is here," Brimley said. "Let's start with his report."

The little man stood up and cleared his throat. More than any other person in the room, Marion Fredrich looked like someone out of his element.

"While Professor Kritzmer and I regard what happened to our colleagues as unfortunate, the interlude since the accident has, in fact, given us the opportunity to install some new software and at the same time give further study to some of the peripheral considerations of our salvage effort."

China Porter slumped back in his chair. "For Christ's sake, Fredrich, knock off the damn double talk. Get to the point."

Fredrich braced himself. What little color there was in his face drained. "I believe," he said, "that you will find we now have improved our ability to communicate with personnel working below at the actual salvage site. Camera commands, ROV commands, and personnel response will all be handled on the same frequency. In addition, the new WMO software should enable us to give your divers a more accurate forecast on the timing and frequency of the cluster or swarm quakes."

They say that the only dumb question is the one a person doesn't ask. So I asked the one that had been bothering me. "For us newcomers, what is the SOP on swarm quakes?"

Being the new guy on the block, I thought it best not to elaborate on my theory that God had screwed up on three of his inventions: tornadoes, earthquakes, and sharks. Thus far I had been unable to find any redeeming value in any of them.

"Any intensity over 2.12 and a frequency interval of five or more, we bring everyone to the surface," Brimley said.

"Did anyone record the measurements the night the *Hedgehog* disappeared?" I asked.

Brimley went to one of the charts and pointed to an area marked with four red pins. "This is coordinate five-K, Elliott. This is the area we were searching when our difficulties began."

"How big is the area indicated?"

"Each of the colored sectors is nine square

miles. We have already given coordinates four-K immediately east of five-K and four-F and five-F, north and west of the target, a pretty thorough going-over." As an afterthought, he added, "Absorption sonar gives us some reason to feel that the five-K sector looks promising."

"Thus far we have isolated two distinct anomalies, Mr. Wages," Kritzmer said. "Unfortunately, the swarm quakes curtailed our dive activities for several days prior to the onset of the bad weather and the *Hedgehog* incident."

"You're referring to topographical anomalies?" I asked.

Luke Brimley reached over and turned on the overhead projector. "Check out this sonar profile of a rather long and unusual configuration in the 295.0-to-310.0 range of the five-K. The day we took these readings, we were obtaining a complete absorption pattern with the exception of the area designated in red."

The object Brimley was referring to appeared to be in some sort of a depression, a ditch or perhaps a trench. Whatever it was, it was completely inconsistent with the topographical profile of the surrounding terrain. The anomaly was curious enough in and of itself, but what made it all the more so was the fact that it was near the center of the swarm-quake activity.

"What kind of depth are we dealing with in that area?" I asked.

Brimley squinted at the readings. "Surrounding terrain eighty feet, no more. The ditch we think we've located is an unknown. This whole area is a ridge with a minor plateau configuration. On either side of it, it drops away fast. Now we think there might be a depression right in the middle."

"The top of an underwater mountain range?"

"Possibly," Fredrich said. "There is sufficient reason to suspect that we could be dealing with some sort of crustal anomaly in this region as well. Thus far our tests have been inconclusive."

When he said that, I looked at the little man in a new light. He was actually trying to be helpful and explain the incongruents.

"What Marion theorizes," Brimley said, "is that we are dealing with a section of the ocean floor where there is strong evidence of tectonic action."

"That would be the case throughout this region," Fredrich said, "but for some reason it is far more in evidence here."

"The situation becomes more clear when you see it from this angle," Brimley said. "This is a computerized side-section profile of the area where the anomaly exists. Note how there is almost a pie-crust configuration."

As he explained, Brimley pointed to different features of the five-K site. "Here is the dome that brings the ocean floor to within eighty or so feet of the surface, and here is the area immediately surrounding that dome. So far, Dr. Fredrich has supervised the placement of two monitor probes into the area beneath that dome. Indications are that the area beneath the crust is a relatively hostile environment."

I was beginning to understand the problem. Simply stated, both Brimley and Fredrich were indicating that the five-K salvage site sector was, if not downright dangerous, at least damned unstable. In theory, too much activity by Vance's salvage crew—or the resultant impact of the ongoing swarm quakes—could make the salvage site a risky place to be if the swarm quakes occurred. Bottom line: If Luke Brimley and his cast of divers just happened to be working the salvage site when the intensity of the swarm quakes exceeded 2.12, Cameron and his technicians aboard the *Hedgehog* wouldn't be the only casualties.

To my surprise, China Porter turned around in his chair and asked, "How do you read this, Wages? Think it's risky?"

I shook my head. "Don't know. Let me come back at you with another question. Is there any reason to believe the anomaly in sector five-K is not man-made? Or to put it another way, what else could be causing the anomaly?"

"It could be the sheared edge of or a minute fracture feature in the crustal material," Fredrich said.

"Or it could any one of a thousand ships," Brimley said.

"And up until now the thing that's been holding us back is the equipment we lost on the *Hedgehog*?" I asked.

When both Brimley and Fredrich nodded, I decided there was no better time to ask the question. And there was no better person to start with than Porter. "How about it, China? What do you think happened to the barge?"

The big man shrugged off the question. "How the hell would I know? I was asleep in my cabin. Ask Hew or Kritzmer or Carson. They were on the bridge, not me."

"Why don't you ask me?" Jewel Simon said.

"All right, Jewel, I might as well start with you. What happened?

"First you must understand the magnitude of the influence," Jewel said. "The Bermuda Triangle is powerful. It covers perhaps five hundred thousand square miles, and in the last one hundred fifty years, more than one hundred ships and airplanes have disappeared in this area. In many of those cases, there was insufficient time for the ship's captain or the plane's pilot to even radio a distress message."

I tried to assess the crew's reaction to Jewel even while she was speaking. Porter and Brimley had been around long enough to scoff openly, but be secretly concerned. Eberhard Kritzmer wasn't exactly embracing what Jewel was saying, but he was listening. Fredrich was intolerant, but on the other end of the spectrum, the two divers appeared to be paying attention.

"If an entire squadron of airplanes can simply disappear, along with the two search planes that were dispatched to find them," Jewel said, "then why is it so difficult for everyone to accept the possibility that a simple barge could vanish?"

"What would you have us believe, Ms. Simon? That it was simply sucked up into thin air?" Fredrich asked.

"Why not, Mr. Fredrich? Why not? But instead of being sucked up, as you so quaintly put it, why not sucked down into the depths of the Sargasso."

Packy was making faces at me—faces that indicated she thought that Jewel Simon's old logic circuits needed reconfiguring.

"How do you explain," Jewel asked "the disappearance of the British frigate *Atlanta*? There was a crew of more than two hundred aboard. Or how about the U.S.S. *Cyclops*? No bad weather, no radio messages, no distress calls, and no wreckage. There were three hundred ten men aboard the *Cyclops*. No bodies were ever found. Want me to go on? The *Marine Sulphur Queen*, the *Raifuku Maru*, the *Milton Iatrides*, the *Anita*—all disappeared without a trace."

There was no telling how much farther Jewel Simon would have carried her diatribe. But we were spared when Luke Brimley said, "Fascinating, Ms. Simon, but that's a subject for debate at another time. Ambrose Vance is paying us to locate the U-564. And now that we've completed our repairs, both Captain Porter and I think it would be a good idea if we started earning our keep."

Brimley's words were enough to shut Jewel Simon off. I had a hunch he had done it before. She stopped, closed her file, and inquired if there were any last-minute questions.

As Porter, Brimley, and the rest of the crew filed out of the briefing session, I checked my watch. The time was 09:11. Minutes later, when I stepped out on the sunbaked deck of the *Barbella*, the temperature had already soared into the low nineties.

Of the five divers preparing to make the *Barbella* team's first descent since the disappearance of the *Hedgehog*, I was far and away the least experienced. Brimley and his two holdover divers, Gabe Lord and Kit Bench, were known quantities; they had worked together on a number of different projects over the years. Packy, who also had plenty of dive experience of the salvage variety, was a question mark only in the sense that several years had passed since she'd dived with any degree of regularity.

Gabe, a former Navy SEAL and son of one of the original Navy demolition men, had a long dive history. Luke Brimley had known him for twenty years. He was both dependable and knowledgeable. If there was a chink in his armor, it was that he was getting a little long in the tooth for what Brimley needed to accomplish on this project.

Kit Bench, on the other hand, was the prototypical diver. A young forty, he had nerves of steel and the endurance necessary to tackle a job as complicated as the salvaging of the downed U-564. After two months on the project, Brimley had designated Kit Bench as his lead diver.

I had to give Ambrose Vance credit. He hadn't spared money in outfitting the mission. He had not only hired the best, he had also equipped them with the latest in underwater salvage gear, including APDs complete with continuous telemetry displays in the face lenses. The acrylic shield could be programmed so that the lens displayed data covering everything from a total systems monitor of all life-support data to energy depletion and varying site conditions. Communication with the mother ship as well as other members of the team was accomplished by a closed-loop arrangement that made it possible to gate each receiver. Thus, not only every word, but every sound was recorded on magnetic tape. And as an added feature, the diver riding drag on each dive was equipped with a miniature in-helmet sonar as an extra hostile-detection device. Unlike the others, I was working with some of the gear for the first time.

Brimley had planned the first dive of the day to familiarize everyone with the new system. Although he didn't say it in so many words, he hoped to determine just how much of an asset Packy and I were going to be.

When we went down, Bench led, Packy followed, Brimley opted for the third position in the chain, I was fourth, and Gabe Lord rode drag. At twenty feet, we did our equipment check, and Luke had each of us test the new comsys, which worked like a charm.

Despite Packy's obvious feminine accoutrements, Gabe Lord was referring to us as "the new guys." His continuous barrage of instructions proved helpful, even though the Sargasso was not a new experience for Packy. In comparison with Packy Darnell, I was a rank novice. I just wasn't telling anyone how rank.

As usual, the surface of the Sargasso was nearly stagnant and choked with a tangle of green-brown seaweed known as sargassum. Ten feet below the surface, the sargassum wasn't quite as dense. At a depth of twenty feet, it had thinned still further, but the surface light was completely blocked off. We had immersed ourselves into a world of darkness unlike any I had ever experienced before.

I heard Packy's voice crackle through the headphones mounted in my mask receiver. "How you doin', Elliott?"

I pressed the transmit button and muttered something to let Packy know I understood how to operate the comsys as well as confirm my continuing health. The beam of Brimley's searching halogen momentarily danced across the lens of my mask, and I saw him gesture to Kit Bench to begin the second stage of the descent. Through it all, Brimley and Lord kept up a constant stream of chatter.

"Mark," Lord said.

We each began reciting our vitals. I had used more air than anyone in the group.

"That elongated anomaly that we discussed on the surface should be directly below us," Brimley said.

"Five-K," Bench said.

While we continued the descent, I began reviewing some of the refresher and crash-course research material I had digested after striking the deal with Vance. I remembered one group of photographs taken by the submersible *Aluminaut*, a fifty-one-foot underwater research vessel that could carry three tons of scientific equipment and sustain a crew of seven for up to three days.

On its way to a working depth of nearly ten thousand feet, the *Aluminaut* had taken some interesting pictures near the surface. One of them was of the Bimini Wall—an enormous underwater placement of monoliths with right-angle corners and pillars that would have been impossible for the sea to design and carve by mere chance.

It wasn't the first time I had seen those particular pictures, nor the first time I had shared them with anyone. I'd shown them to Packy the night we signed on with Vance, and she had voiced aloud the question that bothered most of us: If there wasn't anything to this Bermuda Triangle business, how had those formations gotten there?

When we reached the bottom, at fifty feet, I started sweating. The water was both calm and black, with a horizontal visibility of less than five feet. Without the halogens, I might as well have been in one of those caves in New Mexico.

"This is it?" Packy asked over her communication link.

Brimley confirmed that it was, and began issuing instructions. "Reference your CU. Gabe, go with five-K-a. Kit, use five-K-b. Packy, try the next set of coordinates in the sequence; that would be five-K-c. Use your G-H probe, repeat on a ten-plus cycle, and record anything that arouses curiosity."

The team fanned out, and the illumination from their individual lamps was swallowed up in the darkness. I followed Brimley, and watched while he assembled the three piece, thirty-six-inch-long G-H steel detection probe and waited for a signal.

There was no distortion in Brimley's transmission. His voice sounded no different from on the surface. "Gabe Lord identified and numbered this anomaly just before we lost the barge. While we couldn't actually get down here to poke around, we have been able to run an absorption profile on it. So far we don't have anything conclusive."

"Are you saying that it's possible that this is a thin area in the crust?" I asked.

Brimley nodded. "That or something else. If the swarm quakes stay on the quiet side, we may be able to determine what we've got here. Haven't felt one yet today, but this is the area that's plagued with them. Don't see many above the 2-1-2 intensity level, though, and at that level, they're more of a nuisance than a hazard."

"It's when they spike up to a 2-1-5 or up on the scale that they can get a little nasty," Lord said. "Before he died, Cameron recorded one in the 2-1-7-plus range. When that happens, you can get some major shifts. Topographical changes are even possible."

"Avalanches, rock slides, major shifts," Brimley said. "The nasty stuff."

I could hear their descriptions, but in the darkness, despite the high-intensity halogens, there wasn't much to see. On the surface, I had viewed the anomaly profiled via the computer. Now I was standing on it. I started to ask another question, but Brimley held up his hand. His head was cocked to one side as though he was listening to something.

"Hear that?" Brimley said.

I shook my head. I was probably far enough away from Brimley that in the darkness he couldn't see my response.

"I'm getting something," he said. "If what we're standing on is nothing more than an irregularity in the floor at this point, I shouldn't be getting any chatter. If you're getting this transmission, Elliott, lock in .97 on your scanner."

I did, and heard a faint pinging sound. When Brimley increased the volume, the sound was more pronounced.

"Is that it?" I asked.

Brimley withdrew the shaft probe and inserted it again, this time at a point where the ground began to slope away. He listened for several seconds, removed the probe, and tried again at a new location. Then I heard his voice bark out a command to the other divers.

"Mark your coordinates. If you're onto something, stay with it. If you're not, I need some help over here. I've got something, but no discernible profile yet."

Like ghosts, their halogens began to emerge from the surrounding darkness. The lamps were little more than faint and amorphous illuminations in the green black. I could hear the comsys crackling with chatter.

"What have you got?" Bench asked.

"Perimeters?" Packy asked.

That was when I really began to feel that something was going wrong. There was a momentary shudder, and all of a sudden, the floor of the Sargasso began to heave and buckle. There was a hissing sound, then something akin to thunder, rolling, almost deafening.

In rapid sequence came a series of oscillations and vibrations. The first round was just a teaser. On the second pass, I felt both my feet go out from under me and I fell backward amid what had become a horizontal avalanche of boulders, rocks, and massive chunks of coral.

"Goddamn the—" Bench said, but his voice was cut off and there was an empty buzzing sound in the comsys. In an eerie and surreal slow motion, I saw him duck away from a tumbling boulder and somehow spin away from another. Even so, his light went out.

Just as suddenly as the tremors began, they ended. The water was murky enough with debris to render the halogens totally ineffective. For a moment there was static in the comsys. Then Brimley's voice edged through.

"Sound out," he said. "Report in."

"I think I'm in one piece," Packy said, somewhat shakily. Her transmission was strong, but in the absence of light there was no way to tell where she was.

"Wages?" Brimley demanded. "Report."

I pressed down on the send button. "As near as I can tell, I'm still in one piece." I didn't tell him that, to the best of my knowledge, I didn't think any of the debris had even come close to me.

"Kit, where the hell are you?" Brimley shouted.

"Scraping the pieces together," Bench said. He sounded as though he still wasn't certain he was going to be able to find enough to complete the job.

"How about it, Gabe? Report in." Brimley said. "Gabe, damn it, report in."

After a moment of silence, Brimley said, "All right, everyone, fan out. Activate every piece of illumination gear you've got. Gabe may have just had his comsys knocked out, or he could be in trouble. But be careful."

For a moment, the underwater scene with our halogens reminded me of fireflies deep in a forest. One moment you could see them; the next moment you couldn't. The illumination was brief and inconsequential. But at that point, any light was reassuring.

In the meantime, I conducted my own systems check. After ascertaining that everything was still working, I adjusted the beam of my chest halogen to scan the floor of the area ahead of me. At best, the light penetrated the darkness no more than six to eight feet. Beyond, there was the forbidding blackness.

I could hear Bench and Brimley on the comsys. Somewhere off in what sounded like another world, I could hear other sounds I couldn't identify, sounds of the Sargasso.

The mission was starting to come unwrapped. Packy reported an equipment malfunction. Kit Bench had some sort of hand injury, and Brimley himself sounded slightly disoriented.

"Where was Gabe when he last reported in?" I asked.

Brimley checked his log and said, "Five-K-a.

See that green area on your screen? Gabe's code is green."

I checked my mask display. If I was reading the display right, I was less than fifty feet away from Gabe's position. "I'm in the area. So far, nothing to report."

The hundred or so square meters that defined the perimeters of the five-K-a sector marked an area where there was an indication of change in the bottom features. For one thing, there was more light. In all probability, the sargassum on the surface was less dense. Either that, or the shifting and agitation caused by the quake had created a variation in the light-penetration pattern.

The sector where I was operating had the appearance of a beach—a sandy expanse void of ocean-floor vegetation. The ripples and patterns in the sand indicated the drift of the prevailing underwater current and the generally easterly direction of that movement. I switched the halogen's reflector shield to a broad-sweep configuration.

"See anything?" Brimley asked.

"Where the hell are you?" I demanded. "It sounds like you're right on top of me."

"Comin' at you from the opposite direction," Brimley said. "See anything?"

"Not yet. The reduction in surface seaweed cover is giving me an effective eight-to-twelve-foot search arc on each sweep."

"Kit, Packy, see anything?" Brimley asked.

The question was directed at the both of them because they hadn't established contact for several minutes.

"Nothing in my sector," Packy said.

Kit Bench's transmission was garbled. I could hear him talking, but I was unable to make out what he was saying. I was still listening to the exchange between Brimley and Packy when I first noticed a slight depression in the sand. But when I began using the steel prod from the absorption probe to investigate the indentation, I thought I detected movement.

I increased the volume and tried again. The more I stabbed at the sand with the probe, the more it became apparent that the hole was several feet deep and a good twenty or so feet across.

Prior to the dive, Brimley had supplied each of us with a camera. I took mine out and began shooting pictures of the depression. I still had a couple of angles to go when we all heard Kit scream.

The shrill, piercing sound was bouncing around inside my comsys when I heard Brimley's voice asking, "Kit, where the hell are you?"

Brimley's senior diver had lost it. For the next several seconds, there was nothing but confusion. The audio-detection unit indicated Bench's transmissions were coming from a northwesterly direction, which wasn't a hell of a lot of help considering the fact that, because of the anomaly, the compass was spinning like a cheap top. I activated the NV unit to see if I could pick up any kind of infrared image on my lens mask. When I did, I had two hot spots, both converging on the northwesterly fix where the transmissions had originated.

"He's in five-K-d," Brimley said.

In five-K-d, the darkness was blacker then any I had experienced. There was no sign of Brimley, but I shoved the beam of my halogen around until I picked up Packy; she was hovering over Bench. In the sand before them was an object that, from where I was standing, I couldn't quite make out.

By the time I did, I wished I hadn't. It was Gabe Lord or, maybe I should say, what was left of him. The top half of him was there, but the bottom half was missing.

We managed to get what was left of Gabe Lord's body to the surface and onto the deck of the *Barbella*. Brimley was clearly the head honcho when he was leading Vance's troops underwater, but it was equally obvious he wanted no part of being in charge when we were topside.

Porter, Kritzmer, Fredrich, and Jewel Simon clustered around. The questions began the minute we stripped out of our gear. Had we seen what had happened? Had anyone seen what had caused the tremors? Where had they happened? When? How?

Jewel Simon finally pulled me away from the others. "Did you see it happen?"

I shook my head. Now that I was putting two and two together, I didn't like my math.

"We were each working different sectors," I said. "Gabe was at the opposite end of the grid from where I was."

"Surely you saw or felt something," Jewel said.

She had the kind of cold black eyes that bored into a person when she wanted answers. At that moment I wasn't certain I liked the woman who called herself Jewel Simon. She was a bit too insistent.

But I let her take me by the arm and steer me away from where the salvage crew had assembled. In the background, I could hear China Porter trying to establish some semblance of order. After Maydee Hew had covered up Gabe Lord's body, he watched us.

"You must tell me what you saw down there," Jewel said. "Leave nothing out. It's the only way."

"Damn it, Jewel. I didn't see anything. Kit Bench is the one who discovered Lord's body. I was a long way away from whatever happened."

"Tell me what you saw where you were."

"Nothing," I said. "There's nothing down there except sand and an occasional unexplained but equally uninteresting depression in that sand."

Jewel looked slightly exasperated. "Tell me about the depressions—describe them."

"There's not that much to describe," I said.

"The depressions appear to be somewhere in the neighborhood of thirty to forty feet across, and maybe five or six feet deep. I was attempting to do a probe analysis on one of them when Bench discovered Lord's body."

"Twenty to thirty feet across and five to six feet deep," Jewel said. "How many of them?"

"Several. I didn't count them."

"You should have," Jewel said. "Those holes may be far more significant than any gold we recover."

Incident:

Monday, July 11—17:45L

By late afternoon, heavy cloud cover had moved in, and the Sargasso skies deteriorated into a dull, poisonous color. China Porter held the obligatory debriefing session with the entire dive team, then he arranged with Shula Carson, the *Barbella*'s engineering officer, to have Lord's body stored in one of the ship's empty food lockers.

"Want me to have Ritter go ahead and notify the authorities in Miami?" Carson asked. As a warning he added, "If we do, they'll want a full report."

"Then we'll wait until we have a better idea

about what the hell happened down there," Porter said.

Later, when a steady rain settled in, the *Barbella*'s salvage crew was relegated to a host of mundane chores like equipment repair and studying charts, not the least of which was a detailed schematic of the U-564. Brimley came to my cabin with the oversize drawing and spread it out on my bunk.

He studied it for a moment, then leaned back against the bulkhead and lit a cigarette. "Like it or not, Elliott, you just became a little more involved in this whole affair. Losing Gabe Lord puts us in a real hole. From the beginning, I figured it would take an absolute minimum of four divers plus whatever minor contribution I could make to get this job done. Then we lost the two men when the *Hedgehog* disappeared, and we've been operating shorthanded ever since. What happened down there today only makes the situation worse. We lost a hell of a good man, but we also lost twenty-five percent of our salvage team."

For the most part, there appeared to be a shortage on grief. Gabe Lord's death hadn't exactly spurred a monumental outpouring of remorse. I fixed myself a drink, offered Brimley one, and waited for him to continue.

"Actually, the arrival of you and your friend Packy could have given us a diver to rotate, a definite plus. The problem is, it didn't last long enough for us to capitalize on it."

"For what it's worth," I said, "for the next thirty days, I'm all yours. Then Elliott falls back and assesses his position. I've got a thirty-day contract with Vance. That's all."

"That means you're here for the duration." Brimley smiled. "The one thing I have learned since I signed on is that Ambrose Thurston Vance will approve just about anything or any expense that he thinks will get him closer to that bullion—and that includes hiring more divers or lying to the ones he's already got. He'll approve your rotating back as soon as he's found your replacement. The only problem is, replacements take time. There are a hell of a lot of divers out there, but not many divers can handle a project like this one."

I looked at the drawing of the Type VII-C U-boat. "Out of curiosity, just how certain are you that the U-564 is actually down there?"

"Reasonably certain," Brimley said. "Between Hess's journal and the absorption patterns, there's every reason to believe we're already sitting on it."

"I've seen pictures of aircraft sitting on the floor of the ocean east of here. They're sitting right out there in the open like museum displays. Why isn't that the case with this U-564?"

"Two reasons," Brimley said. "One, if the U-564 was sitting out there in open waters like those aircraft you're referring to, she would have been discovered a long time ago. The salvage boys have been hearing stories about a U-boat loaded with gold bullion for years.

"The difference is, people are misled about how easy it is to locate these finds. They tend to forget that most of the ships and aircraft we uncover in the clearer waters west of here are being located in waters that are shallow and free of sargassum. Folks soon learn it's a whole different ballgame here in the Sargasso. A ship can be lying on the bottom in this part of the ocean and no one would ever know it. It doesn't take the swarm quakes that long to cover them up with a couple of tons of silt.

"Two," Brimley continued, "there isn't any doubt in my mind that Hess intended to come back and recover this gold for himself. Either was going to do it for his beloved Führer, or he intended to rip off what was left, take the gold for himself, and head for South America. Either way, you can go to the bank on this one: Albrecht Hess dying before he returned for the gold wasn't part of his plan."

"So just how many people are looking for this pot of gold?" I asked.

"Back in the sixties, these waters were crawling with divers looking for the U-564. But one by one they began to drop off, and the project was all but written off, as a figment of someone's overly active imagination. Then Vance's first crew found the bullion in the harbor at Infante Dom Henrique, and things got serious all over again.

"When it was learned that Vance had obtained what was reputed to be Hess's journal, it was generally conceded Vance had the upper hand in the race for the salvage of the U-564."

"You've actually seen this diary?" I asked.

Brimley shook his head. "Can't say that I have, but Porter claims Ambrose Vance showed it to him."

"Can Porter be trusted?"

"That's not the question. The question is, can any man be trusted when you start talking about one hundred and seventy million dollars in gold bullion?"

Brimley had a point. I thought about whom I would be willing to trust under the same circumstances, and I had trouble coming up with names.

"So," I said, "assuming the U-564 is down there and we can get our hands on her, where's the bullion?"

Brimley shrugged. "No one knows for certain. Hess's journal doesn't indicate exactly where it is. We know how the sub was configured, so we've got logic in our favor. Assuming the gold is actually on board, you immediately begin to reason through what Hess could and would have jettisoned to make room for the bullion."

"For example?"

"For openers, start with the torpedoes and the gear required to move the torpedoes. Along with the crew quarters, those two things take up about eighty percent of the available space forward of the control room. Keep in mind that for all practical purposes, the war was over. Hess didn't need either."

I looked at the drawing of the fantail. "Does the same go for the aft section?"

Brimley nodded. "Consider the situation at the time. Hess's mission had changed. We think Hess was charged with getting the bullion to South America. Under optimum conditions, he would have stripped the U-564 of everything that would have slowed him down. By the same token, taking on all that bullion was certain to slow him down. So what does he do? He dumps everything he believes he doesn't have to absolutely have."

"Including his 8.8-cm deck gun and ammo?"

Brimley nodded. "Uh-huh. And the aft conning tower flak gun."

"Crew and crew supplies?"

"He sure as hell didn't need a full complement of men if he didn't intend to do anything but hightail it for South America."

"So you figure the bullion is in the torpedo storage area."

"And the big battery area."

"Didn't I read somewhere that the Nazis built some U-boats that carried only fuel and supplies?"

"The U-564 wasn't one of them," Brimley said. "According to Vance, Hess describes sinking two Liberty ships earlier in his journal."

"All right," I said. "Suppose we locate and get

to the U-564. How do we get inside to get the bullion?"

"That's the easy part. We've run this whole scenario though our computer models. Assuming we haven't overlooked anything, the U-564 is probably lying on her side. If she's lying on her port side, so much the better. In any case, access can be gained through the main hatch in the conning tower or through the forward tubes. If for some reason those options are closed to us, we can always cut our way through with torches, probably in the area of the aft diesel silencers. The only problem with cutting our way through is the time it will take."

I studied the drawing of the fifty-year-old, 221-foot-long German sub and wondered what 170 million dollars in gold bullion looked like. How many torpedoes, mines, and armaments did a man have to strip out of an old VII-C to make way for that kind of wealth?

Brimley and I discussed the project for another hour or so, until the man saw fit to excuse himself and head topside to check on the repair of several pieces of salvage gear.

Following Brimley's departure, I decided to go looking for Maydee Hew and do a little poking around the *Barbella*. I was in luck. Hew was occupying the captain's chair in the wheelhouse, gazing out at the wall of stolid gray and sipping a cup of coffee. He was alone.

"Hell just got worse," he said when he saw me.

"Meaning?"

"Under the best of conditions, the Sargasso is a bitch," he said. "But on a night like this, she's double bitchy."

I glanced over at the ship's weather gauges and decided Maydee Hew was right. The temperature was still hovering in the eighty-degree range, the air was saturated, the wind was dead calm, and the pressure was falling.

"When one of these sets in," Hew said, shaking his head, "it can last for days. Sometimes it gets so a man can't see his goddamn hand in front of his face."

I played Ain't It Awful with the old boy, agreeing with him and trying to ingratiate myself, before I started asking questions. A few minutes later, Hew quit complaining and started talking about the mission. After that, asking questions was the easy part. Understanding what Maydee Hew was saying when he tried to answer them was the hard part. Finally, I got around to what was really on my mind: the room in the bow, the one with the door locked.

Hew smiled. "That area ain't no concern of yours. That's Kritzmer and Fredrich's business."

"What's the big secret?"

Hew shook his head. "Don't know. Can't say as I care to know either. All I know is, when everyone else hits their bunks and the night watch is the only folks up and about this old tub, you'll find Kritzmer and Fredrich down there playin' with their damn secrets."

"What secrets?"

Maydee Hew laughed. Later, when Shula Carson came on the bridge, I knew Maydee had said all he was going to say.

I introduced myself to Carson, who, according to Vance's chart, carried the designation Engineer behind his name. He was a short man with a soft belly and hard hands. He had the sour smell of accumulated sweat about him and an even more revealing accumulation of grease under his fingernails.

"Did you get in touch with the authorities in Miami?" I asked.

"Radio's out," he said without explaining further.

"A damn radio ain't no good when this shit moves in." Maydee said. "You're in the Triangle."

I would have pressed the issue, but Carson and Maydee lapsed into a discussion about a piece of equipment and forgot all about me. That was when I decided to leave.

Thirty minutes later, I was still on deck, but I had worked my way back to the stern. I was staring off into an encroaching fog and a wall of steady rain that was still pelting the *Barbella* when China Porter came to the bridge for his final inspection of the day. He stopped, lit a cigarette, and slouched against the door to the radio room.

"Well," he said, "now you see what Old Man Vance is up against."

I cocked my head to one side. "Maybe you better explain what you mean."

"Hell, you've seen it for yourself already. Got myself one hell of a crew of loonies and losers, haven't I. Vance and that damn Blanchard fella just keep sending them and I'm supposed to make do—just like you and that Darnell dame or whatever her name is. Vance says I'm supposed to be retrieving a goddamn World War II submarine full of bullion, and he sends me a damn writer and some female. You and I both know women don't belong out here, and even if they did, that Simon dame is enough."

Porter smelled as if he had already had too much to drink. Under the circumstances, I didn't know how fruitful a conversation would be.

"Brimley seems to think," I said, "Ms. Darnell is just what the doctor ordered—another experienced salvage diver."

Porter sniffed, scanned the wall of fog that sealed the *Barbella* in her Sargasso cocoon for the night, grunted, and went below. When I looked over at Maydee and Shula Carson, they were trying hard to look as if they hadn't overheard a single word of the conversation between Porter and me.

I looked at my watch. "Think Kritzmer or Fredrich will be in their playroom by now?" I asked, and Maydee Hew nodded.

He was right. Fredrich was tucked away in his observation room in the bow. I didn't bother to knock, and Marion Fredrich didn't bother to tell me to go away. It seemed to be enough to give me a look of contempt and hope I got the message.

Most of Fredrich's toys were duplicates of the laboratory and darkroom housed midship. The only exception appeared to be a series of specimen jars and photographs of what appeared to be underwater objects and scenes. I made a pretense of ignoring the man and studying his photographs and exhibits. I may have been ignoring him, but I knew he was watching me. When I finally turned to look at him, some of the old white-lab-coat belligerence was gone.

"I saw something interesting down there today," I said, "but I don't think it had anything to do with the U-564."

"Why are you telling me about it?" Fredrich asked with a snort.

"I thought you might be interested. Whatever was down there looked a lot like the picture you've got here on the wall."

Fredrich stood up, turned his back for a moment, then looked at me. "What I do on my own time is my business. Professor Kritzmer has certain expectations and I adhere to them. After that, I am on my own."

I shrugged and pointed to a picture of a depression in the floor of the ocean. "How big is this?"

"Two, perhaps two and one-half meters in diameter."

"How deep is the depression?"

"Approximately one-half meter."

"About eighteen inches then?"

Fredrich nodded. He was becoming impatient. He wanted me to go away.

Instead, I walked across the cabin and looked out the two clear acrylic ports located in the prow. The ports were below the waterline, and there was an H7-X Omni camera on a boom that could be rigged to film the activity out of either port. The camera was outfitted with a 1000-cm telephoto and 445 image intensifier.

"How big was it?" Fredrich finally asked. His voice had lost some of its stony indifference.

"Well, I didn't take time to measure it. But it was somewhere in the neighborhood of ten meters—thirty feet, maybe larger."

"Are you certain?" Fredrich demanded.

"I know what I saw. Why? Is it important?"

Fredrich began fumbling through the keys on his computer. He was trying to bring up the file that would show me just how significant my discovery was. "If you are correct in your dimensions, you may have found it."

"Found what?"

Suddenly the image of a large cephalopod appeared on the screen. "Genus: Manta," Fredrich said. "They are seldom larger than twenty feet from the tip of their wing to the tip of the opposing wing. But if the nest size was, as you estimate, ten meters, that would indicate that the devilfish nest you discovered belongs to a creature nearly twice that size."

"Forty feet?" I asked, and let out a whistle. Then I tried to picture what I would do if I ran into a creature that size. "Here in the Sargasso?"

Fredrich reached over, pulled a battered old journal out of a small bookcase, and began to read.

Later that evening, my brother described a terrible incident in which seventeen of his fellow seamen were lost. His ship, the Eber- esol, *was burning out of control, and the captain had ordered the crew to abandon ship. All thirty-two were being evacuated in two lifeboats. The first of these was progress- ing toward its rendezvous with the* Bunder- shaven *when suddenly the sea was agitated by the thrashing of a giant creature that leaped to a prodigious height and fell down upon the lifeboat, crushing the crew and dragging the wreckage to the bottom under its incredible weight.*

When Fredrich finished reading the passage, he asked, "Do you know where this incident is reputed to have happened?"

"This may not come as a surprise to you, Dr. Fredrich, but everything I've ever read about gi- ant sharks and manta rays would lead me to believe that whoever wrote that passage had been sipping a bit too much of the ship's grog."

"It happened right here in the Sargasso," Fredrich said.

"The way I understand it, the Sargasso covers a lot of territory. Besides, how long ago was that?"

Fredrich scurried about the cabin until he came up with a VCR cartridge. Activating the video, he said, "Look at this."

The momentarily shadowy, half-formed images finally crystalized, and I was able to make something out of them. It appeared to be a diver taking probe samples. Then, while I watched, a shadow entered the picture. It hovered over the diver and gradually darkened the picture to the point that the images became barely discernible.

"So?" I asked.

"Keep watching," Fredrich said.

I did, but I couldn't make out what I was seeing. Then, Fredrich reversed the tape and played it a second time. "There," he said, "see it?"

The second time, I did. There appeared to be a giant dorsal fin, a caudal fin that was significantly larger than any I had seen before. With Fredrich's help, I could make out the details of what looked to be an enormous mouth. The latter sent shivers through me.

"How did you get these pictures?" I demanded.

"Gabe Lord," Fredrich said.

"Who is the diver in the picture?"

"Frank Morgan. He was one of the two diver-technicians who went down when the *Hedgehog* disappeared."

"What you're telling me is the two men who can actually authenticate this piece of videotape are both dead. Is that right?"

"Lord filmed it. I do not know if Morgan was aware of this piece of tape."

"Who else knows about this? Porter? Brimley? Shula Carson? Ambrose Vance?"

"There is a method to my madness," Fredrich said. "No one pays much attention to a salvage ship, Mr. Wages, except on those rare occasions when the crew actually salvages something of value. As long as people view us as nothing more than a bunch of fools employed by Ambrose Vance to find what many consider to be a figment of some crazed soul's imagination, we think we'll be left to our own devices. But if the world were to learn that we have perhaps uncovered an area of the ocean where giant forty-foot manta rays and *carcharodon megalodons* still exist, we could expect to be overrun by expeditions from every walk of life except the scientific world. It would become a circus, and recovery of U-564 would become virtually impossible."

I took a deep breath. Taking Marion Fredrich at face value required a bit of doing. On one hand, he sounded like a fugitive from a grade-B science-fiction movie with his talk of giant manta rays and prehistoric sharks. On the other hand, he was making at least some kind of sense. If the world heard about the *magalodon*, it was circus time for sure.

I had him rerun the video of the diver and shark several times. Each time it was a little more terrifying. "And now you and I are the only ones who know that this piece of tape exists," I said.

Three hours after pulling back the sheets and crawling into bed, I still hadn't drifted off to sleep. I tried telling myself it was the heat, but the temperature wasn't that far from tolerable.

I tried blaming it on the oppressive humidity, but in reality, the generator was doing a pretty good job and the cabin air-conditioning seemed to be holding its own.

Finally, I gave up, went down to the galley, got some ice, fixed myself something to drink, and thought about my session with Fredrich. It had taken me less than thirty-six hours to come to the conclusion that salvage crews, like politics, make strange bedfellows. Up until yesterday, thirteen people had been looking for a downed German submarine where the only indication to the sub's actual location may well have been purposely misrepresented.

I wondered if Hess was the kind of guy who would want someone else to recover the bullion if he couldn't. On the other hand, maybe what Hess wanted wasn't even part of the equation.

Maybe the answer as to whether or not the bullion or the sub would ever be located depended on the magnitude of the disturbance caused by swarm quakes. After living through one, I found it easy to believe that fifty years of that kind of seismic activity could disturb enough ocean floor to hide hundreds of U-boats.

So while Porter and Brimley had their hands full trying to determine the location of the U-564, finding it was only half of their battle. What Brimley, Porter, and the rest of the crew didn't know could prove to be equally disastrous. If Fredrich was right and that piece of videotape was authentic, the *Barbella*'s divers had as much to fear from what was prowling around in the depths of the Sargasso waters as they did from the swarm quakes.

I finished my drink, went back to my stateroom, crawled back in my bunk, and lay there. Later, somewhere in that no-man's-land of half sleep, I heard sounds, but not the kinds of sounds a ship at anchor in torpid waters makes.

When the noises continued, I stepped out in the passageway and tried to determine where they were coming from. I worked my way topside, and discovered that the rain had stopped and that the sounds were coming from the area somewhere near the *Barbella*'s stern. I worked my way aft and found Jewel Simon, wearing a nightgown, seated on the winch housing. With her legs tucked up against her chest, and her arms wrapped around her knees, she was staring off into the darkness. Her hair was wet. There was a thin sheen of sweat on her face, and she was smoking a cigarette. She didn't seem at all surprised to see me. "Can't sleep either, huh?"

I shook my head. "I heard noises. It sounded as if someone was chanting. Was it you?"

She laughed and shrugged her shoulders. "Keep looking in that direction. In another hour or so, you'll see the first traces of light through the fog. It's the best time of day out here."

"Was it you?"

Jewel Simon gave me a half smile. "Did it sound like me?"

I decided to try another approach. "Tell me. How and where does a barge the size of the *Hedgehog* just disappear when it slips beneath the surface?"

"You too, huh? It didn't take you long." Jewel laughed. "Sounds as if you're starting to buy into all this craziness."

She offered me a drag on her cigarette. I took it, then remembered why I had quit. As I coughed, she laughed and moved over so I could sit beside her.

For a while, we were both silent, and I began to reflect on how I had managed to get to the *Barbella* in the first place. Time passed, and two hours later, I realized that Jewel Simon had lied to me. There was no trace of the sun. The fog had closed in on the *Barbella* again, and I decided that Maydee Hew had described what I was feeling when he had said, "I think that this must be the same kind of aloneness that you feel when you die."

At 08:00 hours, we donned our wet suits and hauled out our gear as the *Barbella* crew wrestled the sea sleds to the aft deck. We studied the charts and Brimley announced that, because of what had happened to Gabe Lord, we were going to dive in teams. Packy and Kit Bench constituted one team, while Luke and I formed the other. He further indicated that we would work in such a manner until Ambrose Vance sent us another diver.

"We'll work out of the sleds until we figure out what the hell is going on down there," he said. "Whatever you do, don't let your partner out of your sight."

I was given a crash course in operating one of the *Barbella*'s high-tech underwater scooters, an MD-SH-3, which Brimley indicated stood for Manual Dive Submersible Hydrofoil. The sled was red and white with silver-and-black trim. It looked more like an oversized glass-encased snowmobile with a cockpit canopy than a serious research vehicle.

Brimley walked me through the mechanics and described the functions. "In the nose cone," he said, "you've got the forward-looking sonar, OA sonar, a CCD camera, a 35mm camera, your ascent weight-release control, and your vertical thruster. The controls for each function are on the A panel, the illuminated one in front of you. Everything else is on your B-panel, the one between your legs. Your side-scan sonar, doppler transducer, navigational and emergency transponders—and, of course, the main thrusters and elevator controls—are all there. The red light to the right on your cowling is the indicator for your recovery strobe, and the one to the left is for your RF beacon. About the only thing you don't have is a three-hundred-sixty-degree real-time surveillance capability."

"And that's probably the one thing we need," I said.

Brimley knew I was referring to what had happened to Gabe Lord. "That's why we're working in teams from here on out," he said.

I crawled into the MD and situated myself. It was like sitting astride a torpedo. "What kind of speed?"

"Twenty-five KPH for short periods of time, sustained, twenty. Effective search and filming speed seems to be in the four-to-six range. Your GPQ monitor will give you a pretty good indication of what kind of picture you're getting."

As I ran my hand over the panel A controls, familiarizing myself, Brimley said, "I think there's enough there to keep you from getting bored."

"What about the LS system?"

"Constant monitor, computer-controlled. Watch it. It's completely independent of your sled."

When I saw Brimley signal Kit Bench, I knew the training session was over. Bench and Shula Carson were the custodians of the diving gear, and they were still conducting their final systems check when Luke and I each began shouldering our way into the LS harness. Brimley was reciting procedures for the dive sequence, and I was trying to repeat them.

"I talked to Fredrich last night," Brimley said. "According to him, those absorption probes we conducted yesterday raised a few questions. He says we recorded some suspect readings in five-K-d."

"That's where we found Gabe's body."

"That's also where Fredrich thinks we conducted a series of probes into crustal material that was no more than two meters thick."

"What's under it?"

Brimley shrugged. "Don't know. That's why we're going in there with a couple of augers today. Fredrich thinks there is a good possibility one of those swarm quakes may have covered up what we're looking for."

It was exactly 08:31 when my ride, the second of the two MD-SH-3's, was winched over the side of the *Barbella* into the weed-choked waters of the Sargasso. While Brimley waited aboard his sled, Kit Bench and Packy checked my equipment one final time and gave me the go-ahead.

The sargussum weed on the surface where the *Barbella* was anchored floated in large tangled masses, often covering the surface as far as the eye could see. There were voids, but the combination of haze on sunny days and fog on gray, cloud-covered days made those surface voids all but impossible to detect. Today was one of the latter.

I crawled down from the launch platform on the fantail of the mother ship into the cockpit of the MD-SH-3. Then I pulled the heavy acrylic canopy down, locked it in place, activated the vacuum pump, and waited for the hissing sound of the pressure seal.

I heard Brimley's voice crackle over the I-com, saying "Sync—la-2a. Are you getting a reading?"

When I nodded and gave him the thumbs-up signal, he acknowledged. As my sled started to slide beneath the surface of the water, Brimley circled around me checking my configuration. He nodded a second time and held up his right hand. His index finger and thumb were forming a circle of approval. I took hold of the pistol-grip control stick and watched the red mercury column climb on the thruster speed indicator. At the same time, I was adjusting the left-hand control-operated flaps on the two eighteen-inch horizontal wings. Forward: dive. Backward: climb. I checked my SYM reading, shoved the stick forward, and watched the torpedolike nose of the MD-SH-3 dip toward the depths.

"Wages," Brimley's voice crackled over the I-com, "extend your thruster shield until you get through this first layer of seaweed. It'll cut your power, but you'll be less likely to get anything tangled up in your prop."

I pressed the VTE button twice, activating the shield and extending it to fifty-percent of capacity. The world went from a tolerable gray to an intolerable black. At a depth of no more than ten feet, I plunged into a world in which the sargassum totally subdued the light. I triggered the nose-cone halogen and both wing lights; the light was effective for no more than eight to ten feet. At a phase-one descent rate, I was outdiving my illumination.

"Cut her back one half," Brimley said.

"Slow to .2," I said. Directly ahead of me, I picked up the faint field illumination resulting from the splay of lights on Brimley's sled.

"Passing through fifty," Brimley said.

I checked the cluster of gauges on panel A. I was sliding past the fifty mark and coming up on fifty-five. "Five-five and recording."

"Leveling off, Elliott. Depth: sixty-one."

I looked at my gauges, which indicated two-A or two atmospheres. The PG was calculating the pressure at 29.5 to 30.0 psi.

"How does she look?" Brimley asked. "You should be holding at three hundred thirty-four on all seals. Check for security."

I took off my glove and ran my finger along the cockpit seal. It was dry. "Total integrity. Everything looks fine."

"Rp indicator?"

I ran a scan check on both banks of batteries. "A cell: ninety-seven percent; B cell: ninety-four percent." I noticed when I reported that my voice had taken on a ragged edge.

"Change your mixture," Brimley said. "Or slow your breathing down, you're gulping the mix. If you don't, I'll be scraping you off the ceiling of your canopy."

I shoved the indicator two notches to the left toward the green end of the scale. "Calm down, E. G.," I muttered. Brimley must have heard me because he laughed.

As a precaution, I was measuring the time between each breath. While I watched and counted, Brimley opened the cover shield on his sled to release the probe. When the device was fully extended, Brimley rotated it to the vertical. Unlike the auger probe Gabe Lord had been using on his final dive, the probe on the MD-SH-3 bored into the crust with sound waves.

Finally I heard Brimley's voice say above the din, "I think we're on to something. Looks as if Fredrich was right. I just duplicated Gabe's reading. It looks like we've got a crust that's two, maybe three meters thick, and then some sort of cavern area directly beneath it.

"Okay, Elliott. When you see me run a probe, repeat the operation. I'll record my figures and feed them to Ritter on the surface. When I finish, you replicate the procedure and report your readings independent of mine. That way neither one of us will be influencing the other."

I acknowledged Brimley's command, brought the MD-SH-3 into position, opened both the auxiliary and instrumentation shields, and activated the absorption sonar probe. I was just beginning the countdown when the ocean floor began to shake.

Fortunately, Brimley had already maneuvered his sled into a position directly over mine in order to give me the benefit of the added illumination from his sweep halogens. Unfortunately, that enabled me to see the whole damned area and everything that happened in the next ugly thirty seconds.

"Swarm quakes!" Brimley said "Pull in your probe and get the hell out of there!"

The only problem was, Luke Brimley's warning came about thirty nanoseconds too late to do any good. The floor buckled, the stick of the MD-SH-3 was jerked out of my hands, and the ten-foot-long craft began to cartwheel nose-over-tail along the sandy bottom. The manipulator arm and the probe were still extended, and each time it rolled I heard a sickening grinding sound, the shriek of tearing metal, and the popping of rivets. Finally, something major snapped.

When the MD-SH-3 toppled over into the sand for the final time, the harness snaps released, my head ricocheted back, and I heard what sounded like the distinct and improbable roll of thunder. It was the pounding in my head.

I could smell the acrid aroma of burnt wiring,

and I was aware that there could be a fire. But the bottom line was, I was dazed just enough not to give a damn. It was tough to sort through the chaos. I could hear things breaking and voices screaming over the comsys. But they didn't make a whole lot of sense.

"Damn it, Wages, can you hear me?" Brimley asked.

I reached for the I-com, but my response was all static and noise. Despite the cracks in the acrylic and the loss of integrity in the canopy, I could still see the thrusters kicking up swirling sand and stringy tangles of sargassum. Somehow, I knew I had to marshal my senses enough to try to pull back on the joy stick. But when I did, nothing happened.

Finally, the torrent of seawater did a number on the electronics and I heard the systems begin to shut down. After I watched the lights on the control panel go dark, I looked up and caught a glimpse of Brimley's sled circling over me. He was shouting and gesturing at me, but the I-com had shorted out. The comsys reception was intermittent, and there was no way of knowing what he was saying.

With the cockpit of the MD-SH-3 filling with water, the old Wages survival instincts began kicking in. I took a roll call on body parts, and discovered that all the pieces were still there and, for the most part, still in working order. I reached down, grabbed the D-ring, and released my restraint harness. I had more freedom, but the cockpit canopy was still locked in position. Then I went to the backup on my LS-system and plugged in the auxiliary comsys. I could hear Brimley, but he sounded a long, long way from the action.

When I fumbled with the latch seal and pried the lever up, the handle came off in my hand. Brimley continued to circle, and the lights from his sled lit up my cockpit. To my surprise, Brimley appeared calm.

I still had air, but I was trapped. The MD-SH-3 had taken one hell of a beating, and I was lying on the bottom of the Sargasso, balled up like a wad of paper.

Still visible, Brimley was moving his Terrier MD-SH-3 in for another visual. He played the beam of his swing halogen back and forth over my sled, and when he did, I could assess the damage.

It didn't look good. Ambrose Vance's high-tech pride and joy was in shambles. There was still an occasional spark and a thin wisp of smoke coming from the A panel, but the B panel was burnt out and under water. I didn't need Brimley's lights to tell me how high the water level was creeping. It was already up to the LS panel on my dive suit.

I used the butt of my hand to hammer against the canopy seal in the hopes of disloging it. The acrylic was three eighths of an inch thick, and even though it was leaking like a sieve, I knew there was damn little chance I could hammer a hole in it big enough to crawl through.

I happened to look up again just as Brimley began his second assessment pass. When he did, I thought I saw something gliding above him. By the time it registered that I was seeing something distorted by the loss of what divers call "visual integrity" in the acrylic canopy, whatever it was had disappeared.

Brimley was still on his second pass when there was a second round of swarm quakes. They were of lesser intensity and shorter duration than the first. They lasted for no more than ninety seconds; then the shaking stopped and the sand and debris began to settle. When it did, I had lost contact with Brimley.

There was a prolonged silence, and then the transmissions from topside were coming through loud and clear. I wanted them to know I was still alive. I moaned, complained, even muttered an occasional obscenity just to let the surface know what they were dealing with.

"How long before you can drop that damn winch line?" I said.

"Okay, Elliott, this is Ritter. Bench is already in the water. He's in the fifty-five-K. Keep talkin' so we can home in on you."

"Call Vance," I said. "Tell that money-hungry old bastard that my price just went up."

"Wages, this is Porter. Have you got a visual on Brimley? We've lost contact with him."

"Negative. He was there one minute, gone next."

I wanted to tell them that I thought I had seen something, but I knew no one would believe me.

I hammered against the canopy again, rocked backward, locked my knees, and slammed my feet against the acrylic canopy. It was no use. I had no choice but to sit there and wait.

Consciousness, awareness, and realization came and went. I grabbed hold of reality, then I lost my grip. An eternity later, the area over my canopy was illuminated by two one-thousand-watt flood lamps. At that point, it didn't make a hell of a lot of difference who it was. They had come.

Whoever it was, they were on their knees in the swirling sand outside the crippled MD-SH-3, attaching a cable hook to the D ring on the nose of the sea sled. There was a series of mechanical sounds, and suddenly I felt myself being hoisted toward the surface. I had been too damn close to dying. I was still shaking.

Incident:

"Hell, it's after 20:30. Chuco, how much longer do you expect him to sleep?" I heard a voice say through a fog.

"All I know about concussions is what I read in them books. And what I read in them books says no two people respond to a concussion the same way. He could come out of it in ten minutes or ten hours."

"It's already been ten hours."

"So sue me. It ain't me that ain't followin' the damn script. It's him."

"Well," the first voice said, "give me a call if and when he starts to come around."

There was another period of silence before I

heard footsteps, a door open and close, and more footsteps. It was like listening to an old-time radio show. I was just about to doze off again when I felt someone peeling my eyelid back and holding a light up to it. When I opened my other eye, whoever he was stepped back. He had a surprised look on his face.

"Jesus, man, I was starting to get a little concerned about you," he said. "You've been in here long enough to get people worried."

"In where?"

The little man scowled. "Why, the *Barbella's* infirmary, such as it is. Actually, it's the back of the specimen lab. I guess the guy who designed this tub probably never figured on anyone taking it out in the middle of the Sargasso and administering to the health needs of a couple dozen people."

While the stranger spoke, I rubbed the knot on my head and did what I could to clear away the cobwebs. "How long?"

The little man looked at his watch. "Goin' on ten hours."

"Ten hours! What the hell happened?"

"Doc Fredrich figures you probably did it when the MD-SH-3 was being totaled out."

"Totaled out?"

"Saw it myself when they brought her to the surface. Rolled and wrapped up like a Cuban cigar. Porter's pissed. According to the old man, that's about seventy-five big ones down the

140

tube. Everyone wants to know what the hell happened down there."

It occurred to me that whoever this guy was, he was asking questions I couldn't answer. And since I was lying there in my shorts, and he was standing there staring down at me, it occurred to me that I should be doing something to correct the situation.

When I tried to move, a mean shiver raced up my back and slammed into the base of my brain. My eyes blinked a couple of times, and for a moment or two, I thought there was a chance I was headed for the checkout lane again. So from the supine position I asked, "Who the hell are you?"

The little man had a toothy grin. "Name is Thomas Alva Edison. My mother wanted me to be an inventor, but I'm not smart enough. Nobody calls me Thomas, though. Anyone who's been on this tub any length of time calls me Chuco. I run this infirmary. When I'm not doin' this, I'm helpin' Maydee Hew topside or Fritze Ritter down in the galley. Fritze does most of the cooking, but I help him."

"Ritter?" I said. "I thought Ritter was the radio man."

"Double duty," Chuco said. "Like Doc Fredrich says, we can't have all the amenities if some of us don't double up on the chores."

While Chuco occupied himself polishing up the area, I unleashed a barrage of questions.

"Who was that other voice I heard in here a few minutes ago?"

"Captain Porter. I'm supposed to call him when you start comin' around."

I held up my hand. "That can wait. Before I talk to Porter, tell me just exactly what you heard about what happened down there today."

"I heard we lost Mr. Brimley, if that's what you mean." Chuco wore a blank expression, his voice concealed his emotions. I couldn't tell whether he was grieving or not.

While the little man continued to fuss, I walked over to where my clothes were hanging on the back of the door. Someone had fished them out of my cabin. The last thing I remember, I'd been still wearing a dive suit—a dive suit that had been unceremoniously cut to ribbons and was now piled in the corner. Apparently, someone had overreacted.

Chuco saw me looking at the suit. "We weren't sure how bad you was hurt. Kritzmer warned us not to take any chances."

"What about Brimley?"

"You tell us," Chuco said. "That's what everybody wants to know. We figure you're the only one who knows what happened."

"No sign of him?"

The little man shook his head. "All we know is what we were able to pick up on that tape."

"Tape? Audio tape? You record the transmissions from the dive teams?"

Chuco nodded. "Brimley's idea. He always

figured somethin' got lost in the translation when the divers came back to the ship and recorded their mission details a couple of hours after the fact. That's why he had each of them dive helmets rigged to transmit right into the *Barbella*'s com center."

After I pulled on my pants and slipped into my shoes, I headed for the door, despite a sudden wave of nausea.

"Hey, I'm supposed to call Captain Porter when you come around," Chuco said.

"Porter can wait. I want to hear that tape."

"You probably should take it easy," Chuco said. "According to what I read in them medical books, you shouldn't be movin' around much."

Despite Chuco's warning, I stepped out into the companionway and worked my way up to the first deck. Along the way, I stopped a couple of times and caught my breath. Finally, I managed to thread my way to the B deck Com Cen. Bits and pieces of what had happened in those final minutes had started to come back to me. I remembered watching Luke circle overhead. Then nothing. He had been there; then he was gone.

The Com Cen was unattended. Ritter had opened the emergency channel and left the light on. A simple voice recorder in the voice-activated mode was taking care of business. I looked around until I saw an open reel tape deck; on the table below it was a stack of tapes, each with the word *operations* and a date scrawled across the metal spool of the reel. I found one with the date 07/12 inked on it, and I noted that the take-up side of the reel was almost full. I put it on the drive spindle, hit the rewind button, and started searching for that part of the tape that had recorded those final few minutes before Luke Brimley disappeared. It took a while to find it. 08:47 mark.

> *"OK, Elliott, I've got 'em. Bring her around."*
> *"Roger."*
> *"One-G. Hold her steady."*
> *"One-G. Over Gl, probe activated. Have you got a visual?"*
> *"Roger, I'm right over you. Set her down a couple of yards to your right—"*

At that point, Fritze Ritter's tape brought back the all the terror and chaos of a minute and a half when I thought I was going to die. I heard metal folding and tearing. I heard what sounded like pressure lines rupturing. Then I heard Brimley warning me about swarm quakes.

I played that portion of the tape again. The second time I counted the seconds between the swarm quakes and Luke's warning. The warning had come even later that I thought it had the first time. I remembered the pain and the confusion and then Brimley's Terrier circling over me. Hearing it now, for the second time, I realized that his voice was surprisingly calm.

I was beginning to remember now how Brim-

ley had circled over the disabled MD-SH-3 after
the swarm quakes finally subsided. The beam
of his sweep halogen was pumping sporadic
flashes of light into my darkened cockpit. Then
I remembered the water and how it had started
creeping into the control pod. I remembered
the futility of butting my hands against the clear
acrylic canopy. I remembered Brimley's MD-
SH-3 Terrier circling overhead. Finally, I remembered seeing something over him.

There was what seemed to be a prolonged
and unexplained silence on the tapes, and then
the second set of swarm quakes hit. I remembered counting, trying to remain calm, estimating time, and counting to ninety—the same as
the first series. There was more noise, more
chaos. Then I remembered a period of silence
and the dirt and debris beginning to settle.

There were fragments of communication
from the people on the surface. As near as I
could make out, someone wanted a salvage
crew in the water immediately. Then I heard my
voice. It was brittle and tinny, maybe on the
verge of panic, when I asked how long it would
be before they dropped the winch line.

The response was measured and cool. The
voice of a man in total control. "They're already
in the water. We'll have you out of that thing
and on the surface in no time."

When the tape finished, I sat there for a moment before hitting the rewind button with the
intention of playing the tape a second time. If

nothing else, I had remembered one thing: I had indeed seen something over Brimley's Terrier prior to the second set of swarm quakes. The problem was, what had I seen?

I slumped into the chair in front of the console and hit the rewind button. As I was preparing to listen to the tape a second time, I heard footsteps in the passageway. When Packy walked in, I breathed a sigh of relief.

"Elliott," Packy whispered as she knelt down beside the chair and peered into my eyes. "Are you all right? Chuco said you were still a little shaky when you left the infirmary."

When I nodded, my head hurt, and I promptly vowed to be more verbal and less physical in future responses. "A little wobbly, but all in one piece. How did you find me?"

"Chuco said that you started to come around about thirty minutes ago, that you began asking questions, and that when you learned Fritze Ritter made audio tapes of each of the dives, you indicated you were heading for the Com Cen."

"Have you heard the tape?" I asked.

Packy shook her head. "I can listen to that tape anytime. The question is, how are you?"

"Pride's a little wounded and I'm a bit confused. But I guess that's to be expected when you reduce a piece of equipment like the MD-SH-3 to a pile of rubble the first time you get behind the stick."

After a moment, Packy asked, "Did you hear about Luke?"

When I shook my head, she said, "No luck. Kit and I both searched. We were down there almost two hours. The only thing we recovered was the sled."

I felt sick to my stomach. I didn't even know Brimley, but somehow I felt responsible for his disappearance. I wanted someone or something to blame. Since I had neither, I sat there, wondering what I could have done to change the outcome. "Where's the sled?" I said, intending to check it out.

"Carson winched into the aft hold, where Ritter and Hew could work on it."

The news about Brimley bothered me. I still hadn't figured out whether or not it was wise to tell anyone about the mysterious shadow I had seen just prior to the second set of swarm quakes. If I was right and there was something, we would have fair warning that conditions were not routine and normal down there. If I was wrong, I would be creating doubt in everyone's mind about my stability. My problem was a coin-flipper, and I didn't have a coin.

"Do you know what happened down there?" Packy asked.

"No," I said.

The way Packy was looking at me, I might have said more, but China Porter and Maydee Hew arrived just in time to keep me from saying more than I wanted to. Porter asked the same questions Packy had, and I told him the same thing. He made a couple of inquiries about my health and insisted that I get a good night's sleep before I made out my report. I was grateful.

Back in my cabin, Packy played nurse. She turned back the sheets, made certain I was as comfortable as possible under the circumstances, and waited until I crawled into the shower before she departed.

"Don't forget I'm in the next cabin," she said. "If you need anything, pound on the bulkhead."

I finished my shower and applied a liberal coating of iodine to an assortment of cuts and bruises. After taking a shot of Scotch instead of two aspirin, I pulled on a pair of boxer shorts and adjusted the cabin's air-conditioning, then sprawled across my bunk. Despite one very nasty headache, I decided to check something out. Before I turned out the light, I hauled out the personnel roster containing the names on the *Barbella*'s duty roster. I went over the names of each individual on the list. What I was looking for was the name of someone I could talk to about whatever I thought I had seen just seconds before Brimley disappeared. And that someone had to be an individual who didn't view what I was telling him as a threat to our mission.

I went over the list several times, starting with the old Wages drill of dividing the names into two columns. The first column contained the names of the people actually involved with the salvage effort. The other column consisted of names of the folks who, for one reason or another, appeared to be peripheral to Vance's recovery mission.

In the first column, I jotted down the names of Kit Bench, Packy Darnell, Shula Carson, Fritze Ritter, and China Porter. I was sure the dive crew regarded me as a bad omen. In the two days since Packy and I had joined the team, we had lost two of the four people aboard with dive experience.

The second group, the so-called peripheral contingent, included Eberhard Kritzmer, Maydee Hew, Jewel Simon, Marion Fredrich, and Chuco Edison. I wasn't sure where I should list the name of Mookie Boots. I didn't have him figured out yet.

Then I did something I don't normally do. I made a third column. That list included the names of Gabe Lord, Luke Brimley, Dr. Joffre Cameron, and the two diver-technicians lost when the *Hedgehog* disappeared. All in all, sixteen names—but five of the people were dead. Even that cursory review made one thing painfully apparent, Ambrose Vance's Sargasso salvage effort was a hell of a lot more costly, in terms of human life, then anyone would have imagined.

When I finally dozed off, I was still mulling the names and pieces of the Sargasso puzzle over and over in my mind.

It was sometime in the small hours of the morning when I rolled over and slowly became aware of the fact that someone was in my cabin. Even though I was still wallowing around in the foggy bottoms of a sleep-dulled mind, I had enough sense to slide my hand carefully under the pillow and coil my fingers around the handle of the Mauser. When I finally inched my finger through the trigger housing, I broke the silence.

"Just in case you weren't aware of your plight," I whispered into the darkness, "I have a hair-trigger nine-millimeter automatic aimed right at your head."

I lied, of course. In the darkness, I didn't have the slightest idea where the intruder's head was or even who it belonged to. By the same token, I figured there was no way my uninvited guest could know where I had the weapon pointed. The advantage was all mine.

"Now," I said, "without making any moves that are likely to make me nervous enough to pull this trigger, reach over and turn on the lamp on the desk."

I heard fingers fumble in the darkness. When the light finally came on, I saw Jewel Simon blinking like a lizard caught in a sudden wash of sunlight.

"Will you put that damn gun away," she said.

I sat up in bed. Jewel was wearing that same funny-looking nightgown and an expression that would have made most folks think she was the one who had been awakened from a sound sleep. She reached for a cigarette, and I slipped the Mauser back under my pillow.

"Okay," I said. "Want to tell me what the hell is going on?"

"What happened down there today?" Her voice sounded strained.

"Oh, for Christ's sake, you woke me out of a sound sleep to ask me that?" I was feeling just rotten enough to give the lady a healthy ration of static and a parcel of patented smart-mouth Wages answers when I noticed there were tears in her eyes. Because of that, the answer she got was a shade more civil. "I wish to hell I knew. Porter asked me the same question. One moment Luke was there, circling in the Terrier. The next moment, he was gone."

Jewel shook her head. "Don't you see the similarity?"

"What similarity?"

"The similarity between what happened to Luke Brimley and Gabe Lord. Don't you see it? The gods don't want us here."

She closed her eyes and lapsed into that strange monotone voice again.

There is a choking in the seaweed among the waves where monsters move to and fro—

"Wait a minute," I said. "Damn it, Jewel, what happened down there today had nothing to do with what you call monsters that move to and fro any more than what happened to Gabe Lord."

"Devilfish," she said.

"Mantas had nothing to do with it."

Jewel held up her hand, opened what appeared to be a battered old book of some sort, and began to read. "Devilfish, sometimes called manta, of the family Mobulidae, are found in temperate and tropical waters."

"Yeah, yeah, I know, but just because we're in tropical—"

"These creatures," she said, continuing her reading, "may measure up to twenty-five feet from tip to tip."

"And," I said "if you read far enough, they are harmless to man."

"Are you forgetting the shark's tooth?" Jewel asked. "That megalodon's tooth is seventy-five million years old if it's a day."

"So what are you saying? Gabe Lord was attacked and killed by a seventy-five-million-year-old shark? That's nonsense."

"How can you be so certain?"

Jewel Simon had a point. Some species, scientists claim, have been around since the Earth cooled. I didn't want to admit the lady had hit a nerve. In an odd sort of way, she was right. I couldn't be certain, and I had seen something. Still, at one o'clock in the morning, I saw no need to add fuel to Jewel Simon's mental machinations by telling her about my conversation with Marion Fredrich and the ten-meter nests that appeared in the files of his computer.

"I'm not certain," I said. "By the same token, what happened down there today had nothing to do with irritating the gods. If you want to blame it on something, blame it on carelessness. We should have gotten the hell out of there after the first round of swarm quakes."

Jewel Simon didn't get much for her effort, but she did accomplish one thing. She had given me a fresh perspective. Now I was wide awake and my mind was racing.

Some people say a man can tell when he's been lying to himself because he isn't comfortable answering his own questions. They're right. I was uncomfortable because I had been denying what I saw. I knew what I had seen. I had simply been refusing to accept it because it was too damn hard to believe.

"Tell me," Jewel said. "What makes you so certain the two deaths arn't related?"

"Diving is a risky business," I said. "Salvage diving is at the top of the heap. Things happen down there no matter how careful you are. Pure coincidence."

Jewel Simon wasn't buying my logic. She shook her head. "Suppose you tell me then if you believe the stories you hear about the Bermuda Triangle. Do you believe there is something unusual here?"

"Depends on what you mean by unusual."

"Careful, Elliott. It is dangerous to be flip about something you don't understand."

"Look, Jewel. The last time I read anything about the so-called Bermuda Triangle, authorities were estimating that there could be as many as fifteen hundred uncataloged species of sea life in these waters. If that's the case, I'd be a fool to say that there's nothing unusual going on, but unusual doesn't necessarily mean sea gods and sea monsters."

She leaned forward. "I was there, you know. I was standing on deck the night the *Hedgehog* disappeared. I was there again when Gabe Lord died. Today, it was Luke Brimley. Don't you see? We are dealing with powerful forces that do not want us to disturb that which we have no right to disturb."

"You're referring to the bullion?"

"The bullion is only part of it," she said.

Jewel Simon obviously believed what she was saying. The more we talked, the more her voice became a hiss. When she closed her eyes, I knew that she was seeing a parade of demons and specters none of the rest of us saw.

I stood up, and she moved closer to me. She cried and I put my arms around her. Her voice was fragmented. "I see visions, Elliott, terrible visions. I see these visions every night, and not in my dreams."

When I woke up, Jewel was gone. When her middle-of-the-night crying jag had finally subsided, I put her down in my bunk, covered her with a sheet, and lay down beside her. It didn't take long for the crying to stop. Not long after, she whimpered a couple of times and collapsed into a deep but fitful sleep.

For whatever reason, Jewel Simon did a lot of talking in her sleep. She said some things I'll remember and some others I'll be only too happy to forget, but she made me realize that, for some, the Sargasso demons were very, very real.

While I shaved, while I got dressed, and while I went looking for China Porter, I thought about the previous night. I knew how I was going to handle my report. Until I had a chance to talk to some of the other people involved with the previous day's dive and give the matter further thought, I would say nothing about seeing the mysterious shadow I'd seen just prior to Brimley's disappearance.

I found China Porter in the *Barbella*'s galley. He was talking to Shula Carson. Somewhere between the previous evening and the dawning of the new day, interrogating me had become a lesser priority. Porter had a new problem.

"How the hell did it happen?" he said.

Carson shrugged. "Don't know. First thing this morning, Ritter and I went out to check on the one remaining sled to see if it needed any repairs after yesterday's mission. That's when we discovered it."

I had heard most of the conversation from the passageway outside the galley. When Porter saw me, he motioned for me to come in. "Shula tells me someone sabotaged the one remaining Terrier last night."

"The sled Packy took down?"

Carson nodded. "Same one. I checked it when we retrieved it yesterday. There didn't appear to be anything wrong with it. Everything was intact. This morning it looks like someone took a sledgehammer to the A and B instrument panels. Every damn gauge, dial, and indicator has been smashed. All of the onboard systems are out."

"What about the recorder system?" I asked.

"Destroyed like everything else," Carson said.

"What are you getting at?" Porter asked me.

"Would the mission tape pick up anything from one of the divers after they had exited their sled?"

Carson frowned. "Why?"

"I saw Brimley just seconds before that second round of swarm quakes hit. He was there one minute and gone the next. But if I understand what you're telling me, if he tried to tell us what happened, it wouldn't be on the mission tape, but it might be on his recorder."

"Except that the recorder was destroyed along with the rest of the instrumentation," Carson said.

"See what I mean?"

"Wait a minute," Carson said. "Are you insinuating that someone destroyed the recorder on Brimley's MD-SH-3 just so we wouldn't know what he recorded?"

"I don't know what I'm insinuating."

Porter frowned. "Let's see if I follow you. You think someone may have destroyed the recorder on Brimley's Terrier to keep us from hearing his last transmission?"

"Something like that."

Carson slumped back in his chair and drained the last of his coffee. "It still doesn't make a whole lot of sense."

"That's because we don't have all the parts yet," I said.

Carson rummaged back through the delays. "The second or third day we were here, there was a fire in the radio room and we lost communications for damn near a week. One man was burned so bad we had to send him back to Miami. A couple of weeks later there was another fire—this time in the galley—in the middle of the night and not a damn soul anywhere around. Just like the first one, no explanation and nothing to prove it wasn't an accident.

"Two weeks after that we lost the *Hedgehog*. In that one, we lost Cameron, two good technicians, and about half of our salvage gear. The worst part of that one was, half the damn crew saw it happen and the best explanation I can get out of any of those clowns is it disappeared."

While Carson enumerated the *Barbella*'s woes, Porter lit another cigarette. "Two days ago, we lost Gabe Lord. Yesterday, we lost Luke Brimley. Any more of this shit and I'll start thinkin' like that goofy Simon bitch. She thinks the whole mission is jinxed."

"What about the Simon woman?" I asked.

"She claims this is due to the curse of the Triangle."

Porter laughed. "The only influence the goddamn Triangle has on any of this is it attracts loonies like her and that clown, Fredrich. If Vance had allowed us to pick our own crew, we'd already have that damn bullion and we'd be making arrangements to turn Hess's U-boat into some kind of underwater amusement park."

Incident:

We spent a good part of the afternoon trying to piece Brimley's wounded Terrier together. Most of the work was done on the aft deck, in the sun, until a big-bellied mass of ominous gray clouds moved in near the supper hour. Not long after that we could smell the rain in the air. It never was a matter of if the rains came; it was simply a matter of when.

As the day wore on, both Shula Carson and Kit Bench became more talkative. I learned that Porter was openly critical of the two Germans, Kritzmer and Fredrich, and that on at least two occasions he had asked Ambrose Vance to have the two men flown back to Germany. The way

Shula told it, Vance had refused without giving his captain a reason. His refusal rankled Porter.

Jewel Simon was another problem. "She was okay at first," Carson said. "But she's gone off the deep end with all that talk about monsters and us disturbing the gods."

Bench's sentiments were pretty much the same. "If she hasn't cornered you already, she will."

I did a lot of listening, and whenever there was the slightest pause in the conversation, I took the opportunity to spur the talk on with more questions. I figured that that was as good a time as any to get some straight answers concerning the *Hedgehog*. I decided that neither Shula nor Bench was the type who would buy into Maydee Hew's disappearance story.

"So," I said, trying to sound only half interested, "what did happen to the *Hedgehog*? Surely there was some attempt to salvage it."

Shula Carson, who had been devoting most of his efforts to rewiring the Terrier's console, stopped and pointed to the wheelhouse. "I was standing right there, not more than ten minutes before it happened. Hew is right about one thing. That damn fog was so thick you could have cut holes in it with a knife. Cameron and the two technicians had been alerted an hour or so earlier because of the intensity of the swarm quakes. But when the quakes hit, the three of them were still on the barge, taking care of last-minute details.

"The only reason I was on deck at the time was because I had been working with Frank Morgan. He was one of the technicians. He'd been complaining about a piece of equipment and wanted me to take a look at it. So when they winched it aboard, I came up on deck to take a look at it.

"Since day one out here, Porter has been pretty damn adamant about us gettin' right on it anytime there was something wrong with the salvage gear or the dive equipment. He's got a thing about down time."

"The next thing we knew," Bench said, "the *Hedgehog* was gone."

"That's the part I don't understand," I said. "Why wasn't there some effort made to find *Hedgehog* then?"

Bench looked at Carson before he answered. I had the distinct impression that he wasn't at all eager to admit what he was about to reveal. "The swarm quakes lasted most of the damn night. When they finally quit along about dawn, Shula sent Luke and Gabe down."

"And?"

Bench hesitated, then shrugged. "They said they couldn't find anything."

"You mean they couldn't find the bodies."

"Kit means that, when Gabe and Luke debriefed, they said they couldn't even find the damn barge," Carson said.

The minute Carson spoke up, Bench busied himself with the panel wiring. I had the feeling

Kit Bench would have preferred to drop the conversation right then and there.

"Let me get this straight. You're telling me that you're in eighty, maybe ninety feet of water, and the next morning you can't locate a ninety-foot-long supply barge that went down just a few hours before?"

Carson braced himself. "That's exactly what I'm telling you. Both Brimley and Lord said they sorted through that damn forest of elephant weed and sargassum for hours with four different dives. They didn't find nothin'. There wasn't a trace of that damn barge."

"Three days in a row," Bench said. "They never found nothin'."

"Any theories?"

Shula Carson sniffed, lit a cigarette, scanned the low-hanging cloud deck, and exhaled. "Once I asked Brimley what he thought happened. He said he believed one of them swarm quakes was strong enough to shift some of the bottom around and cover it up."

"Wouldn't absorption sonar take care of that?"

Bench suddenly looked like a man who had been backed into a corner. He was avoiding eye contact. When Shula flipped his cigarette overboard and turned back to the control panel, I knew I had gotten all they were willing to give—and probably a whole lot more than they felt comfortable revealing.

In my final analysis, Kit Bench and Shula

Carson were no different from anyone else who had been witness to something as bizarre as the disappearance of the *Hedgehog*. Neither wanted to look like a coward, and neither wanted to look foolish. If they said any more on the subject, either or both was possible.

When it started to sprinkle, I headed below. By the time I scampered down to B deck and Packy's cabin, I could hear the rain hammering on the deck above me. Shortly after that, the lights flickered a couple of times and the *Barbella* was plunged into darkness.

I groped my way to Packy's cabin and knocked. By the time she answered, she had located a candle. She was still fumbling around for a match when she opened the door.

"How are you feeling?" she asked.

I waited until the flame on the candle flickered to life and she extinguished the match before I motioned her toward the rear of her cabin and her bunk.

She arched her eyebrows and smiled. "Don't you ask a girl if she wants to get undressed first?" she teased.

"I want to play what-if," I said.

Packy was wearing a pair of shorts and a tank top. She sat down on the bunk and curled her long legs under her. "What if what?"

"Just follow what I'm about to tell you. Every time you can't buy what I'm saying, stop me."

She nodded. In the candlelight, she looked like a candidate for any number of games, none

163

of which fell under the heading of *what if.*

"I've just spent the better part of the afternoon listening to Shula Carson and Kit Bench. I asked them about the *Hedgehog*. They claim Porter sent Brimley and Lord down to recover the bodies of Cameron and the two divers the morning after the *Hedgehog* went down."

"And?"

"No luck. Not only were they unable to recover the bodies of the three men; they were likewise unable to locate the *Hedgehog*."

A smile played with the corners of Packy's symmetrical mouth. "Eighty feet of water and they can't find a ninety-foot-long salvage barge? Come on. I'll admit it's dark down there, but not that dark. How long did they wait before they went down?"

"Several hours. Bench claims they had to wait out the swarm quakes." The glow from the candle danced in Packy's eyes. The smile had faded. "And you want to know what I know about swarm quakes? You've already been through a couple."

"And I was too busy to take notes."

"They're not usually as severe as the ones we've been experiencing. Usually the ones here where the *Barbella* is anchored are nothing more than peripheral quakes, sort of like small explosive charges along the edge of the plate action."

"I thought this kind of thing was confined to the circum-Pacific belt—in other words, just along the plate boundaries of the Pacific."

"Your friend Dr. Fredrich explained it to me," Packy said. "And the way I understand it, the eastern arm of the circum-Pacific belt loops around north of Venezuela and heads into the Caribbean, not far from where we are. The swarm quakes then are the result of conflicting plate action." Packy held her hands out horizontally with the tips of her fingers touching each other. Then she rubbed them back and forth. "According to Fredrich, it's not a lot of friction, but it's enough to generate a bunch of these so-called swarm quakes."

"Enough to cover up a ninety-foot-long salvage barge?"

"Enough to wad up an MD-SH-3 like a cheap cigar, but probably not enough to bury a ninety-foot-long salvage barge."

I studied Packy in the flickering light. The silence was a giveaway. When I cleared my throat, she started to laugh.

"All right, Elliott, I know that look and I've heard that throat-clearing routine before. You want me to do something, right?"

"Do you believe in vibrations?"

"Which kind? The kind we've been having with the swarm quakes or the psychic variety?"

I kept my voice low. "I want you to check a couple of things, and I'm not exactly sure where to start."

"Like?"

"I want you to get a look at the *Barbella*'s log.

I want your interpretation of the log entries on the night the *Hedgehog* disappeared."

"What specifically am I looking for?"

"You've spent a lot more time on ships than I have. You know what to look for: swarm-quake intervals, number, intensity, who recorded the information, and—"

"Why me?"

"Like I said, you'll know if the entries are on the up and up."

"And while I'm doing that, what will you be doing?"

"I'm going down to take another look around."

"By yourself?"

"I can handle it. Nothing you've said so far convinces me that a swarm quake could stir things up enough to swallow up a fully equipped ninety-foot-long salvage barge."

As bad as it was, the weather was playing to my advantage. Shula Carson and Kit Bench had obviously worked long after I had gone below. They had rigged a tarpaulin over the ravaged Terrier so they could work in the rain. But the on-again, off-again performance of the *Barbella*'s malfunctioning generator had finally discouraged them. Finally, Porter instructed Ritter to shut down the ship's main engines until the problem could be diagnosed. That was all it took. By early evening, most of the crew had grown weary of the darkness and retired to their cabins. There was a candlelight poker game in the galley. With Maydee Hew at the helm, I had the aft hold area all to myself.

Even though I was operating in the dark, I pulled on the exposure suit, a hood, boots, and an alternate air source. The chest-mounted IP had the depth gauge, compass, thermometer, SPG, and a modular NV computer designed for night dives. Just before I went over the side, I disconnected the recorder and the connection to the Com Cen.

I groped my way along the hull of the *Barbella* until I was midship and reasonably certain no one on the bridge would see the wash of my halogen before I activated it. I was already in a tangle of sargassum and choke weed, and I had to peel away the clinging broad leaf plants from my fins.

Orientation was my first problem. I had slipped into the water from the *Barbella's* stern and worked my way around on the starboard side to a point where I could see the mooring lights on the bow. If there was anyone on the bridge, I had to hope they were either napping or otherwise engrossed, I was splashing around more than I had intended. I had purposely stayed to the windward side of the *Barbella* so that I would be upwind from the craft and all the more difficult to see. The way I figured it, if Maydee Hew was on the bridge, he would have had to have been on lookout to the windward side to see me—a scenario that didn't seem too likely considering the time of night and the weather.

I checked the time and logged it into my dive computer. It was 23:41. Then I went over my gear, resecuring my BCD and utility belt. I exhaled, began deflating my BCD, and at a depth of fifteen feet, activated the beam halogen mounted on my equipment harness. The blackness sucked up the light less than six to eight feet in front of me.

At the 30.50 depth, I stopped for a second time, actuated the PDD sonar, waited until I had a display, and selected a random 3-2-1 and 2-2-3 pattern. I doubted if Kritzmer or Fredrich had an auxiliary generator in their little playroom in the bow of the *Barbella*, but I didn't want a random ping arousing their suspicions. If I had my druthers, even Packy wouldn't have known I was down there.

At the 23:52:41 mark, or eleven minutes and forty-one seconds into the dive, I made my first systems check. I was in forty-seven feet of Sargasso soup and the horizontal visibility wasn't much more than zero. Above and below me was an undulating jungle of gigantic rystmus grass and an endless tangle of sargassum.

At the 00:07:17 real time, or twenty-six minutes and seventeen seconds into the mission, I took another set of readings. I did an agonizingly slow 360 sweep and took PDD readings every thirty degrees. Bottom line, nothing. Then, more out of frustration than anything else, I triggered a sweep beneath me. I got nothing in return. At the sixty, ninety, and 120 intervals there was no interception.

I knew there had to be a bottom down there somewhere, but where the hell was it, and why wasn't I getting a reading?

The constant data update in the lens was a distraction, so I closed my eyes and tried to reason my way through the information I already had. Then I did an absorption profile, and repeated it a second time when I couldn't get a reading on the first. I was falling into the trap of repeating everything twice, and some checks three times. When you do that, you don't access new data. I was losing my orientation. To reorient myself, I made certain the audio was disengaged, and pressed the illumination bar on the data pack. That was when I did a double take. My DG was indicating eighty-one feet, and if I could believe the readings on the PDD, there was nothing beneath me but more of the same. According to Porter's charts, I should have been on the bottom.

For the next several minutes I tried threading my way through a complicated underwater jungle of twists, links, and disorder. I was getting discouraged. Up looked like down; horizontal looked like vertical. Most of the time, my chest-mounted halogen wasn't effective beyond a range of three or four feet. To top it off, I was still getting nothing from the PDD, and at the forty-minute mark, I was ready to buy Gabe

Lord and Lucas Brimley's version of what had happened to the *Hedgehog*. They were right. It had disappeared because there was no bottom.

I was running out of time when I switched the sweep on the Ind-Son to 180 degrees and monitored the tiny screen for the data results. It was on the third sweep that I noticed something. I increased the horizontal scale on the beacon five degrees and repeated it. Now there was no doubt about it. I was picking up a definite anomaly. It appeared to be no more that two-hundred feet directly ahead of me.

On the fourth scan, the return signal indicated the depression could be as long as a mile, and maybe more. At that point I couldn't tell whether it was a crevice created by the swarm quakes, a ditch, or a natural depression. I threaded my way through another hundred feet or so of tangled sargassum, and suddenly found myself in an opening with as much as ten to twelve feet of horizontal visibility. When I looked down, I realized that I was staring down a minimum thirty-to-forty-foot decline—and that there was something at the bottom. I got down on my hands and knees and clawed at the sand. No more than a foot down, I ran into solid rock and coral. Hello, big crevice. That baby wasn't on Porter's charts.

E-time stood at 00:39 and I was fast closing in on an hour. I did a couple of quick calculations on my computer, and decided I had everything I needed to finish what I had started.

It didn't take me long to figure out what I had stumbled into. It was certainly long enough to hide the *Hedgehog*, and it was wide enough. When I bent down to clear away the sandy debris, I found it was deep enough. I kept digging, and found a montage of buckled and splintered plank decking entwined in a tangle of rusting steel cables. The deck angled away from me at about a ten-degree pitch, and each time I took a step, the sand and debris billowed up around me. At the bottom of the incline was a mound of oversized crates, barrels, and containers. I played the beam of my lamp across the legend on one of the containers; the words "*Hedgehog* consignment" were stenciled in black letters along the side of the wooden container. I caught my breath and straightened up. I had started with one question and now I had an answer to it. The only problem was, now that I had answered the first one, I had more questions.

I used what time I had left to plot coordinates, and make certain I had a solid position fix. Then I dug out the small infrared 35mm camera to take some shots of my discovery, just enough to make certain I had solid proof. I squeezed off twenty-four frames in rapid succession, and was just getting ready to reload when I heard the first warning signal. I glanced at the gauge on my PDD, shoved the camera back in the equipment pouch, and started for the surface.

I surfaced about three hundred yards from the *Barbella* and began swimming. When I got to it, I crawled up on the dive platform, pulled off my fins and mask, unbuckled my tanks, and crawled back aboard ship through the dive gate on the stern. The rain was still falling, but it had been reduced to little more than an irritating drizzle.

By the time I had pulled off my exposure suit and stowed my gear, I had determined that whoever had taken over the midnight-till-dawn watch was busy logging sack time. A single chart light beamed from the wheelhouse—and the fore and aft navigational lights were the only indication the ship had power. I could hear the hum of a small standby generator, and wondered if that was all the *Barbella* had going for it.

After pulling on a pair of swim trunks and a T-shirt, I started forward. The Com Cen was empty, and the receiver switch had been locked in the open position. Ritter was slumped over the chart table, snoring.

My tour around the rest of the ship didn't take long, and it was thirteen minutes past the hour when I finally got back to my cabin. Packy had curled up on my bunk. She was asleep. The illumination came from two candles.

I reached down, touched her on the shoulder, and kept my voice low. When she opened her eyes, she stretched like a big cat. She was inching her way back into reality.

"What time is it?" she finally muttered.

When I showed her my watch, she pointed to

172

the thermos bottle on the nightstand. I opened it and poured each of us a cup of coffee. It was thick and black and hot. She rubbed her eyes, took a sip, and finally managed a small smile. Even then, her voice was thick with sleep. "Find anything?"

I shrugged. "For whatever reason, it looks like Luke Brimley and Gabe Lord lied."

"You found the *Hedgehog*?" She sounded surprised.

"Right where Maydee Hew said she was when she disappeared."

Packy's face was mostly frown. "I don't get it. Why would—"

"That's the big question. Now I'll ask mine. Did you get a look at the log?"

She padded barefoot across the cabin and picked up what appeared to be an oversize cloth-bound journal. It was the *Barbella*'s log. She rifled through the pages until she found what she was looking for, and held it out to me. "Read this," she said. "It's the entry the morning following the *Hedgehog* incident."

Both Carson and Hew insist there was nothing to indicate that the salvage barge was in any kind of trouble at the time of the incident. Both men reported being in contact with Dr. Cameron and his two subordinates just moments before the onset of the second wave of swarm quakes. There was no prior indication of any problems.

Carson further stated that because of the intensity of this particular cluster of quakes, the Barbella *was bobbing about in the water for the entire ninety-to-120-second duration of the second round of quakes. He further indicates that because he believed the* Hedgehog *to be secure at the time, his attention was focused on the trailing GMQ unit which had been deployed earlier that day for the specific purpose of measuring seismic activity. Carson says that he looked up only when Second Officer Hew informed him that the* Hedgehog *had disappeared. Carson claims he heard nothing and when he asked Maydee Hew what had happened, all Hew could do was indicate that the* Hedgehog *had disappeared.*

"Whose handwriting is this?" I asked.

Packy shrugged. "Don't know. I wondered the same thing. But I can tell you this much. It isn't Porter's. I compared several of the signed-off entries in the bridge log. Porter has unique handwriting."

"Anything else?" I asked.

Packy nodded. "Flip over a couple of pages. See the one dated May seventeenth? That's Porter's summation of Lord and Brimley's search for the Hedgehog."

Lord and Brimley reported that there was no trace of the barge, its contents, or crew.

Packy folded her arms across her chest. "So, Mr. Wages, what do you make of that?"

I pointed to the equipment bag I had dropped just inside my cabin door. "There's a roll of thirty-five-millimeter film in my camera that says either Brimley and Lord weren't looking all that hard or they were lying."

Packy looked perplexed. "Same coordinates?"

"Same coordinates," I said.

"I didn't know Gabe Lord that well," Packy said. "But Luke Brimley didn't strike me as the kind of man who would lie."

"You knew him before?"

"I knew his reputation," Packy said. She stood up and started to pace about the cabin. "Why would they lie about finding the barge?"

"Maybe they really didn't locate the wreck," I said.

Packy looked at me skeptically. Then she took the log and rifled through several more pages. "Brimley and Lord went down on the eighteenth, twice on the nineteenth, twice on the twentieth. Then Porter called a halt to the search on the twenty-first. With most of the dive supplies on the *Hedgehog*, they'd started running low on air."

"Let me ask one of those off-the-wall questions then," I said.

"Go ahead."

"Does it seem curious to you that Kit Bench was never involved in any of the dives? Why were Brimley and Lord the only ones doing the diving?"

When Packy started rifling back through the pages of the log again, I asked, "What are you looking for?"

She was frowning. "I was checking to see if for some reason Porter had relocated the *Barbella* since the night of the *Hedgehog* incident."

"And?"

"No record of it," she said.

"So where does that leave us?"

"Frankly, Elliott, all it does is leave us with a lot of unanswered questions." She was holding her coffee cup with both hands as she moved across the room. She sat down on the bunk next to me and crossed her legs. The candle highlighted the shadows on her face. "You're supposed to be the puzzle-solver. What do you make of all of this?"

I didn't know how to answer her question— not because what we had learned during the past few hours pointed in any one direction, but because it pointed absolutely nowhere. At that particular moment, I couldn't see that we had learned anything except that the supposedly long-lost *Hedgehog* was no more than eight hundred yards from the *Barbella* in approximately 120 feet of water. Why Brimley and Lord had reported that they had been unable to locate it made no sense at all.

Finally Packy sighed. She looked tired. She gave me a peck on the cheek, took one of the candles to light her way, and headed for the door. "Let's call it a night." she said.

I waited until I heard the door to her cabin close and the lock click. Then I leaned back across the bed. Moments later, the candle flickered and the cabin went dark.

For a moment or two, I thought about trying to find Shula Carson to see if I could lend him a hand with the balky generator. Then I figured it could wait until morning. I pulled the sheet over me and tuned out the world.

If you've ever been awakened out of a deep sleep by the acrid smell of an electrical fire, you know exactly what I'm talking about. I rolled over with the irritating smell of burning wiring assaulting my senses. But I was still so groggy, so trapped in the webby confusion that goes with the journey from the world of sleep to the world of consciousness, that I didn't react.

When the word *fire* finally did register in my brain, I rolled off the bunk and groped my way through the sticky darkness to the door of my cabin. The door was still cool and I opened it, but the passageway was choked with smoke. I dropped to my hands and knees, and was working my way toward Packy's cabin, when I heard her shout.

"Elliott! Elliott!" The second time her voice was choked off by the smoke and she began coughing.

I put my arm around her, turned her back

toward the stern where the smoke appeared to be less dense, and shoved her along the passageway ahead of me. We stumbled up the stairs to the A deck and out into the Sargasso night. It was still dark. The rain had deteriorated to a drizzle and the fog was settling in again.

It took several minutes, but we were finally able to clear our eyes and get our breathing under control. When we did, I glanced toward the wheelhouse and saw Porter, Carson, and Ritter milling around the entrance to the Com Cen.

Hew was emerging from the radio room with a fire extinguisher. The smoke had combined with the encroaching fog to create some kind of ethereal scene in which the crew of the *Barbella* appeared to be only half human.

Beyond them, looking down from the bridge, was the rest of the *Barbella*'s salvage contingent: Kritzmer, Fredrich, and Jewel Simon. There was no sign of Kit Bench or the one they called Chuco.

I pushed my way past Porter and peered into what was left of the *Barbella*'s radio room; it wasn't much.

"What happened?" I asked.

Porter grunted. "Who the hell knows? Ritter tells me the shortwave is out; the high-frequency stuff is kaput. The ADF is gone and the MOR and VOR equipment is fried. We can't even transmit on the Gee."

"What about the loran?"

"Gone," Carson said.

"How the hell are we going to get help?" Packy asked.

Porter looked defeated. "The way it stands now, we're dead in the water until Ritter can put something together and patch us through to Miami."

Incident:

Moments later, Eberhard Kritzmer arrived on the scene. He glared at Porter, brushed past him, and stepped into the still-smoky Com Cen. If possible, his face appeared even more bulbous and his voice even more strident than usual.

He started with a derisive laugh, then shook his head. "I wonder what our illustrious employer and benefactor would think of this turn of events, Captain."

"It was an accident, damn it," Porter growled.

"This entire salvage mission is turning out to be one monumental accident, isn't it, Captain."

Shula Carson stepped forward. "We've been

having electrical problems most of the night," he tried to explain. "We lost a bearing in the diesel generator and fried—"

"Have you considered employing a backup unit?" Kritzmer said. There was a venomous dimension to his voice.

"The backup unit was on the *Hedgehog*," Carson explained. "We don't have much to work with. Until we can get the main diesels repaired, all we've got to work with is the auxiliary unit on the stern. That'll keep lights on the bridge and in most critical areas—but we'll have to shut down the refrigeration units, most of the galley gear, and the power to all the cabins."

"The ship's laboratory must have power," Kritzmer insisted.

Porter stepped forward. He towered over the German. "Know somethin', Kritzmer? I'm a hell'uva lot more worried about keepin' us alive and afloat until Ritter and Carson can get us powered up again than I am keeping you and Dr. Fredrich amused in that so-called laboratory of yours."

"We have several rather rare specimens—"

"Forget your damn specimens, Kritzmer. We're out here to locate that U-564; everything else is secondary."

"Including keeping us alive, Captain?"

"I wouldn't push it, Professor," Carson said, "not unless you can prove you weren't on the A deck when the fire started."

Kritzmer stiffened. "Is that an accusation, Mr. Carson?"

"Call it anything you like, Doctor." Porter's voice was edgy. "The fact remains the fire broke out in the Com Cen sometime between 04:00 and 05:00 this morning, and at that time, Ritter and Carson had the standby generator shut down. In other words, Doctor, there was no power. Now if I haven't made myself clear enough, let me put it another way. I get real damn suspicious when there is an electrical fire and no power to spark it."

Kritzmer wheeled and started for the door of the Com Cen. He pushed his way past Carson and Ritter, stopping only when he was far enough away from Porter that the *Barbella*'s captain no longer posed a physical threat.

The German's voice was icy. "Do you have any idea how long we must be inconvenienced by your crew's incompetence, Captain?"

Shula Carson was the one who answered. "If we've got all the parts we need, we could have her up and running by nightfall. If we haven't got 'em, Fritze and I will have to try to make them."

Porter waited until Kritzmer had departed before he turned to Packy and me. "Kritzmer isn't the only one I'm concerned about, Wages. Where the hell were you this morning?"

Porter was in the driver's seat. That's the luxury of having something go wrong in the middle of the night; you can accuse anyone you have a mind to. In the middle of the night, damn few people have an alibi.

I waited while Porter lumbered over to the blackened console of the comsys, picked up a charred tape reel, examined it momentarily, then dropped it back on the plotting surface near the burned-out RF unit.

"Maybe neither one of you were anywhere near it, Wages, but I have to ask anyway. Did you see or hear anything? Voices? Noises in the passageway outside your cabin? Anything un-usual? The smoke alarm?"

I looked at Packy. She was shaking her head.

"The smoke alarms didn't go off in either of our cabins," she informed him.

Porter grunted and turned his attention back to what was left of the *Barbella*'s radio gear. Lit-tle beads of sweat were working their way down from his temples, and his matted gray hair was damp with the heat and humidity. The more he assessed the damage, the more his dull brown eyes narrowed. When he turned and walked out of the Com Cen, I followed him.

I followed Porter down to the *Barbella*'s galley. There was enough power to light the stairways, but for the most part, the interior of the *Barbella* was a series of dark corridors and even darker corners.

A bleary-eyed Kit Bench was hunkered over a cup of thick, black coffee that smelled like it had been reheated one too many times. Porter fixed himself a cup of the same and eyed me.

I had nothing to lose so I fired the first volley. "What the hell is going on here?"

If I had been cataloging them, I might have classified the first look as one of contempt, the second as a bit more conciliatory, and the third as recognizing the fact that I was damn near as big as he was and that the old bully tactics probably wouldn't work. Still, that wasn't going to keep him from trying.

"I got a question for you, Wages. Just who the hell are you? What are you doing here? Why did Vance hire you?"

"That's three questions," I said, straddling the seat across from him.

Bench's head popped up. His bloodshot eyes danced from Porter to me, and back to Porter. With Porter and me glaring at each other, the galley was no longer the place to catch forty winks. Bench stood up, looked appropriately disgusted, and trudged out without speaking.

"Ambrose Vance hired me on the recommendation of a mutual friend," I said. "Now I know why. He hired me because you aren't getting the job done—it's as simple as that."

Even in the limited lighting of the galley, I could see Porter's face color. His jaw tensed. I had the feeling he was use to hitting things he didn't like.

I leaned forward, keeping my voice low. "Just exactly how much of all of this have you reported to Vance?"

Porter listened because he was curious to find out where I was coming from. Vance had dropped me right in the middle of what was proving to be a tight little community. Outsiders weren't welcome.

"Vance knows everything," he grunted. "If I don't report it—you can bet your sweet ass one of his stoolies aboard this miserable tub will."

"When did you tell him about losing the *Hedgehog*?"

"The morning following . . ."

"How did you explain it?"

"I blamed it on the cluster quakes—check the log."

"Will the magnitude of those quakes that night support that kind of damage?"

"What difference does it make? When they occur in clusters like that, anything over a magnitude of 3.0 can make the water boil."

"Where were you the night the *Hedgehog* disappeared?"

"In my cabin. Why?"

"After the cluster hit, why didn't you report to the bridge?"

"Why the hell should I? Shula Carson was on watch that right. We'd been experiencing those damn cluster quakes ever since we put our anchor down. Besides, Carson's an old hand, he knows what to do in a situation like that."

"When did you learn that the *Hedgehog* had gone down?"

"The next morning."

"You mean to sit there and tell me you lost three men and a ninety-foot-long salvage barge with a good share of your gear on board and your crew didn't bother to inform you until the next morning?"

This time Porter didn't come back at me. I had just asked him the question that didn't have an answer. Finally he said, "What's all this mean to you? How big of a cut are you in for?"

Submariners have an expression when they're trying to get from one place to another in the cramped confines of their ship. That term is "make a hole." To Porter's dismay, I had just made a very big hole in the scenario he had been spinning for Ambrose Vance.

"Where I come from, there's an old saying, Porter: Never give a cokehead any responsibility."

Porter stiffened. Under most circumstances it would have been imperceptible, but it was there, the tightness in the jaw, a slight twitch in the eyes, the slightest bit of flare in the nostrils. Deception and cocaine don't mix. Sooner or later the user gets careless. "You didn't come to the bridge that night," I said, "because you couldn't come to the bridge."

Porter chewed on his lip. Suddenly he was a whole lot less belligerent, less bellicose. Suddenly he was smaller. The shoulders sagged and there was a corresponding loss of antagonism in his voice. He started to protest, saw the futility of it, and looked away. The eyes were empty.

I cleared my throat. "When you came to the bridge the following morning, Carson reported what had happened. The only problem was, he relayed it just like Hew had described it, and you were still stoned—stoned just enough to buy it."

"You'd have a hell of a time proving that, Wages."

"Would I? I don't think so. I've been going through the ship's log. On at least three different occasions since the *Barbella*'s been anchored here, you were too incapacitated to fill out the log. Carson signed your name. What's more, I suspect I can prove that it's been Shula Carson who's been covering for you for a long time."

Porter glared at me. "So what happens now?"

"When did you figure out that Brimley and Lord had lied to you when they said they were unable to locate the wreck of the *Hedgehog*?"

"I'll use your words, Wages. I'm a cokehead, not a fool. It had to be down there. We were in less than one hundred feet of water. I don't care if this is the Sargasso; ninety-foot-long barges don't just disappear."

"Why didn't you take them into custody, report them to Vance, have him recruit you a fresh crew, and go on about your business?"

Porter fumbled in his shirt pocket for his cigarettes. The hand emerged with the cigarette, a butane lighter, and a pronounced shake. For a brief moment the darkness in the galley gave way to the light of a red-orange flame. He exhaled, and leaned forward again.

"For some time now I've been convinced that Brimley and Lord had to have friends in their little venture," Porter whispered. "Now that you've got pictures . . . I've got the proof."

"How so?"

"First Lord. Then Brimley. Someone killed them."

"Someone or something?"

Porter laughed. "You sound like that Simon dame got to you with all that talk of giant manta rays and prehistoric sharks. She's loonier than a goddamn spar fish."

It seemed like as good a time as any. I decided to tell Porter about the final minutes before Brimley disappeared. "I still don't know how this fits in with all the rest of what we know. But moments, maybe even seconds, before Brimley disappeared, I saw something."

"What do you mean 'something'?" Porter grunted.

I shook my head, "I don't know what I saw, but I saw something—something moved—it was fleeting, but I—"

Porter cut me off. "The way I've got it figured, Brimley and Lord were in this with someone. Now that it appears we're close to locating the U-564, I figure someone is starting to get a tad excited, and maybe a little greedy. First Brimley and whoever figured there would be one less split if they got rid of Gabe Lord. Then the same logic worked in getting rid of Brimley. What the hell, they wouldn't be the first divers who died 'mysteriously' in this damn part of the ocean."

While I was still ruminating on Porter's theory, he took one last drag on his cigarette and doused it in his coffee. He may have been following the white line, but what he said, with certain reservations, made sense.

"Maybe a few of the pieces just came together," I admitted.

"For you maybe—but I still got the same question, Wages. Where the hell do you go with all of this?"

Porter was asking the big question. I wasn't sure where I was going with it. It would have been easy to dump everything I had learned in Ambrose Vance's lap, pick up my check, and cozy up with Packy back aboard the *Perpetual Motion*. But—then I would have to live with myself and the realization that Vance had received, at best, a halfhearted effort for his money. That didn't mesh well with the old Wages code of ethics.

So what did I do? I asked Porter another question. "What about the fire in the Com Cen?"

"Out-and-out arson," he sniffed, "no question about it. Whoever it is, they got us right where they want us. Vance has filed all the necessary papers. People know why we're out here. No one expects us to maintain any kind of contact with the outside world unless we ask for help. We're out here for one purpose—and one purpose only. The maritime authorities think we're combing the bottom of the Sargasso for a fifty-year-old sunken U-boat. If they don't hear from us for days on end—in their book there's nothing to be alarmed about—we're just busy."

I didn't like what Porter was saying.

He lit another cigarette. "Think about it, Wages. First Lord. Then Brimley. Last night we lost power; this morning a flash fire takes out our communication gear. Hell, we're sitting ducks for someone."

In what little light there was, I could see that Porter still wasn't quite sure where I stood. His face was creased with an expression carved out of distrust. When I said, "We've got work to do," and he heard the tone of my voice, he breathed an almost audible sigh of relief.

After my session with Porter, I went topside to check the weather. I could have saved myself the grief. The *Barbella* was still mired in a thick, greasy fog that made it difficult to see from one end of the ship to the other. From the stern where Carson and Ritter had been working on Lord's battered Terrier, I was barely able to make out the outline of the wheelhouse. And since the reverse would be true, I knew that whoever was on the day watch was unable to see me. I decided to use the opportunity to see if I could learn anything by going over the sled

Brimley was using when he disappeared.

In size and cockpit configuration, the MD-SH-3 Terrier was an updated version of the one I had piloted. The A and B console controls had been modified, but were laid out in the same fashion. Even the cockpit canopy as configured in much the same manner. Ritter had earlier said that these same modifications were being made in all of the underwater craft to facilitate the movement of divers from one unit to another.

While I studied the cockpit layout in the Terrier, I tried to recapture the fleeting image of Brimley circling overhead. The images refused to crystallize. Had I blinked? Did I black out? If I did, how long was I out? And . . . what happened? One moment Brimley was there; the next moment he wasn't.

It was bit easier to buy Porter's theory on the Gabe Lord. Lord was working in a sector by himself. He could have pulled a disappearing act with little or no difficulty. Disappearing wasn't the problem. The question was, where the hell did he think he was going after he bailed out? There weren't a hell of a lot of a places for a man to hide in the middle of the Sargasso. Either way, what happened wasn't in the plan. No one plans to die.

I examined the gasketing around the canopy seal, checked the batteries, and looked for some sort of sign that either Brimley, the craft, or the combination of the two had been in some sort of distress. If the signs were there, I couldn't find them.

I was still poking around, looking for something to hang my theory on, when I heard footsteps. Maydee Hew emerged from the shroud of fog like an apparition. As a concession to another day of sticky heat, he was barefoot and had stripped down to an old pair of cut-off wash pants secured with a piece of cotton rope. For a man of his vintage, he was surprisingly muscular, and he walked with a grace that belied his years.

"You got the same questions I got, huh?" he said. "What da ya figure happened to old Brimley? Think it was the same thing that got Lord?"

I didn't laugh, but that didn't stop him.

"Don't suppose it was one of them giant devilfish Jewel Simon is always talking about, do ya? Or maybe one of them prehistoric sharks she claims is out there? Course, maybe it ain't nothin' more than the Sargasso. They's folks out there that says once the Sargasso claims it— they ain't no man what can have it back."

Hew didn't require much encouragement. I had the feeling that he would talk as long as anyone would listen. My first question was designed to elicit a detailed description of what had happened.

"You said you, Carson, and Dr. Kritzmer were on the bridge the night the *Hedgehog* disappeared?"

Hew nodded. "All at one time or another."

R. Karl Largent

"Exactly what happened?"

Maydee Hew leaned against the fuselage of the Terrier and scratched his chin. The proliferation of stubble hadn't quite progressed to the point where anyone would call it a beard.

I tried to get him started. "Cameron and his two technicians had been working on the barge most of the day. Is that right?"

"Yup," Hew confirmed. "Cameron reported that something 'hit' the barge and knocked some of his instruments out of whack. He told Porter he was getting some bogus readings . . . and he wanted one of the divers to check it out."

"Go on."

"Carson went down to the galley and got Brimley. He told him about Cameron's request. Carson said he figured Brimley would send Lord and Bench . . . but Brimley went himself. They looked the hull over, located the damage, came up, got some tools, and set about fixin' it."

"Did they say what kind of damage they found?"

Hew shook his head.

"What kind of tools did they want?"

Hew laughed. "The usual—the welding stuff; the acetylene tanks and some torches."

"Did they say what caused it?"

"I reckon that whatever they found must have been the damage caused by whatever it was that Cameron heard hit the barge." Hew sounded like a nineties version of Yogi Berra.

"Two questions," I said. "Was the barge moving when Cameron heard whatever he heard? And did you ever hear Brimley and Lord describe the damage?"

Hew looked at me. "Yeah, the barge was moving, all right. Back then we was trailing the bottom-profiling sonar from the *Hedgehog*. We had been towing it back and forth in sector five-K all day long."

"You're familiar with these waters, Maydee. Can you think of anything the *Hedgehog* might have hit?"

"Shallows, a reef, an outcropping—or maybe one of those monsters down there Jewel Simon is always talkin' about." Hew laughed, just in case I had missed his attempt at humor.

"Wouldn't the trailing sonar have detected any bottom anomaly big enough to damage the hull?"

Hew smiled. It was crooked and all the teeth weren't there, but it accomplished his mission. "If'n you was me and you knew there weren't nothin' down there in the way of bottom stuff that could have bumped Cameron's barge hard enough to do damage, what would you think?"

"I might think Jewel was right," I admitted.

The sessions with Porter and Hew had given me something to think about. I went back to my cabin, fumbled around until I found a candle, lit it, and sat down to record what I had learned in my journal.

First there was the actual time when Hew,

Carson, and Kritzmer had recorded the disappearance of the *Hedgehog*. According to the *Barbella*'s log, that was 18:42 on May 17.

Then there was the matter of the weather. The last recorded surface weather observation had been taken at 18:00L. At that time the *Barbella* was experiencing what is known in meteorological parlance as an X condition. An X condition simply means that from any given unobstructed viewing point, the viewer is unable to see any further than fifty feet either horizontally or vertically.

That raised two more questions. First, where was the *Hedgehog* tethered in relation to the *Barbella*'s wheelhouse? Second, under the circumstances, how much could be seen from the wheelhouse?

Hew maintained that he had contact with Cameron and his crew "just moments" before the barge disappeared. Did "just moments" mean five, ten, even thirty minutes? Obviously, there was no clear-cut answer—at least not yet.

At that point I turned my attention to the swarm or cluster quakes. What impact did they have on the barge's disappearance? A 3.0 quake on land would have been of little consequence. But this wasn't land—it was water, and water was a different story.

It all went back to one of those painful lessons from my youth. My father had sent me out to break up some concrete on an old patio. After thirty minutes of getting nowhere by giving it everything I had with my then-150-pound frame and my father's twenty-pound sledge, Pappy Wages came to my rescue. He simply set up a constant tapping motion, and it wasn't long before the concrete began to crack and crumble.

The same was true for the cluster quakes. If they were severe enough and happened often enough, sooner or later they were going to trigger some kind of chain reaction. The question was, was the magnitude and frequency of the May seventeenth cluster quakes enough to sink a ninety-foot-long salvage barge? I figured the insurance folks would be debating that one for years to come.

I drew a line down the middle of the page, from top to bottom. Then I listed the quakes, time, and weather in one column, and started a second list of factors in the other. Hew had indicated that the *Barbella* had been towing the barge through the five-K sector while the barge in turn trailed an absorption beam sonar to profile the bottom. In sequence, the first round of cluster quakes occurred, closely followed by a second. Somewhere in there, Cameron reported his problem. That was where my interpretation of what had happened became just a little too subjective. How big did something have to be to notice that a ninety-foot-long salvage barge weighing a good twenty tons had hit it?

Cameron must have thought that the incident

was significant; otherwise he would not have requested a damage report.

So where did that lead me? Answer? Nowhere.

I decided to take another approach. I checked off the list of names: Cameron, Ryder, Miller, Brimley, and Lord. They had one thing in common. All were missing and all were presumed dead. In the margin of column B, I scribbled a note:

Find out where Bench was at the time of the Hedgehog's *disappearance.*

Then I jotted down a few more questions. These were the afterthoughts; the unorganized what-ifs and the could-it-possibly be questions. Why did Cameron and his technicians stay aboard the *Hedgehog*? Did Brimley and Lord really think they had the damage to the *Hedgehog* repaired? And why, on subsequent dives, as Packy pointed out in the ship's log, did Brimley and Lord report that they were unable to locate the *Hedgehog*? It was a puzzle, and I was getting nowhere fast.

I slumped back in the chair and scanned my notes. I knew I wasn't any closer to coming up with concrete answers, but I felt better. I had the feeling that some semblance of order was starting to emerge from the chaos. Looking back, if I hadn't been indulging myself in a fit of self-congratulation on getting organized, I might have been aware of what was happening.

It all started with the feeling that the cabin, which had become progressively more stuffy without the air-conditioning, was becoming unbearable. I was sweating and the air was heavy. I looked out the porthole and saw that we were still wallowing in slate-gray air that clung to the thick glass and sealed off the world beyond. That was why the dryness in my throat should have been a clue.

Seconds later my eyes began to tear and itch, and before long, I was coughing. From there it went downhill fast. There was a stricture in my throat and I started gagging. Then I saw the first drop of blood splatter on the surface of the table where I had been making notes.

I staggered across the room, grabbed the doorknob, and started yelling for help. The door was locked. My fingers went numb as I tried to fumble with the latch. There was another spasm, a sharp, searing pain in my chest, cloudy vision, and my head began to throb. I had been in big trouble before—but I couldn't recall getting there any faster.

At that point the panic was already starting to set in. I knew if I didn't get help and damn quick, Mama Wages's boy, Elliott, was going to be in the kind of trouble he couldn't get out of.

I went to my knees, slumped against the door, and began pummeling it with my fists. I was shouting, but no sound was coming out. I started retching again, and this time a torrent of thick red mucus gushed out on the floor of my cabin. The room was beginning to spin.

The last thing I remember was someone trying to push the door open—but the weight of my body was wedged against it and they weren't making much progress. Then there were hands and shouts and lots of weird noises. I was making a hole on my way out.

There was a touch-and-go session with reality: lights, then no lights, retching, a pain in my chest, in my stomach—and then the welcome feel of a clammy kind of coldness on my body with someone forcing cold water into my mouth.

I coughed and gagged. Then I was rolled over on my stomach and the water was being used to stop the burning in my eyes.

Then, as if whoever was doing all these things knew it would, the burning sensation began to subside. Enough water had been forced down a throat that already constricted in rebellion that I had no other option than to throw up. It happened again and again. But for the first time I was hearing voices that made partial sense.

One of them was familiar—the other wasn't. There was a third and perhaps even a fourth voice—but they didn't matter—because they were off in the distance—shouting—disconnected—all unreal. I rolled over, didn't like the way it made me feel, and rolled back on my stomach again. My throat burned and my eyes, even though I was trying like hell, were refusing to open.

"Keep pumping the water down him," I heard one of the voices say.

"What about yours?" someone else shouted.

"I need help over here," a distant voice pleaded.

"I can't get a pulse," another complained.

"I think Wages is okay," the voice directly over me declared. I tried to force my eyes open to tell them they were all wrong—that I wasn't even close to making it. When I did, the vision blurred—and the words came out, sticky, thick, and unrecognizable.

"Give Maydee some help," someone shouted. I heard scurrying sounds—and then what sounded like someone dropping to the deck and making frantic breathing sounds.

Suddenly there was another voice in the chaotic montage; this voice was strident, panic-stricken—ushering in a string of redundant and frustrated expletives. "Damn it, no, damn it, no—no . . ."

Finally I managed to get one eye open to a slit-shaped, blurry image of a world that was completely devoid of color. It was a major accomplishment that was accompanied by a cauterizing kind of pain, and all I could see was the sooty tones of nothingness that I had been looking at out of my porthole when it all began.

When I forced the other eye open, the fragments of the nightmare began to coalesce. Now they were more than voices. Now they were images attached to the discordant sounds.

I recognized Fritze and Shula. They were working, almost hesitantly, around another prone figure—a smaller figure—a figure that was also moving.

Finally I was able to make out the face of Jewel Simon leaning over me. At the moment I wasn't the slightest bit interested in reading anything into her expression. I was too damn busy being grateful I could make out the worried details of her face.

Finally I heard Shula say, "I think she's starting to come around." That was when I realized that Packy Darnell had been through the same ordeal.

Then, out of the corner of my eye, I saw Kritzmer get to his feet. There was a stoic kind of finality to the gesture.

I saw Fredrich and Porter approaching with the sickly yellow wash of light cast by an incandescent bulb being energized by the standby generator. Kritzmer looked almost human. "There was nothing I could do," he said flatly.

I looked down at the place where Kritzmer had been kneeling. It was Kit Bench. He wasn't moving.

It was almost midnight when Porter and Kritzmer walked into the room. Porter slumped into a chair at the end of the galley table, while Kritzmer was content to remain standing by the door. The situation had changed. It dictated co-operation. Despite their differences and for whatever reason, the two men had decided there was strength in numbers. For the moment, at least, they had joined forces.

"How you feelin'?" Porter inquired. He sounded too weary to really care.

I replied with what I hoped would be interpreted as a semi-revealing grunt aimed at conveying discomfort. The same question posed toward the equally groggy Packy earned him little more than a furtive glance.

"Kit Bench didn't make it," Porter said. "Fredrich claims he never even got a pulse."

"What happened?" I finally asked. I was surprised at how weak my voice sounded.

"Internal hemorrhaging," Kritzmer said. "Mr. Bench bled to death."

Packy blinked back at the two men. For some reason she didn't look as bad as I did. She had a towel draped over her shoulders and looked vulnerable—but not any more vulnerable then she did the night she arrived aboard the *Perpetual Motion*.

"Does anyone know what happened?" she asked, her voice barely audible.

Porter reached in his pocket and produced a small vial. He set it on the table. "What do you know about cyanide?"

When Packy shook her head, Kritzmer said, "Hydrocyanic or prussic acid. It probably came from the sodium cyanide or the potassium cyanide my colleague, Dr. Fredrich, uses to test his subsurface samples."

Porter nodded toward the small vial sitting on the table. "We found it in the air-conditioning vents directly over Ms. Darnell's cabin."

"That stuff could have killed us," Packy said.

"If the generators had not been down, our perpetrator's clumsy efforts might not have been so effective," Kritzmer said. "HCN boils at 25.7 degrees centigrade. The air-conditioning ducts became incubators. As the dampness accumulated, it accelerated the potency. You were fortunate. A few milligrams of hydrogen cyanide can be fatal."

"Whoever it was, they meant business," Porter explained. "Like Kritzmer says, our not having any power played right into their hands. With the passageways dark except for a few strategically placed security lights, it was a piece of cake for someone to move around, remove and replace the access plate on the vent system in the B-deck cabins, and stuff these under the doors." Porter held up some towels.

"It would appear that they were taken from the ship's supply and linen room near the C-deck crew quarters," Kritzmer explained.

"There ain't much doubt about the son of a bitch's intentions," Porter said. "You were supposed to be dead by now."

"You found it in the ducts over Packy's room?" I asked.

Porter nodded. "I had Ritter and Carson

comb the area. There is an access door and a service trap in the ventilating system just above the door to Ms. Darnell's cabin. The way I got it figured, with no air movement to speak of in the ductwork, the heavy HCN molecules drifted to the low spots in the system. That would be the ventilators."

"Mr. Carson thinks you were the fortunate one, Ms. Darnell," Kritzmer said. "Your vent was partially closed. Otherwise, I'm afraid you would have been the one that received the brunt of the hydrocyanic onslaught."

When Packy heard that, she burst into tears, and Kritzmer continued slowly. "Instead, it was Mr. Bench who suffered the consequences."

By any stretch of the imagination, I wasn't feeling good, and I knew I wasn't on top of my game. Nevertheless, I pushed myself up to the table and started asking questions. My voice was scratchy and my tongue felt thick. "Have you checked to see where everyone was when this happened?"

Kritzmer nodded. "It's likely that the cyanide had been in the vent ducts no more than fifteen to thirty minutes before it started to boil. We know that Dr. Fredrich keeps the material stored at between thirty-five and forty-five degrees Fahrenheit and that the ambient temperature in the vents at that time would have been somewhere around ninety degrees Fahrenheit. So the only question is, how long did it take the hydrocyanic acid to reach the 78.2-degree-Fahrenheit boiling point?"

As I reached across the table and poured myself another glass of water, Kritzmer took out a small notebook and began rifling through the pages. "I have not had the opportunity to interrogate everyone, Mr. Wages, but it would appear that this misfortune occurred somewhere between 16:30 and 17:00 hours."

Packy came up for air. "Misfortune seems a bit of an understatement for what happened, doesn't it?"

Kritzmer wasn't fazed by the snarl. "From approximately 15:30 until Captain Porter apprised me of the situation, I was in my A deck stateroom with Dr. Fredrich. We were going over the printouts from yesterday's dive."

"With no power?"

"A small impediment in the form of insufficient lighting should hardly be grounds for not doing one's work, Mr. Wages. Would you not agree?"

"Then you're Fredrich's alibi and he's yours?"

"It would appear so, would it not, Mr. Wages? Does that bother you?"

It occurred to me that accusing either Kritzmer or Fredrich would have been a whole lot like saying that the butler had done it. The not-so-dynamic duo was just a bit too obvious. While it was true they were eager to claim what rightfully belonged to dear old Deutschland, claiming it had started with Ambrose Vance, the bottom line was, if Vance didn't line his pockets with the remainder of the gold from the national treasury of Francisco Franco, the Kraut contingent didn't stand to gain much.

"What about the rest of the crew?" I asked.

"We haven't had time to talk to all of them yet," Porter admitted. "Carson and Ritter were working on Brimley's Terrier. I could hear the generator."

"What about Chuco?"

"I know for a fact that he was in the galley most of the day. With Fritze spending all of his time working on getting the diesel and the diving sled repaired, we've been keeping Chuco busy down there."

"Jewel?"

"She's the one who discovered that something was wrong. She was on her way to her cabin when she smelled the bitter-almond odor. If she hadn't alerted us, Bench might not be the only victim."

"I want out," Packy said. Her voice was small and tortured. Still, the words surprised me.

Porter scowled. "Until Carson and Ritter can get us powered up again, ain't none of us goin' nowhere."

Incident:

Friday, July 15—03:40L

I woke up in the wee hours of the morning feeling, if not actually decent, at least tolerable. My throat was still sore, a condition that Chuco assured me from reading his books in the *Barbella*'s make shift infirmary was to be expected.

"You're gonna feel like a piece of shit for the next couple of days," he had proclaimed, and twelve or thirteen hours into the ordeal, he was right.

I rolled over, hit the light switch, and waited. Nothing happened—the room was still dark. I lay there for several minutes, listening for the telltale sounds of the *Barbella*'s generato... Again, nothing. Finally I admitted to myself that this was that special kind of spooky and deafening silence we tend to experience when our world quits working and we have to make do with pieces.

After what seemed like an eternity groping for a flashlight, I found one, and permitted myself the small luxury of enough light to find clothes and get dressed. Through it all, I was convinced I could still smell the bitter-almond aroma of the cyanide, and I was happy to get out of my cabin and away from the smell.

Any vessel, especially an incapacitated one the size of the *Barbella*, affords a minimum amount of places to go. In the middle of the night, that situation is compounded. I worked my way aft, past Porter's quarters, the kitchen, the ship's dining area, the wardroom, the diving locker, and out onto the rear deck near the winch.

If anything, the fog was thicker and the visibility further reduced by the darkness. It was as if the world ended just a few feet beyond my reach. I stood at the railing, gazing out into the nothingness, listening for the sound of the Sargasso. If there was movement, it was infinitesimal.

From there I decided to find out who was on watch, and I headed for the bridge. It turned out to be Kritzmer's taciturn associate, Marion Fredrich.

The moon-faced little man had managed to situate himself in such a fashion that he was able to capitalize on every amenity in the wheel-house. Despite that, his lab coat was soiled and wrinkled, he needed a shave, and even in the sinister light of a flickering kerosene lantern perched on the loran, he managed to look just slightly less than harmless.

There was nothing personable about Marion Fredrich. His high-foreheaded, puffy face hid behind heavy glasses, and his dull brown eyes were lifeless. They reminded me of the eyes of a derelict. His empty stare was the kind I had learned to associate with street people; they mirrored a special kind of hopelessness.

"Couldn't sleep," I admitted.

He glanced at me, acknowledged my presence with a slight nod, and proceeded to finish his cigarette. The ashtray betrayed him. It had been a long, lonely, unnerving night for the little man, and the stale smoke from the previous cigarettes still lingered in the super-saturated air. Already he was lighting another.

"Long night, huh?"

Fredrich flinched as though he was surprised I had a voice. Finally he nodded.

I looked around the wheelhouse, then gazed into the fog for several minutes before I tried again. "Heard whether or not there was any progress on the generator repairs?"

Fredrich shook his head. I wasn't sure how to interpret that, no progress on the repairs, or—no, he hadn't heard. He turned away, like me beguiled by the fog. Finally, he endured the agony of verbalizing what had probably been on his mind before I interrupted the wheelhouse tranquility.

"What is it like down there?" he asked. He slid into the question, like a man who wasn't certain he wanted to know.

My response was the wrong response—probably because I didn't particularly feel like rhapsodizing. "It's there," I said, "like everything. Some days are better than others."

When Fredrich grew silent again, I realized it had not taken much to shut him off. He was still there—but he had withdrawn. From his perspective, he figured he had made his overture—and I had cut him off. I knew I would have to wait several minutes before I tried again.

"I'm curious, Marion," I finally said. "What's in this Sargasso thing for you? I get the feeling you couldn't care less about Vance's treasure quest. It's hot and sticky. I figure you can probably think of a hell of a lot of places you'd rather spend your time than the Sargasso."

When the little man finally looked at me again, I thought I saw a spark of interest. But when he spoke, his voice sounded distant and detached. "I've never actually been down there," he said. I knew he wasn't registering a complaint; he was simply stating a fact.

"You have your videotapes," I reminded him. "In some ways that's even better. The camera records things your eyes miss down there." At that point I was thinking about the videotape footage Gabe Lord had shot of Miller and the assortment of oversized Sargasso denizens that Fredrich still assured me only he and I knew about.

Fredrich's voice had a lingering brittleness. He squinted into the fog, and at first I thought he was praying. Then the words began to filter out.

"You see, Mr. Wages, the form of the creature is fluid. Through my viewing port in the forward observation port, I have seen the big one focus his eyes directly upon me. He is magnificent. He does not lose sight of his prey for even a fraction of a second. I have seen his ballet, his infinite grace, the indescribably beautiful brute force he exhibits. Then I realize that his function and purpose have not changed in more than one hundred million years. I am witnessing, I tell myself, the consummate killing machine."

I had the feeling Marion Fredrich had just revealed more of himself than he realized. "Would you even be here if it were not for Dr. Kritzmer?" I asked.

"I would not be anywhere," Fredrich said.

"I don't understand."

"One could say that he saved my life."

I waited to see if Fredrich intended to elaborate. When he fell silent again, I pressed on. "Were you observing through your forward port the day Brimley disappeared?"

The moon-faced man nodded.

"Did you see the one with the big fin?"

"Are you talking about the great shark?"

"Yes."

"I see him every day. He is always there. He watches me. He sees everything."

It wasn't until Fredrich revealed that information that I realized how warped and twisted his perspective had become. He actually saw his role as that of the creature's protector.

Earlier he had indicated that he did not want others to know about his find, not because others would come to seek out the shark, but because they would simply make the search for the U-564 all the more difficult. That, of course, had been his subterfuge, his own attempt at acceptable dissimulation.

Now the question was, did Kritzmer's assistant, the little man in the wrinkled white lab coat, feel strongly enough about protecting what he had witnessed in the Sargasso waters to kill?

With the exception of Cameron, I could construct a scenario at least superficially logical in which Marion Fredrich was systematically attempting to eliminate the divers who threatened to uncover the U-564. For him, the equation was simple: no discovery—no one descending on the dive site.

I went over the list: Lord, Brimley, Bench, Ryder, and Morgan. And if it hadn't been for a fortuitously closed air-conditioning vent, Packy

Darnell's name might well have been an addition to that list.

It was at that point in our exchange that Fredrich seemed to get a grip on himself. He glanced at me, cleared his throat, made an empty and pointless comment about the *Barbella*'s continued lack of power, and took down the ship's log to record his 05:00 entry. Even then he seemed a bit too distracted to write. I watched him light another cigarette, scribble one or two comments in the book, and set it aside. He appeared to be unable to concentrate.

At that moment, my assessment of Marion Fredrich was that while he lived on the ragged edge of reality, I wasn't looking at the kind of man who would put a vial of cyanide in the ductwork to protect his prehistoric friends in the Sargasso.

I left the bridge, worked my way back to the radio room, turned on my flashlight, and looked over the charred remains of the *Barbella*'s Com Cen gear. Everything seemed to be pretty much as it had been after the fire was extinguished the previous morning. I was no authority on such matters, but from where I stood, most of the gear appeared to be beyond repair.

I was engrossed enough in rummaging through what was left of the Com Cen that I did not hear Porter come up behind me. "If you hadn't come' pretty damn close to buyin' the farm in that cyanide incident yesterday, I might be askin' you if you had returned to the scene of the crime."

"Nothing that diabolical," I said. "Couldn't sleep."

Porter grunted and pushed past me. In so doing he stepped out of the thin strip of gray-silver illumination that constituted a foggy-morning Sargasso sunrise. Then he turned on his flashlight, panned the room, and directed the beam of light into my face.

"You still look like shit," he said.

"I feel like it too. I've been up on the bridge talking to Fredrich."

"Good. You probably kept him awake. Otherwise the little creep probably would have propped his ass up there on the bridge all night and slept. Can't help it, though. We're runnin' out of people to put on watch."

"How long have you known Fredrich?"

Porter hunched his bull shoulders. "He's part of Kritzmer's baggage. As far as knowin' him, I don't. Kritzmer dragged him aboard. Neither one of their names appeared on the original crew roster when I signed on for this godforsaken mission . . . and they damn sure weren't aboard the night we sailed. Two days out I got a call from Ambrose—that's when he informed me he had hired Kritzmer as some kind of concession to the German government. Seems the Krauts had two things on their mind. One, they wanted to make damn certain they got their share of whatever we recovered, and two, they wanted to be equally sure no one did anything to desecrate the graves of those poor sons of bitches that went down with the U-564."

While I tried to assess what Porter was telling me, I was also trying to decide whether or not he was one of the people aboard the *Barbella* I could trust. If we were going to get out of this thing alive, I knew I was going to have to have some help. That meant I had to trust someone. Porter was one of the candidates.

I took Porter by the arm and steered him out of the charred radio room into the damp air on deck. He gave me a curious look. "What the hell's with you, Wages?"

"We need to talk in private."

I think my reply must have surprised him. He studied me for a moment, then turned and headed down the ladder toward his quarters. He motioned for me to follow.

When we were inside, he closed the door, lit the hurricane lamp, motioned me to a seat next to his desk, and busied himself pouring each of us a couple of fingers of bourbon in old jelly glasses. He handed me one, but I declined. He shrugged, poured the two together, and bolted the contents.

"You know what I decided, Wages? A man only needs three things in this shitty world: a woman, some bourbon, and an occasional snort. All of which goes to show you just how goddamn bad it is out here. Thirteen weeks without a woman, been out of the dust for better than two weeks now, and all that's left is this sorry-ass cheap bourbon."

With that, he lit his usual cigarette, sat down on his bunk, and rubbed his forehead. When he wasn't trying to massage away the demons, he was squinting at me, trying to decide what I was all about.

My first volley surprised him. "How long would it take Carson and Ritter to piece together one of the sea sleds so I could go down to take a look at the *Hedgehog*?"

At first he didn't answer. He cocked his head to one side. Finally he said. "Suppose we could get one of the sleds ready and . . . suppose you went down to inspect the wreck of that damn barge—what's that accomplish?"

"I have a theory," I said.

Porter leaned back. "Let's hear it."

"I talked to both Kritzmer and Hew about what happened that night."

"And?"

"According to Kritzmer, the first series of swarm quakes occurred just after he informed Carson he had hit something in the water."

"Go on," Porter said.

"The second set of swarm quakes occurred after Brimley and Lord had inspected the damage. It was at this point that Cameron informed the bridge that he was powering up the *Hedgehog* and would be coming in alongside the *Barbella* so they could secure the barge for the night."

"That would be the procedure," Porter confirmed. "Brimley had us tow the *Hedgehog* on those initial sweeps because the screws on the barge created such a racket that it interfered with the readings on the sonar array the old tub was dragging."

"Sometime and somewhere between the time and space Cameron indicated he was coming in, he reported that he'd either *hit something or something had hit him*."

Porter nodded. "That sounds more like Maydee's words than somethin' Cameron woulda said."

"This is where something gets lost in the translation," I acknowledged. "Cameron doesn't indicate that the collision was all that alarming, yet he requests the bridge to dispatch divers to make a damage assessment."

I had Porter's attention. His body language gave him away. He put out his cigarette and leaned into the conversation.

"This raises more questions," I said. "One, what made Cameron think that whatever he hit had caused enough damage that it needed to be inspected? Two, what's out there that, if you collided with it, would cause enough damage to be of any real concern? Which brings up the third question. Why did Cameron ask Kritzmer to send out divers from the *Barbella*? Ryder and Morgan were also divers. If that's true . . . getting Brimley and Lord in the water to inspect the damage was the long way around the barn."

I could tell from Porter's expression that he hadn't caught up with me yet.

"Now," I went on, "Brimley and Lord get in the water, they conduct a damage assessment, surface—and request some tools. What do they request? Well, among other things, acetylene torches. I specifically asked Maydee Hew if they requested any welding equipment. He said no."

Porter got up and poured himself another drink. He leaned against his wall locker waiting for me to continue. "So you figure Brimley and Lord did what?" he finally asked.

"I think they made damn sure the *Hedgehog* went down."

Porter started to laugh. "For Christ's sake, Wages, even I can see the holes in that theory. You want me to believe that Cameron called in Brimley and Lord to make certain the damn barge sank? No way. Why would Cameron stay on board the damn thing if he knew it was going to be scuttled?"

"I don't have all the answers yet," I admitted.

"Sounds to me like there's quite a few of 'em you ain't got nailed down," Porter said.

"That's why I want to get a better look at that barge."

"And that's why you want me to have Carson and Ritter get one of the sleds ready?"

"Actually, I want two things. A working sled is one."

"What's the other?"

"Brimley had the stateroom next to yours. I

want to get in there and look around. Then I want to get a look at Brimley's contract, the one he signed with Ambrose Vance."

Porter walked to his desk and opened a small door above the desk that revealed the door to a safe. He twisted the dial for a couple of seconds and the door opened. He reached in, and when his hand emerged, he was clutching a small stack of papers.

"Nifty little hiding place," I said.

Porter grunted. "Vance claimed he bought this tub from a some guy in South Africa. Said the guy used to smuggle diamonds, but gave it up when he discovered he could make a hell of lot more money packin' powder." He threw the stack of papers on his bunk. "There's a copy of Brimley's contract in there somewhere. Ain't no need to read it, though. They all got the same deal: half of one percent of whatever we recover."

"Same for you?" I asked.

"It might be a little different cut for me," Porter admitted. He wasn't smiling, which, I figured, was another way of telling me it wasn't any of my business.

"Same contract for Cameron?"

Porter nodded. "Cameron and Brimley were in for half of a percent of whatever we brought up. The non-essential personnel signed on for something less. Kritzmer's and Fredrich's deal is with their government. Anyway you slice it, if that damn U-564 contains even half of what

Old Man Ambrose thinks it holds, everyone on this tub has got themselves a one-way ticket to the good life."

"How about it? Do I get a look at Brimley's cabin?"

Porter dug in his pocket and produced a key. "Here," he said, "this'll get you into any damn stateroom or cabin on this ship."

"What about the sled?"

"I'll talk to 'em" Porter said.

With Porter gone, I went over Luke Brimley's personal belongings. They failed to shed much light on his role in what was happening aboard the *Barabella*. If Brimley had his own agenda, or was part of some sort of a sinister plot, there was nothing among his personal effects to point to it.

The one item that I found intriguing was his resume. The document was no more than one page in length, but it contained a history of the major salvage projects he had worked since his early days in Naples. It took me less than an hour to determine that either Luke Brimley didn't have what I was looking for, or I wasn't looking in the right places.

By the time I had finished, it was almost 09:00 and the sun had finally managed to burn off some of the fog that had been enveloping the *Barabella* for the past several days. The visibility was all the way up to a sixteenth of a mile by the time I started aft.

Both Ritter and Carson were working on the

Terrier. The doors to the aft hold were open, and everything appeared to be buttoned up but the craft's canopy.

Ritter looked up, squinting into the silver glare of a bright fog. "Porter tells us you found the wreckage of the *Hedgehog*."

"It was there all along."

"How come Brimley and Lord didn't find it?"

"You never find anything if you don't look in the right place," I said. I didn't smile, and Ritter didn't catch on. I figured it would come to him after he had a chance to digest it.

"Who's goin' down with you?" Carson asked.

"Nobody's riding shotgun," I said. "I'm going down to take a look at the *Hedgehog* to see if there is anything we can salvage."

"The power plant on the *Hedgehog* is similar to the *Barbella*'s diesels," Carson said. "If we could get the injectors out of that baby down there, we might be able to get this one fired up."

I glanced up at the five-ton hydraulic crane perched on the *Barbella*'s stern, then back at the winch. "What's the capacity of that little gem and how much cable have we got?"

Carson was beginning to get the picture. "I can rig up a hundred-fifty-foot cable."

"Enough to hoist that generator?"

"That and then some," Shula said. "Where is she?"

"She's lying down there in about ninety feet of water. I'll have to look around to see if we can get to the power plant, though."

At that point even Fritze Ritter was beginning to get the picture. "You'll have to torch her loose. She's bolted to sixteenth-inch steel plate and she's ground with four-inch-long steel pins and cable. Plus—you'll need something to cut through the lines."

Shula Carson led me back to the *Barbella*'s engine room and showed me how the *Hedgehog*'s diesels would be bolted to the decking. "You'll have to cut here and here," he said, pointing. Then he indicated where the fuel lines could be cut. "Know how to operate a torch?" he asked, and I indicated that I did. "It's more than a one-man job. You gonna have help?"

I explained that with the untimely death of Kit Bench, the *Barbella*'s salvage crew had been reduced to two divers. One experienced—and one not so experienced. He was talking to the one with the lesser experience.

"What about the Darnell dame?" Carson asked.

"We can't take the chance. Fredrich says the cyanide tore her throat up. If she does any diving now, the air mixture in those cylinders can't contain even a trace of carbon monoxide or oil vapors. The slightest hint of contaminant in her tanks could open up every blister in her throat. One hundred feet down in the Sargasso is no place for a seizure."

At approximately 10:30 hours, Fritze Ritter and I manually winched the Terrier over the stern and down into the water. Then, while Shula Carson went over the contents of the equipment locker on the sled, I verified the accessibility, and in some cases, working condition, of each item. There was a spare dive light, a night-vision camera, spare film cartridges, spare air, additional weights, auxiliary straps, O-rings, some CO_2 cartridges, a tube of suit cement, an assortment of bulbs for the sled and diver lamps, batteries, and a 150-foot long, five-thousand-pound nylon test line.

Then Carson gave me the final check. He checked off each item as he went over the list; gear bag, weight belt, BCD, backpack, regulator with SPG and alternate air source, wrist compass, depth gauge, PCD computer, chest-mounted halogen, watch, and E-time indicator.

"Remember," he said. "Your life support system in the personnel pod of the Terrier is not working and your 21T cabin-mounted air supply is not functioning. We don't have the parts to repair it. As far as air goes, you've got what's in your tanks and the pony. Watch your mission time. Your E-time is one hundred twenty minutes max—and that's only if you don't get too excited down there. If you have any trouble at all, release the Corsican flag—I don't know what the hell we'll do about it—but at least we can start wringing our hands.

"Remember to attach the D-ring the minute you dismount from the sled—and be aware that the L-line will probably get in your way, but if ·

you have any trouble it may save your ass.
You're on beacon fifty-five, stay on it. We've got
the standby generator hooked up so we can get
a constant pulse. The one thing we can't give
you is radio contact. The minute you go below
the surface, we break voice contact and you're
on your own. And—I almost hate to bring this
one up, Wages, but you realize that you're it. We
don't have anybody we can send down after
you."

Actually, I was doing fairly well until Carson
laid that last one on me. Then I did a slow swallow.

It was 19:10 when I jumped into the water,
slid into the cockpit, straddled the saddle of the
Terrier, made one final check of the sled's onboard systems, and purged my ballast tanks. At
that point the Terrier began to slide beneath the
moss-covered, weed-green surface of the Sargasso.

According to my PCD, I was already
breathing at an accelerated rate.

I had learned a little about what to expect
from the Sargasso from previous dives. There
wasn't much action in the water and with little
mixing going on, it was a whole lot more like a
biological desert than a landscape teeming with
millions of life forms. The clumps of sargassum
weed played host to what marine life there was
and the small fish, crabs, and shrimp didn't
stray very far from them.

The more I thought about it, this dearth of

smaller marine life made it all the more curious that Fredrich reported spotting both the giant mantas and some unusually large six-gill sharks through his viewing post in the *Barbella*'s observation bow.

So much for the theory of the food chain.

The clumps of sargassum became more frequent and started to blend in with the swaying forest of elephant grass. When that happened, my world went from dark to darker and I plunged through a thermocline into decidedly colder waters.

Despite the mind-numbing tangle of rystmus weed and hyndra, the combination of an efficient preprogrammed NV computer and an ultra-accurate DDG guided me to within a few hundred feet or so of the depression where the bottom profile gave way to the thirty-or-forty-foot drop-off.

I parked the Terrier, crawled off, hammered a six-inch steel pin into the rock formation on the lip of the drop-off, attached the O-ring, looped the rope through it, and scaled down to the wreck of the *Hedgehog*. On deck, I worked my way past and around piles of debris toward the superstructure where the two-story wheelhouse, engine room, and crew quarters were located. The wheelhouse had been crushed by the shift of deck equipment sometime during the sinking. Immediately behind and to the rear of the wheelhouse was the engine room where the *Hedgehog*'s diesel was located. Behind it was a wall and a room with a sink, a head, and an adjacent area with two narrow bunks. Beyond that, there was an enclosure just outside the combination crew quarters and engine room where someone had rigged a shower head. There wasn't much left of any of it. The rest of the deck was littered with wreckage and rubbish: crates, barrels, a tangle of cables, a couple of welding tanks, and a diesel fuel tank. The latter had been dislodged and there was a rupture in the tank. A thin stream of diesel fuel was still bleeding from a violated seam near the bottom.

From the looks of things, the *Hedgehog* had slipped into a trench that cut at a severe right angle through the five-K sector. I played the beam of my sweep halogen into the depth of the trench beyond the bow of the barge and watched the white-yellow light get swallowed up by the blackness. Without the charts, there was no way to tell how deep or long the trench actually was.

I crossed from port to starboard, swam up what proved to be no more than a ten-percent incline, and looked back. From that vantage point I stabbed the beam of my halogen down into the trench again. On the starboard, near the stern, the ship was wedged against a large ridge projecting out from the rocks at the edge of the ravine. I knew that in all probability it wasn't Marianas Trench situation where I was staring into something 36,000 feet down. Nevertheless, it was black and foreboding, and because of the limited visibility, it was one of those places that gives you the feeling that it's a long—no, make that a hell of a long—way to the bottom.

I worked my way back through the rubble to a point about midship, shimmied over the side, and began to examine the port hull of the *Hedgehog* just below what had been the waterline. A demarcation line of rust, barnacles, and lime deposits gave a good indication of just how long the old girl had been surviving in these waters. I took out the camera, snapped a couple of pictures for reference, and began to work my way from midship toward the bow. I still hadn't found anything to support any of my theories.

Because I thought it would be easier to move on around to the starboard, I swam out and around the bow, working the beam of my light in an up-and-down movement along the length of the hull. So far, what I was certain would be there, wasn't.

By 030 E-time I had worked my way to a point where the sweep of the deck was starting back toward the stern again. A tangle of rusting steel cables had looped over the side, paradoxically some of what had to be the very salvage equipment the *Barbella* would need when her diesels were repaired.

Twice during the port-side inspection I had gotten the nylon lifeline tangled in deck debris. And because it was too short to allow me to conduct the same inspection of the starboard hull, from midship on back to the stern, I decided to disconnect it and loop it over one of the mooring cleats. That gave me the freedom of movement I needed.

I was just about back to my starting point when I found what I was looking for. Suspicion confirmed. Proof positive that in the hands of the right man, an acetylene torch can cut one hell of a hole in the hull of a barge. This one was about eight to ten feet long and a good twelve inches in width. They had cut through the skin, the baffle, and the plate—the way a good salvage diver learns to do it.

It didn't matter much whether it was Brimley or Lord, or both of them; they had done a number on the *Hedgehog* and they had done a lethal job. The hole was just forward of midship, just below the waterline and angled so that any kind of draft or forward movement would force the old girl to take on the maximum amount of water.

I flooded the hole with the light of my chest-mounted halogen and started taking pictures. I had the feeling that before Ambrose Vance was through wrestling with his maritime insurance company, he was going to need every last one of them.

Getting sufficient evidence to prove that Brimley and Lord had actually contributed to the sinking of the *Hedgehog* took care of one matter. That was the easy part. Finding a way to salvage some of the parts from the barge's diesel power plant was an altogether different matter. I swam back to what was left of the superstructure and inspected the structure where the *Hedgehog*'s diesel was housed. As near as I could determine the housing was constructed primarily of timber, as was most of the decking where the big power plant was mounted. The only place where I could see that steel plates had been used was where the unit had been installed—and that was primarily for reinforcement. The mounting had been accomplished with what appeared to be four-inch steel bolts at something approximating twenty-four-inch intervals along a flange on the base. Studying the situation in what my DI was indicating was 111 feet of water, I was begining to doubt that the barge's power plant could be recovered.

The way I saw it, the only way to remove the bolts was to torch them out. It was obvious that whoever had initially installed the unit on the *Hedgehog* had never imagined a scenario where the unit would have to be salvaged under water.

Having determined that any effort to salvage the whole package was probably doomed to failure, I checked my gauges, calculated that I still had something close to forty minutes of bottom time left, and worked my way topside, under one of the beams, where I could get to the valve cover and at the injectors.

The area was confining. There were less than thirty-six inches of clearance between the engine's cover plates and the roof of the diesel shed. All of which meant I had two new problems. One, it was going to be damn difficult to get leverage on the cover plate bolts, and two, I had to be careful I didn't damage any of my diving gear. Complicating matters even further was the fact that I would have to exit the engine shed and return to the Terrier for the tool kit.

I curled my way down, snaked out of the enclosure, and started for the sled.

That was when I saw it.

It was bigger than a damned semi and there was no mistaking its intent. It was coming straight at me. All I could see was mouth and teeth and those cold, dead, black eyes. I was face to face with a giant-size version of what has been called the consummate killing machine.

From that point on, every response was pure reflex.

Incident:

Friday, July 15—14:33L

Somehow I managed to veer to my right and he missed me on the first pass. Even then, he managed to get close enough that his sandpaper hide abraded through my dive suit. I rolled over, righted myself, and watched a thin pink-red cloud of blood billow out from an abrasion on my right forearm and another on my right leg where the hide was gone.

There was no time to conduct a damage report. I was focused on what appeared to be a narrow space between the edge of the barge's deck and the rocks supporting it.

I made it just in time to look back and see the creature pitch its massive bulk into the steel plates of the barge. I felt the carcass of the old ship shudder and begin to slip sideways. When it did, the beast looped up and over and crashed into it a second time. On the second pass I was looking straight into the big bastard's mouth. It came within inches and my regulator, caught on an outcropping, was ripped away. When that happened, my face must have scraped along the same outcropping because my mask was knocked off, the salt water assaulted my eyes, and I ended up groping in the darkness for my mask and regulator.

Apparently it wasn't checkout time. I fumbled around, located the mask, held it with one hand, and cleared the skirt with the other. Finally I was able to slide it back over my face.

The regulator was an altogether different problem. It had become lodged behind the handle of my bone knife. Getting it back in place wasn't easy. When I did, it didn't work and my first inclination was to think it was fouled. I pulled it out, twisted it, and put it back in my mouth a second time, only to suck in and swallow the bitter-salt taste of the Sargasso. The second-stage hose had been severed.

With chest pounding, I reached back and grabbed the pony tank. Shula Carson had rigged it with its own regulator and sleeved it to my primary tank. I pulled it out, straightened the hose, turned the valve, and felt the first surge slam into my chest.

Just as I did, the monster crashed into the

heavy timber deck of the barge, and I felt the ninety-foot-long ship shudder as it slipped further into the crevasse. I had learned a long time ago that objects underwater appear to be some twenty-five percent or so larger than they do on the surface. Even with that, the beast was the biggest thing I had encountered. In the washed-out light of my halogen, it appeared to be mostly slate gray in color with a white underbelly and a torpedo-shaped head with a blunted, slightly upturned snout. I counted gills: six instead of the conventional five. I estimated the length at somewhere in the neighborhood of thirty-five to forty feet.

When the creature came directly at me, its mouth was a good seven or eight feet across and there was one hell of a terrifying display of row after row of fist-sized, jagged teeth.

The mind does funny things at a time like that. I had a flashback to something I had read by a French scientist who claimed he had snared a giant Great White off of the Great Barrier Reef in the early sixties. The man reported that it was twenty-five feet in length . . . a record. I had news for them. This one was bigger— a hell of a lot bigger.

The creature circled one more time and made another pass less than five feet from where I was hiding. I got the distinct feeling from the look in those insensate eyes that the big bastard was telling me he wasn't through with me.

I glanced at my E-time indicator and checked

the reserve on the pony tank. The situation was getting a bit sticky. If the prehistoric juggernaut didn't find himself another diversion in the next seven or eight minutes, I knew I was going to be in a heap of trouble.

From where I was hiding between the wreck of the barge and the ridge of the ravine, I watched the monster cruise in ever wider circles. The attack frenzy appeared to be over.

At one point the beast disappeared into the undulating confusion of elephant grass and didn't return for what seemed like an eternity. I started to get my hopes up. Then without warning, it reappeared directly overhead, seemingly intent on diving straight for the Terrier. It attacked the sled just as I had seen tiger sharks attack a wounded seal. The sand and bottom debris billowed up as the giant jaws clamped over it. The beast thrashed violently, oversize jaws locked in an improbable death grip on a fragile fiberglass sled.

Within seconds the giant had reduced the Terrier to a tangle of wiring and broken body panels. Within thirty seconds the sled had all but disappeared the way millions of dolphins, sea lions, and seals had fallen victim to the same kind of eons-old violence.

Somehow I managed to retreat even further into my hiding place along the ravine and under the barge. I had every intention of staying there until the fury subsided again, regardless of the amount of air left in my tank.

When the behemoth emerged from the churning clouds of sand and rubble, I had the impression it looked assuaged. At first I figured it was nothing more than my own hopes and fears getting the best of me. But the beast's eyes were no longer hooded, and the side-to-side body agitation was clearly less pronounced. It made several more passes over the barge and then disappeared into the disorder and disarray of the Sargasso weed.

I seized the opportunity. I glanced down at the E-time factor on my instrument console and tried to calculate my ascent time. I was already seven minutes into the pony—and I hadn't even begun to think about getting out of there.

That was when I felt the earth start to tremble again, and realized I was experiencing the halo effect of the swarm quake. I felt the *Hedgehog* shift. Then it started to slide. It hung on the edge of the ravine for what seemed like an eternity and protested. Then it screamed some sort of final and terrible epithet and pitched down into the blackness. Finally, all there was, was silence.

I stayed there for a long period of time. Too terrified to move, I crouched in that jagged outcropping, well aware that I was breathing too fast and that I had lost what little cover I had. It would have been sheer folly to move; so I concentrated on remaining motionless.

All the while I was trying to calculate the distance from where I was, still hiding on the ridge below the edge of the ravine, to what looked like the slightly safer cover of the elephant grass. I was guessing the distance at less than fifty yards. But fifty yards across a stretch where there was no sargassum or plant life presented the six-giller with the only opportunity he needed.

Still, I knew that, if I could make it to the tangle of sargassum, rystmus weed, and God knows what else growing in that thick, green, inviting underwater jungle, I had at least a fraction of a chance.

At the moment, it was damn little consolation that the shark, with one major exception— keenly developed olfactory sense—was working with the same handicap I was. Plus, there was another big factor. I was bleeding and he wasn't. That put him one up in the seek-and-find or, in my case, swim-and-hide game.

By the time I checked my E-time factor again, I had run out of options. A couple of fast calculations told me I'd need somewhere in the neighborhood of twenty minutes to get to the surface. I had, at the most, twenty-three minutes to accomplish that feat. If my shark friend was still in the area, what little margin I had left was going to be used up in a big hurry.

I moved as fast as I could to the cover of the sargassum, timed my ascent, and counted off every second. I rotated in a slow 360-degree circle trying to keep an eye open for the six-giller. With a horizontal visibility of little more than four or five feet in the thick of the sargassum, I was all too aware that the big, ugly bastard could be no more than a few feet away from me at any one moment and I wouldn't know it until it hit me.

I paused just long enough to do my count at sixty-six and thirty-three feet, each time checking the E-time and monitoring the DG. When I broke through to the surface, I got my second break. I was surround by sargassum. If that prehistoric killing machine was still cruising around beneath me, it was going to be tough for him to spot me. I kept my legs as motionless as possible, scooped surface sargassum along in front of me and began working my way toward the *Barbella*. Every inch of the way I was wondering how Porter was going to react to the fact that the last of the sea sleds was lying in pieces no more than fifty yards from where the *Hedgehog* had really finally disappeared.

I swam around to the stern, crawled up on the dive platform, took off my mask, and looked back down in the water. There it was. I saw the huge dorsal fin rise above the surface as the giant six-giller cruised defiantly to within fifty feet of the stern.

There was no one there to see it but me. Even with the heat and the oppressive humidity, I was shivering.

It was 19:30 hours when the last of the *Barbella* crew finally stumbled into the galley. I found myself situated across from Shula Carson, Eberhard Kritzmer, and Marion Fredrich, while Fritze Ritter and Jewel Simon sat beside me. Maydee Hew, Packy, and Chuco had gotten there early. They were sitting at the far end of the galley table. Mookie and the captain were the last to arrive. As a whole they looked defeated and dispirited. The heat, the fear, and the uncertainty were taking their toll.

Carson had managed to round up two hurricane lamps. The flickering light constituted the room's only illumination. At the same time, somewhere in the background, I could hear the laboring sounds of the ship's last standby gas-fired generator. It occurred to me that the lamps and the generator were about the only things on the *Barbella* that still worked.

I had spent what was left of the afternoon with Porter, reporting what I had found aboard the *Hedgehog*. Now there wasn't any doubt. The sinking of the *Hedgehog* had been a conspiracy. And even though we didn't have answers to questions like who and why, Porter decided to gather everyone for the briefing.

He leaned forward with his hands on the table. Unshaven and wearing a stained T-shirt, he looked like anything but a ship's captain. "Listen up," he said. "I think most of you know that I sent Wages down to take a look at what was left of the *Hedgehog* earlier today. It was a long shot, but we thought he might be able to recover the injectors off of the barge's engine."

Kritzmer cleared his throat. "Everyone here finds it strange, Captain Porter, that our divers repeatedly reported they were unable to find the remains of the barge, only to have Mr. Wages locate it on his second dive."

As Fredrich, sitting beside his colleague, nodded agreement, I pushed the sector map across the table at Kritzmer. There was a red X in the northeast quadrant of five-K. "It was there all the time," I said. "There's a general downslope in that area. Everything appears to funnel into a deep trench that runs diagonally through the sector."

Fredrich understood. "And because of this bottom configuration, the action of the constant swarm quakes only exacerbates the situation. Correct?"

"Exactly. Eventually, everything slides into that trench."

"Then the salvage of diesel parts is not feasible?" Kritzmer asked.

When I shook my head, Ritter asked, "Can't we get to 'em?"

"Afraid not. That last series of quakes shook the barge loose. It slipped deeper into that trench."

"How deep?" Packy asked.

"I don't know," I said. "I didn't have enough light to work with and that trench, however deep it is, is not on the charts. It could be another one hundred or so feet—or it could be a thousand. With no power, there's no way of telling."

"There are some ranges," Fredrich said, "in this part of the ocean where depths exceed three thousand feet. Since this particular area is uncharted, we could be dealing with depths that exceed our dive capability."

"Wait a minute," Jewel said. "Are you saying that if we can't get to the barge we aren't going to be able to repair the *Barbella*'s engines?"

Porter nodded. "We need the injectors out of the barge's engines."

"Then we are prisoners here," Jewel said.

Porter looked like a man who had already been stretched to the limits. "This is the situation," he said without theatrics. "There are eleven of us. We're stranded in the middle of the Sargasso, and if that isn't enough, one of us is a murderer."

Porter hesitated before continuing, but none of the others knew what to say. They didn't even protest the fact that Porter had called one of them a murderer.

Finally he said, "Wages and I are in agreement. First, we think everyone might breathe a bit easier if we posted some kind of around-the-clock security in addition to the bridge watch. Second, we're going to conduct a search of the *Barbella* to see if we can't find something that will point us toward Kit Bench's killer."

Kritzmer bristled. "Quite obviously, Captain Porter, your rather pedestrian little search and interrogation plan does not include Dr. Fredrich or me. Correct?"

Jewel laughed. "Everyone gets the same treatment, Professor, even you."

Porter spoke up again. "I'm going with the people I know I can trust. At the moment, that's Wages, Shula Carson, and me. If I need backup, I've got this." He laid a military-style .45 on the table in front of him. Even in the semidarkness, the weapon looked imposing.

There was a long silence before Kritzmer leaned back in his chair. "I am not easily intimidated, Captain. Suppose Dr. Fredrich and I decide not to cooperate. What do you and your associates propose to do about it?"

Porter didn't flinch. He reached into his pocket and threw the ammo clip on the table. "I propose, as you put it, to blow your fuckin' head off, Herr Kritzmer."

"It would appear, Professor," Jewel said, laughing again, "that it would be in your best interest to cooperate."

"First Officer Carson will handle the security tonight," Porter said flatly. "And Wages will relieve him at 06:00 hours tomorrow morning. In the meantime, Wages and I will start the cabin search. We're starting, Kritzmer, with you."

Kritzmer closed his eyes. Porter had won.

"It's agreed then. We'll take the first-deck staterooms in order. That means Kritzmer, Fredrich, Brimley, and Lord. When we're through with those, we'll move down to the B

243

deck and pick up Wages's cabin, along with Miss Darnell's, and Kit Bench's stuff. Sooner or later, we're going to uncover something that's going to crack this thing open. Just in case someone didn't understand, no one returns to his cabin until I give you the okay."

It was Jewel Simon who pushed herself away from the table first. "Elliott," she said. "Before you get started, I must talk to you."

I waited for the room to clear. "It's your nickel."

"Not here," she said, glancing around at the shadows. "Can we go topside?"

I followed Jewel down the passageway, up the steps, and into another pallid Sargasso sunset, a twilight study in foreboding grays. Jewel lit a cigarette, puffed nervously, and turned to face me.

"Tell me. Who does China suspect?"

The question surprised me. "We're all suspects."

"Does he think I was trying to get rid of the Darnell woman?"

"Somebody was," I said.

"I heard what he said the night you and the Darnell woman came on board."

Whatever Jewel Simon was driving at had been carved out of the same shadowy images that had fostered her earlier observations of ancient effigies.

Porter had referred to her as the "witch of the Sargasso." The indictment was harsh, but as I stood there looking at her in the toneless grays of approaching night, I could understand where the *Barbella*'s captain was coming from. Her wide-set eyes, broad forehead, and high cheekbones were shadowed by thick brown-black bangs that made her look both mysterious and hard at the same time. Her permanent-pout mouth was narrow, thin, and completely void of sexuality. Her movements were quick and jerky, and she smoked like an edgy teenager— as though she lived in fear of being caught.

"It would be only natural to suspect me. After all, it was cyanide that killed Bench, and I know—"

"Know what?"

"All about cyanide. Back in the days when I thought life had a meaning and purpose, I knew I didn't have what it takes to become a doctor; so I entertained some idyllic notions about becoming a pharmacist. That was going to be the way I made my contribution to mankind."

"Worthwhile ambition. What happened?"

"I discovered that fucking the pharmacology professor was a whole lot easier than listening to the horny bastard drone on and on in a lecture day after day. I got the grades I needed. The problem was, I couldn't pass the state pharmacopoeia exams when it came time to get my license."

"So you ended up here—a project administrator on a salvage ship stuck in the middle of the Sargasso."

"Hey, I could add two and two. According to Vance, the only skill I needed was the ability to count a few boxes of provisions, order more when the supply got low, and keep track of things."

"And for that you're in for one quarter of one percent of whatever Porter recovers, right?"

"Not a bad deal," she replied. "The best part of it is Old Man Vance didn't even ask me to lie down. He hired me because of what I had between the ears instead of between the thighs."

Even before Jewel Simon finished, I had the feeling that someone or something was overhearing our conversation. Because of the long shadows and the configuration of the *Barbella*'s layout aft of the burned-out Com Cen, there were areas aft of and between the stack where anyone could have been hiding. I took out my flashlight, used the winch to scale myself up on the roof of the dive locker, and probed into a few of the nooks and crannies, but came away empty. Either my imagination was working overtime, or whoever was doing the listening was more adroit than I was.

"See anything?" she asked.

I shook my head and jumped down. When I did, she turned my hand over and ran her fingers over the skin abrasions where I had had my encounter with the six-giller. The salve Chuco had supplied had proved to be at least a temporary ablution—a layer of gauze covered the rest of it.

"I did not kill Kit Bench," she said. "Nor did I have anything to do with the rest of the strange occurrences that have been going on aboard this floating nightmare."

I would have been better off if I had let the matter die there, but for whatever reason, I'd never learned the subtle art of keeping my mouth shut. I squeezed Jewel's hand, told her not to worry, and headed down to meet Porter.

Rummaging through first Kritzmer's and then Fredrich's cabins turned up nothing of significance, which was to be expected. Even though Porter had insisted that everyone remain topside until after we had searched their cabin, it seemed rather obvious that, if you expected to discover something incriminating, you did not first warn the suspect that there would be a search. If there was anything the German contingent did not want us to see, they could have found an excuse to go back to their cabin and hide it.

Brimley's cabin was a different story. Porter uncovered a journal, and I found a series of schematics tucked away in the rear of the wall locker of the man Ambrose Vance had hired to be the dive master of the *Barbella*. Porter put the journal in his pocket and we spread the drawings on the small table. They were hard to see in the lamplight. The first was a drawing of the MD-SH-3 sea sled that I had been piloting the day Brimley vanished in mid-water. There was a another drawing of the modified Terrier sled, and then one of the *Barbella*.

"Mean anything to you?" I asked.

Porter shook his head and handed me the bulky journal. The last complete entry was dated "July 8" at the top of the page. Two previous and two succeeding pages had been torn out. There were no entries after that. In the front of Brimley's journal, I found four snapshots. Three of them were exactly what you would expect to find in a journal kept by a loner like Brimley. There was one of a young Brimley with his arm around a heavyset, middle-aged woman standing on the lawn of an imposing-looking brick structure. Another was a snapshot of Luke standing beside a two-door Pontiac Grand Am, and the third was Brimley standing in front of a nondescript but obviously home-made camper mounted on the back of a Dodge pickup truck.

"Look at this last one," Porter said.

It was a snapshot of a group of people in bathing suits kneeling in the sand. All of the people in the picture were tanned and athletic-looking. I turned the photo over and read what had been scribbled across the back.

Bill Lord's retirement party
Lauderdale Salvage,
June 14, 1991

"Lord?" I said. "Suppose he was any relation to Gabe?"

"Them divers is a close-knit bunch." Porter took the snapshot, stuck it back in the journal, and started to put it away. That was when I noticed some portion of the picture was missing.

Porter shrugged and continued going through Porter's papers. "May have been a picture of some bikini-clad bimbo that Brimley didn't want his wife to see."

"Brimley wasn't married."

Porter gave me an indifferent shrug, fumbled around in his shirt pocket until he found his cigarettes, lit one, and dropped down into the chair sitting in front of the small writing desk. He opened the small center drawer, rummaged around, and pulled out a packet of papers. On top of the stack was an envelope containing a copy of the same brief resume Ambrose Vance had handed over the night I accepted his offer.

Luke Brimley, 46, Boston, single,
Lauderdale Salvage, 11 years, certified,
D.I.D., Op. Lic. 45987, contract date 2/25/94:
Blanchard ver.

"Know anything about this guy Blanchard?" I asked.

Porter nodded. "Everybody in the salvage business anywhere south of Lauderdale and all the way down through the Keys knows Chester Blanchard. President of Lauderdale Salvage and"—Porter was holding up two fingers, close together—"one of the good old boys. I hear he's buddy-buddy with your friend Ambrose Vance. His son's also in the business Named Ringer."

I sat down on Brimley's bunk and stared at the brief resume. The name Blanchard was rattling around in my head like a couple of marbles in a boxcar, but I wasn't having any luck making the connection.

Porter snuffed out his cigarette. "Seen enough? One more to go, then we'll call it a night."

Gabe Lord's cabin turned out to be no more interesting than Kritzmer's or Fredrich's. The man had few personal possessions and even fewer personal papers. He did have one thing in common with Brimley, however, and that was the fact that he was "Blanchard verified."

Again, it was Porter who went through the personal effects, while I confined my exploring to the wall locker, shelves, nooks, and crannies of the former diver's cabin. The only item of interest as far as I was concerned was something I happened to uncover in a drawer in the bottom of Lord's footlocker: a revolver. It was a well-oiled, chrome-plated .32. There were no shells. I slipped it back in the little chamois sack just like I'd found it, and tucked it back in the drawer. If and when we were able to get the *Barbella* back to port, the authorities were going to be all over this tub like a homely hooker. The last thing I wanted to explain was a chrome-plated .32.

It was pushing 22:00 hours when Porter decided to give up for the night. He headed for the bridge to check with Shula Carson, and I headed for my cabin.

The twelve-by-fifteen stateroom was stuffy and, for the most part, damned unpleasant. The prospect of spending another sweaty night tossing and turning on a too small bunk was anything but appealing.

Everything was backward, even my routine. First, I fumbled around in the darkness and splashed some Scotch in what felt like a glass before sitting down on the edge of my bunk. Then I lit the candle.

I amused myself by peeling off the layer of gauze in the two places where the six-giller had abraded away some precious Wages epidermis. I examined the wound and discovered that it was still tearing, and slapped the gauze back on to protect it.

I stripped down to my shorts, opened the two ports over my bunk, snuffed out the light, sat down, and sagged back against the bulkhead. The name Blanchard was back again.

Porter had referred to him as the well-known president of the Lauderdale Salvage Company. But the name conjured up something different to me. The problem was, I couldn't remember what or why.

How long I sat there or just how alert I was when things started to happen is subject to debate. I do know I was still lying across my bunk with my back propped against the bulkhead when I first remember hearing something.

I was in that foggy arena of half sleep when I realized that the door was slowly being opened. I could hear someone. I could feel someone. But in the darkness I couldn't see a damn thing. Disadvantage Wages. Disadvantage intruder. Disadvantaged or not, he still opened fire.

My brain recorded one or two bright orange flashes and firecracker-like explosions. The latter sounded like air rushing back in to fill a vacuum after a blacksnake whip had sliced through to open the wound. More disadvantage Wages. Because now there was pain like a thousand bee stings.

There were two shots, and the interval between the two occurrences was probably no more than a nanosecond, but it sure as hell seemed longer. The first shot creased my shoulder and spun me around. The second missed altogether.

I headed for the basement, tumbled off the bunk, and fell to the floor in the darkness. The intruder was still there, but he—or she—didn't know where I was. His only option at that point was to start spraying the room with bullets, and that option had its disadvantages. Bullets have a tendency to ricochet indiscriminately when a room's primary construction material is steel.

I was relearning an old lesson. It's difficult to bleed, keep your mouth shut, and not whimper when you're hurting. I waited for the inevitable. Instead I heard the door shut. If there were footsteps in the passageway, I missed them.

I got to my knees, groped around in the darkness for my survival kit, and fumbled through it until my fingers wrapped around the handle of the Mauser. I was still in the squeeze and hope position when my door opened again and the beam of a flashlight danced thru the darkness.

"Shit," Maydee drawled. "You all right, man?"

It took me a moment to regain my equilibrium, and I was just getting to my feet when Packy appeared at the door of my cabin behind Hew. Hew spun around and jammed the beam of light in her face.

"Elliott!" she screamed. "What happened?"

I mumbled a few obscenities and finally blurted out that some heat-crazed bastard with a suspect pedigree had fired two shots at me.

"Are you hurt?"

Hew was dancing his flashlight over me, looking for gory indications of just how bad I was hurt. When he saw the crease in my shoulder, he informed her it was just a scratch.

It didn't take Packy's nimble fingers long to probe the extent of the damage. "It doesn't look too bad. Anywhere else?"

I pointed to the stretch of irritated skin that extended on a line from front to back just under my left arm. "The second one missed."

Packy shook her head. "Too close for comfort."

"Shit," Hew said, "a miss is good as a mile."

With Packy's assistance, I got to my feet. "You must have seen or heard something" I said to them.

Maydee shook his head. "All I heard was them shots—two of 'em. That's when I came runnin'."

"That's all I heard, Elliott," Packy said. "I took something to make me sleep. I probably wouldn't even have heard anything short of gunshots."

Hew went to get the first-aid kit, and Packy went to the sink, dampened a washcloth, cleaned the area around the shoulder wound, and inspected it. "At least it's clean, but I'd have Fredrich look at it."

"You're certain you didn't hear anything other than the two shots?" I asked.

"Like what?" Packy said.

"It was dark. There's nothing on our doors to indicate who is in what cabin. Unless the gunman knew his way around a hell of a lot better than I do in the dark, he couldn't have been too sure which cabin was which."

Packy was still mulling that one over when Hew returned. He had Porter in tow. "Maydee said somebody took a couple of shots at you," Porter said.

When Hew pointed to the superficial hole in my shoulder, Porter sniffed. "Damn near missed." After he appraised the wound, he lit a cigarette and looked at Packy. "You were next door; did you hear anything?"

"Other than the gunshots?"

Porter nodded. "Yeah, noises, voices, anything that might have . . ."

Packy shook her head, and Porter scowled. "By the way, neither of you have seen Kritzmer, have you?"

"It's not my night to watch him," I grumbled. At that particular moment, Eberhard Kritzmer was the least of my concerns.

"Fredrich has been lookin' for him. Says he's been all over the ship and he can't find him anywhere."

"When's the last time anyone saw him?" Packy asked.

Porter had to think for a moment. "On the bridge. He was lookin' for a lantern."

"One thing for sure," I groused. "He didn't go far."

I wasn't concerned about Kritzmer; someone had taken a couple of shots at me. At the moment I was a great deal more concerned about who had thrown my door open and started pumping bullets into my darkened cabin than I was about the whereabouts of Eberhard Kritzmer.

"How do you feel?" Porter asked me.

"Just a wee bit testy," I said. "But I tend to get that way when people start shooting at me."

"Do you feel good enough to help us look for Kritzmer?" Porter asked.

I figured I had gotten all the sympathy I was going to get; so I decided to cooperate. "Sure," I said, "why not?"

Incident:

The forward hold on the B deck was full of an assortment of crates, barrels, and boxes. Hew and I opened the ones that appeared to be big enough to put a body in, especially an oversize ton of self-pronounced importance like Kritzmer, and then resorted to the cargo manifest to determine the contents of the smaller containers.

We were rewarded for the extra effort when we located one small crate of assorted flashlights. Maydee found one to his liking, extinguished his lantern, and left it in the crew quarters. As it turned out, Kritzmer wasn't in the crew quarters either.

After the crew quarters, Maydee continued his search in the machine shop, while I sifted through what had been stored along the walls of the engine room. If Eberhard Kritzmer was or had been in either area, voluntarily or otherwise, there was no trace of him.

I worked my way back into the passageway just as Maydee emerged, and we headed for the aft hold that had once housed the *Barbella*'s assortment of sea sleds and diving gear. There wasn't anything left of the former, and no one to use what was left of the latter.

I had already looked in the obvious places, and had begun shoving the beam of my lantern into corners where light hadn't prevailed for a while, when I heard Maydee stop, catch his breath, and mutter some half-muted obscenity. By the time I turned around and saw what the old boy was looking at, I had to do my own breath catching. I sucked it in and held it while my stomach did a slow roll. All of my hastily constructed, half-cocked theories about what had or had not happened to Eberhard Kritzmer were suddenly subject to extensive reformulation.

From all indications, the man responsible for seeing that the German government got its share of whatever Ambrose Vance's crew turned up was through being responsible for anything. Kritzmer's throat had been cut wide enough, deep enough, and long enough to be devastatingly fatal. Yet the curious thing about the body was the very obvious smell of bitter almonds.

"Holy shit," Maydee muttered. "They damn near cut his head off."

I was still struggling to get my stomach under control when I heard voices on the A deck above us. A light poked down in the hold, and there stood Carson and Porter. Shula Carson saw what we did and turned away.

Within a matter of minutes, Hew managed to round up a couple of sheets to put over Kritzmer's body, while Porter sent Carson to locate Fredrich. Moments later the whole ship had earned about Kritzmer's fate. Both Jewel Simon and Packy had the courage to assess Kritzmer's fate. Chuco and Ritter didn't.

"Do I smell cyanide?" Jewel asked after examining the body, and I nodded.

"With all that blood," Packy asked, "why use cyanide?"

Jewel bent down and studied Kritzmer's wounds. She ran the light back and forth as she assessed the extent of the slash across the German's throat. "I learned just enough in my anatomy classes to be dangerous."

"And?" I said.

"For a wound of that magnitude, there isn't all that much blood."

"How long would it take for the aroma of bitter almonds to disappear?"

Jewel shrugged. "A few hours, maybe longer. It varies. Why?"

"Think about it," I said. "If we hadn't discovered the body when we had, we would have figured that—"

"The knife wounds killed him," Jewel said.

All of a sudden I found myself theorizing what was happening with one of the people who would least appreciate the chain of logic. "Follow my rationale, Jewel," I said. "There are still ten of us left on board the *Barbella*. There's Porter, Carson, Packy, Fredrich, Fritze Ritter, Maydee Hew, Chuco, and Mookie, plus you and me. That means the odds are nine to one. If I was the killer, I wouldn't want the other nine people gaining any satisfaction or strength from the fact that they had me outnumbered."

"I don't follow," Jewel said, shaking her head.

"If all the victims were killed with one gun, or one knife, or with one modus operandi, it would be natural to assume that there was only one killer. Right?"

Jewel frowned. "I still don't see what you're driving at."

Porter had been listening. "So we're supposed to think the killer is working with someone."

"Exactly. If we hadn't discovered Kritzmer's body when we did, the aroma of the cyanide would have been lost by morning, and we might very well have been looking for someone that we figured had to be strong enough to overcome a man the size of Kritzmer and then carve him up like they did."

It was Shula Carson who introduced the

other possibility. "Or maybe Kritzmer's killer *is* working with someone."

What was left of the crew of the *Barbella* retired somewhere after midnight with Maydee Hew assuring everyone that we could expect the fog to be gone in the morning. "I can feel it in my bones," he said.

Porter grumbled something about any kind of change in the weather being an improvement, then reminded me that I was scheduled to relieve Shula Carson at 06:00.

Even though I didn't put much stock in what Maydee felt in his bones, I did think I could see a kind of silver halo to the fog. It was easier to believe that what we were actually seeing was nothing more than luminescent traces of the moon visible through the supersaturated air that had been choking us for days.

I escorted the two women back to their cabins, advised them to lock their doors, then thought far enough ahead to throw the beam of my flashlight around the darkest corners of my own room before I entered.

Inside, I peeled out of everything I had on, rummaged around in my locker until I found a dry bathing suit, put it on, and doused an old cotton T-shirt with a liberal dose of rubbing alcohol.

I poured it over the bandage and let it soak through and sterilize the gauze where the bullet had creased my shoulder. Then I dabbed at the

two abraded skin patches where I had had my
encounter with the six-giller. I let out an involuntary whistle and decided the latter was a bit
touchier than the former. Suddenly I found myself reverting back to a page out of those hot
summer nights of my childhood. I took the
alcohol-soaked cloth and rubbed it over my
face, arms, chest, and legs to cool myself off.
For a moment or two, I damn near felt human—
and for a moment or two, I was young again.

That was when I let out a sigh and slumped
back against the bulkhead. Since I was momentarily into self-gratification, I wished I had one
of Cosmo's Havanas and a couple of fingers of
Scotch over shaved ice. As it turned out, my fit
of fantasy was just enough to distract me and
just enough to let my guard down.

"Mr. Wages," a small man's voice suddenly
said.

I sat upright, slid my hand under the pillow,
and coiled my fingers around the broom handle
of the Mauser. For some reason there was a tiny
sliver of light beyond the black-on-blacker sil-
houette of the intruder, and I had the Mauser
aimed right at it.

"Your door was open," the man said.

"Like hell it was."

"I have to talk to you."

It was a good thing that whoever was standing there in the darkness hadn't come through
that door with guns blazing. If it had been a pro,
I would have been dead in the water by now. As

it turned out, I managed to get the Mauser and the flashlight pointed in the same direction at the same time. Advantage Wages.

"I—I," Mookie stammered, "gotta talk to to you."

"Under the circumstances, you could get your head blown off," I said with a snarl. "I'm getting sick and tired of people just barging into my room without knocking."

Mookie stood there. I threw the beam of the flashlight at him and made sure he wasn't packing a gun. When he saw that I was, he swallowed hard.

That was when I realized that Mookie Boots wasn't what I thought he was. How long had I been on the *Barbella*? Four days? Five days? Sad, but true. Up until that very moment I couldn't have told you what Mookie Boots even looked like. Now, in the unflattering white-yellow wash of a flashlight, Mookie didn't look all that good.

Mookie Boots was one of those pencil-thin kids with long hair the color of thistle weed, and the standard-issue vacuous eyes of nineties youth. He was part of that generation that had mastered the void expression. He stood there, clad in what had become standard attire for the *Barbella*, dirty cotton undershirt and oil-stained jeans.

I noticed something I hadn't noticed before: Mookie had tits, not imposing tits, but the kind that girls scissored from the Mookie mold were proud of—unflattering, and decidedly unfeminine. Standing there in the dark, Mookie Boots was no threat. If anything, she was the threatened.

"Can you get us out of this?" she asked.

At that point I realized I still had the Mauser pointed in her direction. I laid it down on my bunk and motioned for her to sit down. She moved with the clumsy, stilted grace of youth; practiced insolence, part pout, part fear.

"I'm scared," she said. "I wasn't scared until I started to figure out what was going on."

"Maybe you better tell me."

"Will you go with me?" she said. "I think there's something you should see."

I followed Mookie Boots through a labyrinth of corridors and passageways to the A deck forward of Porter's quarters. There were six staterooms; the two located closest to the bow were adjacent to the shower and the head. Mookie stopped in front of A-2, fumbled with a set of keys until she found the right one, unlocked the door, and went in. She anticipated what I was going to say, because she said, "I know you searched this earlier, but there is something I want you to see."

She stood to one side and allowed me to pass. I flashed my light around the room. It didn't look any different from the way it had a few hours earlier.

Mookie Boots opened the door to Brimley's wall locker and pointed to a stack of papers.

"That's what I wanted to make sure you saw."

I wasn't sure what China Porter's daughter was getting at, but I picked up the stack of papers and started rifling through them. Near the bottom of the stack there were two envelopes. Both were addressed to Mr. L. Brimley, Apartment 313, 2474 Seagate Drive, Miami, Florida. The return address was that of the Lauderdale Salvage Company.

"There," Mookie said. "That's what I mean."

"So?" I asked.

"I think Mr. Brimley was letting someone else in on where we were conducting our salvage operation."

"Last night, your father and I decided to search some of the cabins. In Kit Bench's room we found a picture of a group of divers. It was taken at the Lauderdale Salvage Company. I thought it might be significant, but your father tells me that sooner or later every diver up and down the east coast of Florida ends up working for Lauderdale Salvage."

Mookie sat down on Brimley's bunk. She looked uncertain. "When I signed on, Porter told me I was responsible for seein' that the divers had everything they needed. I was always runnin' here and there, gettin' stuff for them. Sometimes I helped them get ready for their dives, sometimes I did their laundry for them. It was when I was doin' laundry that I found this." She held out her hand. In it was a tightly folded piece of paper. "It's a radiogram—or maybe I should say it's what's left of the piece of paper the radiogram was written on."

proceed (stop) schedule confirmed (stop) penguin departs 07/08 at 23:00 hours (stop) expect to be at designated coordinates A.M. of 07/11 (stop) no further communications anticipated (stop) implement (stop) proceed (stop) running back (stop) pussy cat (stop)

"Does Fritze know what this is all about?" I asked.

Mookie shook her head again. "Porter made it a practice to put the Com Cen on open channel after 20:00 hours each night. Everyone knew how to work the radios so we was free to contact anyone we wanted to—anytime we wanted to—as long as it was after 20:00."

"Didn't anyone keep a log?"

"I never did," Mookie said, "and I don't know anyone else that did either."

I wondered what else I had overlooked.

Mookie went back to Brimley's wall locker, opened the drawer below the area where the clothes were hanging, and produced a two-pound cookie tin full of jeweler's tools and an assortment of small batteries and two small containers. The containers were identical. They had been purchased from Clayborn Marine Supply in Miami. According to the markings on the boxes, both cartons had at one time or another contained A-44JT Random Impulse Transponders. I showed them to her.

"Transponder?" she asked.

"A little electronic gizmo used to locate someone or something, works on a relatively simple principle," I said. "Someone sends out a signal, this little device captures it and fires it right back, thereby informing the sender where the device is located."

Mookie's eyes widened. "It wouldn't be too hard to find somebody if they were wearing something like that, would it?"

"A body doesn't wear these. A thing does."

"Like a ship maybe?"

"You catch on quick. This little device strategically placed somewhere on the *Barbella* would give anyone who wanted to find us a no-fail homing signal . . . it wouldn't matter how closely guarded our coordinates were. Or—" Then I decided not to lay a second possibility on her, one that I hadn't quite thought through yet. Nevertheless, in theory, the same random capture pattern would work if the transponder had been placed on the hull of the downed *Hedgehog*—and could explain why Brimley and Lord put the old barge on the bottom with their torches. It was more than coincidentally close to where we believed the downed U-564 was located.

"When did you discover these?" I asked.

"The day Brimley died. Porter asked me to go down to Brimley's cabin and see if he had an address book or something—anything that would give Porter some idea of who to contact. You know, the next-of-kin thing."

"And you didn't tell Captain Porter about any of this?"

Mookie shrugged. "I didn't know what it all meant. Even then I probably wouldn't have said anything about it—that is, until Bench died."

"What's Kit Bench's death have to do with it?"

"He got the same message Brimley got."

"And Lord?"

She nodded. "Each one was kinda different, but Mr. Lord and Mr. Bench got to talkin' one night down in the galley. They was whisperin' and comparin' notes. I was workin' in the back of the galley, cleanin' fish. They never paid no mind to me."

"Do you remember when that happened?"

The corners of Mookie's mouth turned down. "That all happened the night before Gabe Lord was killed by them swarm quakes."

I tried to thread my way back through what Mookie had been telling me, repeating aloud what she had said and attempting to tie it to what I already knew.

"What do ya suppose those things mean?" she asked, slowly reviewing some of the words or names from the message all three of the *Barbella* divers had received. "Penguin, running back, pussy cat."

After a prolonged silence she repeated the

question she had asked earlier. "Are we going to get out of here?"

"If I have anything to do about it," I said.

"Oh, yeah," she said, "I almost forgot." She reached in her pocket and produced a small Saint Christopher medal. She held it out for my inspection.

"What about it?"

"It was Luke Brimley's."

"And?"

"He was wearing it the morning he took his last dive."

"Impossible," I said.

Mookie cocked her head to one side. "No. He was wearing it, all right. He always wore it when he was diving. When he wasn't diving he left it in that little tray in his wall locker."

I was tempted to dismiss what the young woman was telling me. At the same time, that funny twinge in my stomach was telling me not to. "Why are you so certain he was wearing that medal that morning?"

Mookie was trying to look offended. "Because I'm the one that helps everyone put on their diving gear. Remember?"

When she said that, the picture came back to me: Mookie Boots helping me with my BCD, checking the second stage of the alternate air source, making certain I had my dive tables and slate, and finally, strapping me in the free-flow cockpit of the MD-SH-3. Under those circumstances, she would have known what he was wearing.

"And you're certain he was wearing that particular medal?"

"Yeah, I recognized it. I'm the one who gave it to him. It used to be mine. When I found out he was diving without one, I insisted."

"You're telling me Luke Brimley was wearing the medal you're holding in your hand the morning of his last dive. And you found it in his wall locker when?"

Mookie Boots shrugged. "I don't know. Later. Does it really matter?"

I shook my head. "It sure as hell does."

I don't remember exactly what time I got back to my cabin. I do remember that by the time I checked out for the night, I had pretty well sorted through most of everything I had learned that night two, and in some cases three, times. The problem was, when the pieces of the puzzle were laid side by side, they still didn't add up to the whole of anything.

About the only thing I knew for certain was that when Lord and Brimley responded to Cameron's request for a damage assessment that night aboard the *Hedgehog*, they didn't assess damage, they inflicted it.

Could I prove that? Maybe. Maybe not. It all depended on how those pictures I had taken turned out. With the *Hedgehog* slipping deeper and deeper into that uncharted trench every time there was an outbreak of swarm quakes, it was highly unlikely we were going to get a second chance.

The second thing I tried to work my way through was the content of the radiogram. I read, then reread the copy Mookie gave me several times.

Even though I knew I was probably shooting in the dark, I tried a couple of theories on for size. For example, if Gabe Lord, Kit Bench, and Luke Brimley all received essentially the same radiogram, but at different times, they were all involved in the plot to throw the salvage effort off course.

It could also mean that in sending the message three different times, the sender was trying to confirm something, or that the messages only looked similar on the surface . . . a ploy designed to fool someone who saw similarities and assumed the messages were the same? That fact, if true, raised more questions. Did anyone else receive that same message? Which was another way of asking, was anyone else aboard the *Barbella* involved in these machinations?

By the same token, I realized that even if I had answers to those questions, there were still others, perhaps even more important ones, that I didn't have the answers to.

Question: How certain was I that there really was some sort of a plot? Answer: Reasonably certain.

Question: Was I force-fitting pieces into the

puzzle? Answer: No . . . someone was doing their damnedest to bring Vance's mission to a screeching halt.

Question: If the plot revolved around the three divers, and they were all dead . . . who the hell was behind the deaths of Bench and Kritzmer?

I started to laugh. I realized that if anyone heard me, lying there in the dark, babbling on with my endless questions, he could make the argument that my so-called evidence was all circumstantial. All the evidence except the transponder boxes—there was nothing circumstantial about the transponder boxes found in Luke Brimley's locker.

After mulling over the way Brimley and Lord had handled Cameron's call for help, the radiograms, and the transponder boxes, I worked my way back through the deaths of Eberhard Kritzmer and Kit Bench. Originally I had thought that whoever planted the cyanide in the vent system over Packy's cabin had intended it to put an end to one Packy Darnell. Maybe that wasn't the case. Maybe the killer had a different objective. With Brimley and Lord already dead, maybe the cyanide had been put there to get rid of Bench. But what did that accomplish? Or did the killer hope to get all three of us? If the killer had pulled that off, he would have stripped the *Barbella*'s salvage mission of all dive capability.

That was a possible conclusion, but what was

the motive? No one was going to get the bullion off the U-564 without divers.

I could only mull over a problem so long; then my will weakened and fatigue set in. Despite the muggy heat, I was starting to get sleepy. By the time I turned my thoughts to the sabotaging of the *Barbella*'s diesels and the torch job on the *Barbella*'s Com Cen, my thinking was fuzzy and I was going nowhere. I was stuck with the same old conclusion; there was no other way to read the tea leaves. Someone was determined to make damn certain Ambrose Vance did not lay claim to the treasure of Francisco Franco. And that someone was willing to strand a dozen or so people in the middle of the fogbound Sargasso with no power, no communications gear, and no way out. I had the distinct feeling that Eberhard Kritzmer wasn't the last. There would be more. The question was who?

My last few thoughts before I dozed off centered around Chester and Ringer Blanchard and the Lauderdale Salvage Company. There wasn't much left of my candle at that point, but that didn't stop me from taking out the snapshot of the gang at Bill Lord's retirement party and studying it. It was then that I began to think I could identify one or two people in the picture. The first was Gabe Lord, with a mustache maybe—but the more I studied the picture and thought about it, the more I realized that much was a no-brainer. According to Lord's resume, in his younger days he had been a lead diver for Lauderdale Salvage.

The other was a man in the second row, second from the left, that could have been Kit Bench—but there was no way to be certain.

A third man in the picture had one of those faces that conjured up the old, where-in-the-hell-have-I-seen-him-before question, but I wasn't able to put a name with the face and I decided to go back to the radiograms.

Even though I was exhausted, it was nearly four a.m. when the candle finally died and I drifted off to sleep.

I woke up to something I hadn't seen in days—the sun. It was streaming through the two open portholes in my cabin, accompanied by the incessant buzz of Sargasso flies. I was already sweating, and so far the only strenuous thing I had done was open my eyes.

I splashed some rubbing alcohol on a towel, gave my face the once-over, and then rubbed it on my neck, chest, and shoulders. With any luck at all, I could count on the cooling effect lasting until I got to the bridge to talk to Porter. If I timed it right, he would be relieving Shula Carson just about the time I got there.

When I got to the wheelhouse, I found Carson staring into the Sargasso distance, a horizontal visibility of no more than a mile. At that point, the horizon dissipated into a blurry haze that made it impossible to determine where the surface of the Sargasso ended and the green-blue haze melded into the hot July sky.

Carson sported a three- or four-day-old beard. It was splotchy and gave the impresion that no matter how long he let it grow, it would never be very impressive.

"Long night?" I asked.

"Couldn't get that damn picture of Kritzmer out of my mind." He pointed to a nearly spent can of Sterno and a tin can containing coffee. "That'll curl your dingus."

Shula Carson had yellow-brown teeth, probably the result of his love affair with a generic brand of cigarettes I had never heard of before. His gray-green eyes never seemed to be more than half-mast. Like everyone on the *Barbella*, he needed a haircut. What hair he did have was shoulder length and had been pulled back in a poorly fashioned ponytail.

"Know somethin', Wages?" he said, and I shook my head. "This damn place is beginin' to spook me," he muttered, pointing due west. "Look out there. See anythin'?"

I squinted into the haze and shook my head again.

"See what I mean? Let me tell you somethin'. A half hour ago I was convinced I saw something out there."

"Night watch will do that to you," I said. "Where's Porter? I thought he was supposed to take over the bridge at 07:00."

Carson took a sip of the bitter black coffee,

grunted, and assured me the *Barbella*'s captain would be along any minute.

"So how long have you known Porter?" I asked him.

Shula Carson squinted into the harsh glare of the early morning sun and rummaged around in the corners of his mind. "Let's see," he said. "First time I met China, me and him was doin' a little political penance for bustin' up a bar in Singapore. I guess we had a little too much of his flower friend."

"What happened?"

Carson shrugged. "Hell, you know how those things happen. They thought he was too fried to notice and I saw one of those greasy little monkeys go for China's wallet. He was American. I was American. I jumped in. At the time it seemed like the logical thinking to do."

"How long ago was that?"

Carson rolled his bloodshot eyes back in his head. "Damn near twenty-five years now. You get to know what a man's all about when you're locked up in a cell with him for six months."

"Six months?" I said.

"Hell, you know them damn Singaporians. They'd about as soon lock a man up and throw away the key as they would look at him. Neither one of us had the money to pay the guy for trashin' his bar."

Despite his tendency to mumble, Carson had made the whole affair sound mildly intriguing. It was one of those stories I would probably repeat one day, and it was one of those questions a man asks almost as an afterthought. "So how'd you get out?"

"Ambrose Vance heard about us and bailed us out," Carson said.

"Ambrose Vance," I said. "How long had you known Vance?"

"I didn't," Carson said. "But Porter did. Porter finally bribed one of the guards to get a message to Vance's contact man in Singapore. A couple of days later, this lawyer fella shows up, pays off the man who owned the bar, pays our fine, and hands us a couple of plane tickets. He tells us to get the hell out of Singapore."

"Tickets to where?"

"Miami."

"Then you and Porter have been working off and on for Vance ever since?"

"Mostly off," Carson said. "When Vance found out Porter was hooked on devil dust, he dropped him like a hot potato. I always figured that's why old man Vance didn't hire us to do the salvage job on the *Leichter* at Infante Dom Henrique."

After that, Shula Carson grew quiet, and it didn't take much to talk him into letting me take the bridge until Porter got there. After Carson left, I took out my pen and scribbled a few notes while they were still fresh in my mind. The longtime Vance-Porter connection was new information—and a new wrinkle in all of this. Somewhere along the line, I had gotten the impression that one of the reasons for Vance to hire both Packy and me was because Porter and the rest of the crew aboard the *Barbella* were unknown quantities. Wrong assumption. Vance knew Porter. In fact, he had known him a long time. If Carson was giving me the straight skinny, he also knew about Porter's cocaine addition.

After three days of rain and fog, even in the Sargasso, it was a morning made for looking around. From where I was standing, I could see the *Barbella*'s two lifeboats.

It occurred to me that, if the old girl had been accommodating her original passenger list, two boats would not have been enough. Now, however, with the list of viables dwindling to a mere ten names, it would have been cozy, but all ten could have squeezed into one boat.

I glanced at Shula's coffee tin, decided against trying a second cup, and began to wonder about the feasibility of sending someone for help in one of the *Barbella*'s lifeboats. With provisions such as drinking water, food, shelter from the Sargasso sun, and enough fuel to keep a forty-horse Johnson running, it might just be possible. I took out my notebook for the second time that morning, and began sketching ways that a protective canvas could be rigged over one of the lifeboats.

Jewel's voice took me by surprise. When I turned around she was standing there holding a first-aid kit. "Thought maybe I'd better have a look at that shoulder of yours this morning," she said.

I took off my shirt, sat down, and winced when she peeled off the layer of gauze. She probed, poked, and wrinkled her nose. "Had trouble finding you. I thought Porter was supposed to be here and you'd be in your cabin."

I let out an involuntary yelp when one of her probes dug down into tender tissue, and Jewel Simon actually smiled. It was the first time.

"Figured out how to get us out of here yet?" she asked.

I shook my head. "So far I've considered everything but a signal fire," I said.

"Would that work?"

When the lady said that, a light went off. I crawled down from the bridge and stood next to the gunnel staring at the weed-choked surface of the water. Then I glanced at the anemometer on top of the wheelhouse. Like the water, it was motionless.

From some dark convolution in the back of my addled mind, a far-fetched, slightly cock-eyed idea was taking shape. It had to do with exactly that, a signal fire.

"See if you can find some sort of tub," I said. "The bigger the better."

While the lady scurried off in search of something that would work, I took the grappling hook out of one of the lifeboats and used it to pull several tangled masses of sargassum weed aboard. With it came the budded snarls of dead rystmus and the dried, blackened tips of the elephant grass. While they were lying on the deck in the heat of the sun, a multitude of sea creatures, most of them nameless and unrecognizable, tried to escape in the water seeping out through the scuttles.

"Will this do?" Jewel asked. She had rounded up a large galvanized tray that was used to clean engine parts in the *Barbella*'s engine room.

I scooped up some of the sargassum, made certain that I dumped it in the pan, left Jewel on the bridge, and went looking for fuel oil. I found some in the engine room, took it topside, poured it on the seaweed, and lit it. It worked better than I had hoped it would. Within a matter of minutes we had a cloud of thick, black smoke.

"Okay," I said. "Now we see how long the fire lasts."

Fifteen minutes later it had formed a low-hanging, stratus-shaped cloud over the *Barbella*. Even on a day heavy with haze, the smoke from that sargassum would be seen a long way away.

"Suppose anyone will see that when they're flying over us at thirty thousand feet?" Jewel asked.

"Don't know," I said, "but it's damn sure worth a try. Anyone who does see it is bound to wonder about a fire in the middle of the Sargasso. Keep your eye on it. I'll let Porter know what we're doing."

China Porter's cabin was situated directly fore of the galley and aft of the A deck staterooms. I knocked twice and when he didn't answer, I opened the door. He was sitting at his desk. There was a nasty-looking bullet hole in the middle of his forehead.

Incident:

China Porter, looking for all the world like an unshaved fugitive from a Louisiana chain gang, had taken a slug point-blank. The wound appeared to be almost equidistant between his eyes in the middle of his forehead. There were powder burns around the wound, and the telltale indentation marks where the barrel had been pressed against his forehead. It was as neat and efficient a job of abruptly interrupting someone's life as I had seen.

An infinitesimally small trickle of dried blood had congealed in the stubble of his beard and his eyes were still open. China Porter knew who his killer was—but there was no way he could tell us. The bullet had terminated the information flow so quickly that China Porter's brain had never had time to send the final signal to his life systems.

Now, as I stood there, looking at what was left of the *Barbella* captain, I had even more questions. He was big and strong, and the question had to be, how had the murderer managed to get someone his size to sit there while pressing the barrel of a revolver against his forehead?

Actually, that one was easy . . . the thin white line told its own story. The razor blade and the obligatory straw merely confirmed it.

I reached out and took Porter's hand. The fingers had started to stiffen. The flesh was cold. The color had drained from his face and his mouth hung open. There was no look of surprise. I doubted if there had even been a protest.

There was no way of knowing how long I had been standing there before I heard footsteps coming down the companionway. When I turned around, I saw Mookie. She took one look at me, then at China, and stepped back into the passageway with her hand to her mouth. She almost got the scream stifled. But she didn't—and it reverberated through the ship.

By the time Marion Fredrich and Jewel Simon arrived, I had my arms around Mookie trying to calm her. At the same time, Packy was headed toward us from the other direction. She was carrying the small .32 that I had thought best to leave in Brimley's cabin. Now it was too late. I realized it would have been easier to explain it to the authorities before it had been used to kill China Porter.

Packy handed me the small chrome-plated revolver, took one look at Porter, and turned away. I laid the revolver on Porter's desk, motioned for Packy to take the Boots girl, who was on the verge of panic, up on deck, and turned my attention to Fredrich. Like Mookie, he was close to coming unglued.

"Wh—whe—when did it—it happen?" he stuttered.

Jewel Simon moved toward the body, bent down, and looked into the *Barbella* captain's eyes, looking for signs that would tell her how long Porter had been dead. When she was finished, she looked up. "He's been dead for several hours, Elliott," she said. "Body temp has lowered, the eye sockets are dry, and there is some evidence of pooling—that usually takes a few hours."

Marion Fredrich's curiosity was too much for him. He moved past the Simon woman, reached out, touched Porter's hand, and recoiled. "It is not possible," he quaked. "I spoke to him only a few hours ago . . . after we discovered Dr. Kritzmer's body."

When I turned around, Packy had returned. She was watching us from a distance. "What did you do with the Boots girl?" I asked.

R. Karl Largent

"She's topside. She said she wanted to be alone."

I could see Packy's eyes searching our faces. She looked at Jewel, then Fredrich, and finally me. "Would somebody mind telling me what the hell is going on around here?" she said.

"China Porter was Mookie Boots's father," I said.

Before Packy could react, Fredrich was moving toward her. "You—you were the one with the gun," Fredrich charged. He was looking at Packy.

"That's because I found the goddamn thing laying on the floor in the passageway—outside of your cabin, Dr. Fredrich."

"I have never seen that weapon before," Fredrich sputtered. His hands were shaking.

"I have," I admitted. "Last night in Brimley's cabin. I shouldn't have left it there."

"Who else knew it was there?" Jewel demanded.

"Obviously more people than I realized."

Fredrich was still eying everyone apprehensively when I finally managed to get the crowd out of Porter's stateroom into the *Barbella*'s passageway.

"What—what's going to happen to us?" the German stammered.

"The first thing that's going to happen," I said, "is we're going to round everybody up and meet on the aft deck. Jewel, you find Maydee, Chuco, and Fritze. Packy, wake Shula up—he's in his cabin. Dr. Fredrich, you find the Boots girl; tell her what's happening."

The sun was high in the Sargasso sky by the time I was able to get everyone together. Everyone realized that we were all in it together, but no one could be certain who they could trust.

In the shadow of the winch and the overhang back of the engine room stacks, Shula Carson, Fritze Ritter, and Chuco Edison formed one group, while Jewel Simon and Mookie Boots formed another. The German, Fredrich, had clearly drawn a line between himself and the rest of the crew . . . and Maydee Hew had done much the same. The former distanced himself out of distrust. The latter had probably always isolated himself from the mainstream. Curiously, the initial seven shared a bond that divorced them from Packy and me; they had been together since the beginning. Despite their distrust, they had formed a bond. Only Shula Carson was belligerent; the rest of them were frightened.

"All right, you got us here, Wages," Carson said. "Now what?"

"We're going to pair off," I said. "From now on, no one is alone, anywhere, anytime. We cover for each other, wherever we go . . . whatever we do."

I started by parceling out assignments to Jewel Simon and the young Boots girl.

"Vance recruited you to keep this thing organized—and I don't see any reason to change horses now," I told Jewel. "We've got no refrigeration and no desalinization unit without that standby generator. With no desalinization unit, we've got precious little drinking water. Drinking water gets top priority. Take inventory of everything we've got. Figure out rations . . . then let me know how long we can survive."

Jewel nodded.

"What about you and Hew?" Carson asked.

"No one's above the rules," I countered. "We all know what the situation is. In the last twenty-four hours, the killer has struck twice. Both times, he managed to pull it off right under our nose. The reality is, if he could get to Kritzmer and Porter, then he sure as hell can get to the rest of us."

"You keep saying 'he,' Wages. How the hell do we know the killer ain't one of these women here," Carson demanded. "The way I see it, it could be any one of 'em."

"We don't know," I admitted. "Like it or not, each of us has to think it could be anyone in this room. So from here on out, no one, repeat, no one, works alone. If you're so much as breathing, you're going to have somebody with you twenty-four hours a day. Commandment number one is: Keep your backside covered at all times."

I looked around the room. Only Jewel was smiling. "If you ask me, it sounds a little kinky," she said.

"Kinky or not, from now on, we do everything

in pairs; we eat, sleep, work, always in pairs."

Marion Fredrich was the first to speak up. "You are signing our death warrants," he said. "No matter how you arrange it, you are pairing one of us with the killer."

"He's right, Wages," Carson said. "How do we know who we can trust?"

I looked past Packy at Carson and Ritter. "Look, there's a logic to all of this. I'm pairing you two together because between the two of you I figure we stand the best chance of getting the *Barbella*'s engine up and running. Fair enough?"

Ritter squinted around the aft section assessing other possibilities. Finally he nodded agreement.

"You and Dr. Fredrich will pair off," I said, looking at Packy. "We've got a signal fire to keep going."

Jewel Simon smiled. "I've got a better suggestion," she said. "How about you and me? That could be decidedly more interesting."

"Yeah, Wages," Hew said. "Who's gonna keep an eye on you?"

"I'm on my own."

"Like hell you are." Carson glared. "How do we know you aren't the one behind all of this. None of this started happening till you and that Darnell dame came on board."

"And what about the Kraut?" Hew snapped. "Who's gonna keep their eye on that little creep?"

"Nor do I consider you above suspicion in this matter, Mr. Hew," Fredrich countered.

The wiry little man stiffened. Clearly, Maydee Hew didn't like the idea of being paired with anyone. He was the *Barbella*'s loner. Maydee Hew would have preferred to gamble on his own survival instincts. Paired with Chuco, he wasn't so sure.

"All right now. What's the situation with the diesels?" I persisted.

Ritter pursed his lips. "Maydee and I got her opened up. We was just beginnin' to get a handle on the damage when you called this meetin'."

"So far I ain't seen nothin' we couldn't fix if we could get us some power. We'll have to disconnect the standby generator from the refrigeration unit and haul her down to the aft hold," Maydee said.

"Clear it with Jewel so she knows how long we'll have to be without refrigeration," I cautioned.

I could see Ritter mentally planning the sequence of maneuvers it would take to move the generator.

When Fredrich spoke up, he was voicing a different concern. "We will have to be careful. What little food we have left will spoil in this heat without refrigeration."

"How long will you need that generator?" I asked.

"We won't know until we get a better look at those injectors," Carson offered.

"Put a lock on the refrigeration units when you disconnect the generator," Jewel ordered. "No one opens the units until we get them fired up again."

That was the easy part. From the generator, I turned my attention to Packy and the good doctor. "We're going to have to set up some kind of relay system to keep that smoke signal burning. If we keep that fire burning around the clock, we have a chance. If a plane or ship is anywhere in this vicinity, I want that column of smoke to be a damned beacon . . . got it?"

Fredrich started to protest. "Surely there must be something that I can contribute that is more important than burning—"

I was in no mood to try to mollify the little man. "I assure you, Doctor, if I find something more important, I'll damn sure let you know."

Only Jewel Simon appeared to be amused by the exchange.

"What about the supply ship?" Packy asked. "When is it scheduled to come back through?"

"It ain't scheduled," Carson confirmed. "Unless we call for her—she don't come. No radio—no call."

"But the supply ship knows we are here," Fredrich pressed. "Correct?"

"Correction," Carson said. "That supply ship knows we *were* here. For all the captain of that old tub knows, we found what we're looking for and we've moved on."

"That's why we've got to keep that fire burning," I stressed. "Unless we can think of something a helluva lot better, that column of black smoke is our best hope for getting out of here."

By late afternoon, Carson and Ritter had disconnected the standby generator from the *Barbella*'s refrigeration unit and the four of us—Carson, Ritter, Hew, and I—had muscled the unit aft and down into the *Barbella*'s machine shop.

True to Hew's prediction, the sky remained clear most of the day, and only as sunset approached did we begin to see a few clouds forming on the horizon. That was when I went topside to see how Packy and Fredrich were doing with the smoke signal.

The German was standing at the gunnel with the grappling hook, staring into the black Sargasso water. His hands were blistered and he was sweating. I had the feeling Marion Fredrich had done more physical labor in that one afternoon than he had during the entire mission up until now. A tangle of rystmus and sargassum was strung out on the deck, drying in the scorching Sargasso sun, and next to him was a five-gallon can of fuel oil; it was half empty.

"How's it going?" I asked.

Packy's response revealed decidedly more vigor than it had in days. The cyanide burns were healing. Despite the sunburn and exhaustion, she forced a smile.

"Thought you could use an update," I said.

"We disconnected the refrigeration and running lights, and moved the generator down to the aft hold. We've got power in the machine room. Hopefully it'll be enough to mill the head and deburr the two injectors Carson and Ritter made by hand."

"Do you think it will work?" Packy asked.

"Don't know," I admitted. "I figure it's worth a try. But that's not why I'm here."

Packy waited. "What?"

"Think you're up to a dive?"

She thought for a minute and asked why.

"We aren't going to make it with just the one generator. It's too much of a load."

"When one's all you have," Packy came back at me, "what options have you got?"

"Ritter tells me there's a small service generator on the *Hedgehog*."

"But you said the *Hedgehog* was in a deep trench." I could tell by her expression she was surprised I would even consider it.

"It's a long shot," I admitted.

"Do you realize what happens if the swarm quakes hit while you're in that trench?"

I nodded. There didn't seem to be any point in elaborating.

When Packy looked at me I knew what she was thinking. She took my arm and pulled me aside. "You were down there. You'd know whether it was possible or not. How deep is that ravine?"

"I don't know," I said. "As soon as I get someone to help Fredrich, we'll head up to the bridge and see what we can find. Brimley had this area pretty well charted. We can look at his charts."

"There are more charts and maps down in the photo lab," Packy reminded me. "I'll see what I can find."

I went below and found Packy poring over the charts. When she saw me, she slid one of the charts across the table and stabbed at one of the coordinates with her index figure. "Is this it?"

It took me several seconds to get oriented. I found the coordinates and looked for the chart designator. Brimley had labeled the chart AA-2. On it, someone had penciled in three red X's. They were marked K-3, K-5, and K-7. I recognized the K-7 sector as the place where the bottom anomaly was thought to fit the profile of the U-564. As it turned out, it fit the profile . . . but it wasn't the U-564.

I drew a line from where I had surfaced on my previous dive to the anomaly and estimated the distance at less than half a kilometer. The K-3 and K-5 sites were even further away.

"Is there any reference to the *Hedgehog* in his dive notes?" I asked.

Packy scanned the notes for a second time. "He gives some depth figures along what appears to be a pressure ridge," she said. "Then it appears to drop off." She was pointing to two lines that ran parallel with the K-7 mark. "Depth readings at 87.0, 89.0, 97.7, 99.3, 103.1, then it skips several intervals before it picks up again at 94.4, 97.6, 97.6—and then we get an upsweep."

"Slope or drop-off?"

Packy shrugged. "It's a matter of semantics, isn't it?"

"The question is, is there enough of a slope that whatever is down there eventually, with the help of the swarm quakes, ends up in that crevice or ravine?"

Packy shrugged. "That's the way it works in theory."

I decided to try a different tact. "Did he note any difference in temperatures?"

She shook her head. "Not on the charts, and I don't see anything in his dive notes. You don't think that's where the submarine is, do you?"

"I do," I said.

"Then why didn't Brimley indicate as much on the chart?"

"That's just one of the things I haven't figured out about this whole damn affair," I admitted. "For some reason, when Cameron asked the divers to check what happened to the *Hedgehog* the night it went down, all Brimley and Lord did was torch big enough holes in it to make damn certain it did go down."

"Why?"

"That's the second half of the question. I don't have all the answers, but I have got a theory. Let's say Brimley, Lord, and Bench were all in-

R. Karl Largent

volved in some kind of scheme—a scheme to sabotage this salvage operation."

Packy frowned. "Why do that? No one makes any bread until they hit the mother lode."

"Or—instead of picking up fractions of shares, someone decides they want the whole banana."

"But I still don't—"

"Try this one on for size. Brimley and Lord sink the *Hedgehog*. Then, the next day, when Porter gets his act together and learns that the *Hedgehog* has disappeared, he sends his divers down to look for it. Four separate times they go down, on three consecutive days. The last two times they even take the underwater video scanners—that way, Porter can see for himself—no *Hedgehog*. What Porter sees is what he believes to be several hundred square meters of Sargasso bottom where he has been told the barge sank. But that's not where the barge sank."

"How can that be?"

"This is all still a theory," I reminded her. "But let's say Brimley and Lord return to the *Barbella*, tell Cameron they've repaired the damage, and wait. What have they got to lose? There's certainly no risk. If for some reason the damage is discovered before the barge sinks, Brimley and Lord can say they just plain missed that damage. But all of a sudden, they get their second break. The first, of course, was when Cameron thought he hit something and requested a damage report. The second was when the second round of swarm quakes hit. You've seen what happens; the water gets a little agitated, and that's all it takes . . . suddenly the *Barbella*'s salvage barge is history."

"Can you prove that?" Packy pushed.

"Some of it. I took pictures. I figured Vance would need those pictures when he filed either charges or insurance claims. Either way he was going to need proof."

Packy appeared to be caught up in it now. "Go on," she said. There was a curious kind of caution in her voice.

"The next morning, China Porter awakens from his dream-dust state of mind and hears Maydee Hew describe what happened. 'It just disappeared,' Maydee tells him, and Porter's mind is fried enough that he puts being in the Sargasso, the Bermuda Triangle, and what Maydee is telling him together. Then, when he sends the divers down and they report that they can't locate a ninety-foot-long salvage barge, Porter starts to believe it."

"But how did Brimley and Lord conceal the fact that the barge was down there?"

"They didn't have to conceal it. If you look at the chart again you'll see what I mean. Where is three-K, five-K, and seven-K?"

Packy looked at the chart. "Like you said, starting with seven-K, approximately a half a kilometer from here and back."

"Which tells you what?"

Packy Darnell looked at me, then the chart, then back at me again. "There's only one way.

The *Barbella* was moved without telling Porter or making an entry in the log."

"Exactly, if you're looking for the *Hedgehog* anywhere within eight hundred meters of the *Barbella*, you're not going to find it. Eight to nine hundred meters makes a big difference when you're looking for something that's only ninety feet long in a forest of elephant grass and rystmus."

"You figure Brimley, Lord, Bench, and who else?" Packy said.

"Bingo. If we knew that, we'd know who the killer is."

"So what's our next move?"

"Our next move is to make damn certain we've done everything we can to get out of here. Ritter and Carson need more time to repair the engine. They need the generator."

"So, how do we . . . ?"

"I talked to Shula Carson about that auxiliary generator on the *Hedgehog*. He believes that the last time he saw it, it was in the storage area behind the wheelhouse. If we can get to it, we might be able to get it out of there and up to the surface."

"The question then is, can we get to it?"

Packy Darnell had just said the magic words. The plural "we" was what I needed to hear.

"I don't think I can get to it without some help," I admitted. "Even then, it's going to depend on how far down in the trench the *Hedgehog* slid in that last series of swarm quakes."

"There's more to this than trying to determine whether or not we can get our hands on that generator, isn't there?"

"The generator becomes the official reason we're making this dive."

When I looked at Packy I had a strange feeling she knew what I was talking about. She turned her attention back to Brimley's charts. She was frowning.

"The question is, do you even feel good enough to attempt it?" I had to ask; I had no way of knowing how much damage the cyanide had done to her throat. By the same token, I had to caution her. "You won't be able to handle that compressed air if there are any open lesions in your throat . . . or if there is any contamination in your tanks. You know as well as I do that twenty-one-percent oxygen mixture we're using can be toxic if we have to go deeper than one hundred feet."

"What about our air supply?"

"We've got seven tanks left, four conventional and three pony. Brimley filled them. My guess it that the tanks are good. After all, Brimley, Lord, and Bench were doing the diving—and they're the ones that we know were involved in this scheme."

"Then what's our next move?"

"We leave Maydee to keep an eye on Fredrich—and vice versa. In the meantime, you and I go back to the dive locker and see what we can put together."

* * *

We found everything we needed. Packy was tall at five feet eight inches, and tipped the scales somewhere around the 140-pound mark, about the same size as Gabe Lord. She was able to use most of his backup gear with few adjustments.

We located a wet suit, a BCD, a backpack, a regulator with SPG, a chest-mounted PCD and swing halogen, and an auxiliary tool kit containing O-rings, straps, CO_2 cartridges, some spare batteries, and two auxiliary nylon lines.

I helped her into her gear, strapped on her shark knife, and slipped the cartridge gun over her shoulder. Maydee helped her down to the dive platform, and I entered the water close behind her. At that point the only question I had was whether or not what was left of the fading sunlight was going to be of any help to us.

I dropped down off the dive platform, cleared my mask, handed Packy her end of the lifeline, and tested the comsys. Our equipment was identical except for the fact that I was carrying a few extra tools that I hoped would enable me to free the auxiliary generator.

"Comsys check," I said. "Can you read me?"

Packy nodded. "Affirmative."

"How's your throat?"

"So far, so good."

"Activate your halogen at the thirty-foot level. Give me three tugs on the L-line. Check your gauges and give the comsys another test. Whatever you do, stay in touch."

Packy circled her thumb and index finger, gave me the high sign, and disappeared beneath the sargassum-choked surface. I counted to three, checked my SPG, took one last look at the red sky to the west, and followed.

There was more surface light on this dive than I could recall on either of the previous dives. The tangle of sargassum and rystmus created a surreal landscape of green on green that offered only an occasional and fleeting indication of any kind of life form. Ahead of me, in the shadows and blackness, I could see the pale yellow beacon of Packy's waist-mounted halogen. When she paused, I knew she had reached the thirty-foot check level.

By the time I caught up with her, she was already reciting her readings. "E-time 08:45, d-34.3, 'd' time 67 minus. How do I sound?"

I made a fist of my right hand, touching the thumb to the forefinger. Then I held my hand out flat to give her the "level off and stay at this level" signal before showing her my compass. I reset the single-pulse direction indicator to 090, and watched the electronic beam move right and left as I checked for variation.

"Thirteen hundred to fifteen hundred meters straight ahead," I said. "You lead, I'll ride drag."

Packy was a veteran; she set a pace that would use the minimum amount of air, and navigated through the Sargasso underwater jungle as smoothly as if she had been doing it all her life.

At the 0.19.7 mark we broke out of the dense undergrowth and into the clearing. I remembered reading in one of Jacques Cousteau's book about the territorial habits of sharks. They were most likely, he pointed out, to patrol the demarcation lines along areas where there was an abrupt change in either temperature or bottom habitat. Now, some fifty to sixty feet beneath us, the floor of the Sargasso was suddenly a pristine, uninhabited, almost inviting beach. We had emerged from an area where the horizontal and vertical visibility was no more than a few feet, to a place with visibility up to thirty feet in the rapidly diminishing sunlight. I figured most of the light was due to a thinning layer of sargassum on the surface.

Packy was working her way toward the fifty-foot level when I felt it for the first time. It's an old feeling, one I've learned to pay attention to. I opened the channel on the comsys. The red light on her T-panel began flashing, and she stopped just short of a stand of rystmus weed and coral to look back at me.

I held my left hand in a horizontal position in front of my mask and made a circling motion with my right hand.

Packy did a slow 360 rotation. She was searching. "What's up?"

"We've got company."

"Where?"

"Close. I can feel it in my—"

I never had a chance to finish; the giant came rocketing down from its reconnoitering pattern over our heads and went straight for Packy.

"Duck," I screamed, and then added something totally inane like, "Get the hell out of there," as though she needed to be reminded. That "uneasy" feeling had suddenly crystalized into a terrifying, real-world, killing machine that was all mouth and teeth, careening past me, knocking me down, and making one very serious attempt at dispatching my dive partner.

By the time I got to my feet, Packy had escaped into a growth of rystmus and elephant grass and the oversized shark was circling, marshaling its forces for another charge.

"Packy, damn it, can you hear me?"

I heard a surge of static on the comsys, but no response. Silence, I didn't need.

From where I crouched in the outcropping of coral, I was finally able to get a good look at him. He was as big as a semi . . . maybe longer; mostly gray, huge dorsal fin, six gills, and nasty enough to eat a pleasure cruiser. He went into the undergrowth, thrashed about, emerged, eyed me, and began to circle directly over my head again.

I braced myself against the coral and did what I could to get ready. I had made up my mind. If the big son of a bitch came after me, he was going to get one helluva a headache in the process. I slipped the nitro cartridge under the barb on my spear gun, primed it, and waited.

I didn't have long to wait. The six-giller circled, made one pass, and mounted his attack. I felt like that cartoon that depicts a tiny field mouse giving the attacking eagle the bird as its final, defiant act.

This wasn't a case of waiting until the right time to pull the trigger. When the big bastard started down, I fired. At that range I figured I couldn't miss.

The nitro-charged barb slammed into him, there was an explosion big enough to blow out a tree stump, and the Sargasso was suddenly all pinkish and charged with bits of shark flesh.

I had blown away a good third of the marauding giant's head, but I hadn't stopped him. He circled, started to regroup, and I knew I didn't have enough time to reload. I could feel my throat tighten, and I figured there was a good chance I was a man about to take my last breath.

For the record, there is an ethereal kind of deadness in the eyes of any shark—but this one mirrored his own special brand of dispassionate barbarism. He was circling again.

Suddenly I knew what it was like to be a gunfighter—to know that you only had one move—and it better be the right one.

I braced myself—but the creature slowed, backed away, as if it realized that it had to reconnoiter the situation. The initial frenzy was over and the stalking had begun anew. I crouched closer to the rocks and pinned my back against the coral. I could hear the metal walls of my air tanks screech in protest.

The comsys crackled with static. "Elliott?" It was Packy's voice coming at me in fragments and gasps. I looked down at the comsys; the transmit light was flickering. "Where the hell are you?" she demanded.

There was silence on both ends . . . before I heard her voice again. The transmission was breaking up.

"Can't read you," she said. "Are you still in one piece?"

"I—I think—I think so," I stuttered.

"What the hell was that?" Her voice was incredulous.

"Ask Fredrich," I said.

I watched the wounded six-giller swim off into the darkness, return momentarily, then disappear again. There was no way of knowing if the cagey bastard was trying to sucker us or what.

"Do you see it?" she managed.

I came out of my hiding place just long enough to make a quick 360 survey, slide back under the protection of the outcropping, and inform Packy there was wisdom in waiting a bit longer.

Then, because I hadn't thought of it, I tugged on the L-line to make certain we were still together. She gave me a reassuring return tug, and requested readings.

I was still trying to get my equilibrium. "We've got forty-six minutes plus the pony before we have to head for the surface."

"How far are we from three-K?"

"Six—maybe seven minutes."

We didn't leave at the 0:30:00 mark; we waited another three whole precious minutes before I felt confident enough to crawl out from my coral outcropping and scan my surroundings. Fredrich's uncataloged, prehistoric six-giller had exhibited a kind of attack behavior I hadn't witnessed before. Sharks usually attack from a vantage point underneath their victim. On occasion, some sharks will come at their quarry from a horizontal attack angle . . . but this one didn't play by the rules; he circled over, and then torpedoed down on his prey.

The question now was, was the beast mortally wounded? I had blown a forty-gallon hole in its head . . . and it had managed to slip away into the shadows. Someone had said that sharks, like elephants, go to their own private hell to die. I hoped they were right. Whatever the truth was, the creature was gone.

"I've got a fix on three-K," Packy advised. "Think it's safe to move out?"

I had a clearing of one hundred or so yards to conquer before I could get to the cover of the elephant grass. During those one hundred yards, I was going to be a tad too vulnerable to satisfy Mother Wages's only son. I looked up, saw my chance, decided it was now or never, and moved out.

At the 0:35:15 E-time mark, I located Packy, checked over her dive gear, made certain she hadn't dislodged anything, and started for the three-K site. For the next hundred yards or so, we threaded our way through a jumble of coral and undergrowth before we came to another clearing. At that point we could identify a pronounced downslope in the floor of the Sargasso.

"Is this where it starts?" Packy asked.

"This is it," I confirmed. "Straight ahead. The closer you get, the more it drops off. Somewhere down in that ravine is the *Hedgehog*. And if my hunch is right, we'll find something else we've been looking for."

Packy swam past me and out over the yawning chasm that separated the three-K and five-K sectors of the Sargasso. She shoved the beam of her halogen down into the darkness, made several sweeps, and swam back toward me.

I saw the red light blink on my comsys, and locked the transmission-receive switch in the open position. Then I shined my halogen at her. She was circling her arm over her head, then extending it with fist clenched and thumb pointed down.

"I'm going down and take a look around," she confirmed. "Cover me."

Incident:

Minutes later I was listening to Packy's voice crackle over the comsys. She sounded giddy. "Come see what I found," she said. Even with the mirth, I thought I detected a note of irony—as though whatever it was, was too late.

"Read you; give me your DG reading."

"I'm holding at one hundred and thirty-one feet. From the looks of things, one of those swarm quakes must have triggered some sort of minor avalanche. There's one helluva pile of rocks and debris down here . . . and the latest deposit appears to be our beloved *Hedgehog*."

"Readings?" I said, thankful that the *Barbella's* salvage barge had slipped no deeper in the trench than Packy's estimate of another forty feet.

Packy began to spit out the numbers. "E-0:34: 00, d-0:41:30, looks like about one-three-zero. Are you recording?"

"Double check; what's your SPG reading?"

"It correlates, 41:30, now 41:40. Close enough?"

I breathed a sigh of relief. "You look for the generator. While you're doing that, there's a couple of things I want to check on." I said. As an afterthought I added, "Give me a voice check at 00:56:30 E-time."

Packy reached back, disconnected her L-line, and swam toward the stern of the *Hedgehog* where the barge's superstructure was located. At this rate it wouldn't take us long to determine if the auxiliary generator was there—and if it was there, whether or not we had any chance of winching it to the surface.

While Packy checked out the toolshed and the engine room, I worked my way up and over the slightly elevated port side of the *Hedgehog*. When I started down, it was along the hull at a point approximately parallel with where Brimley and Lord had torched through the hull plates and allowed the barge to take on water.

The hull of the *Hedgehog* was a shallow V-type configuration that made it appear as though the design had been some sort of unfortunate compromise. The draft was too shallow for oceangoing applications, and too deep for most river work. I couldn't tell for certain, but it appeared that the draft was no more than six to seven feet.

I located the transponder, detached it, slipped it into my lift bag, and began poking the beam of my halogen around in the debris. If my theory was correct, now it was only a matter of time until I found what I was looking for. The only question I had was was there enought time to locate it, look around, and take a few pictures.

I had been searching just long enough to start worrying whether or not I was off on another wild-goose chase, or on one of those famous flights of Elliott's fancy, when I spotted it. At first it appeared to be nothing more than a piece of junk, some kind of discarded steel-framed tripod with a light on it. I got down on my hands and knees, cleared away the sand, checked the slope of the cat grid, and confirmed my suspicion. It was the navigation light on the fantail of a German submarine. And it was a damned good bet that the submarine in question was the U-564.

The swarm quakes had caused just enough shift in the configuration of the bottom to allow the *Hedgehog* to slip into the trench. Fifty years of that same natural phenomena, frequent vibrations and minor ruptures in the floor of the Sargasso, not some bizarre Bermuda Triangle explanation, had likewise buried the U-564 in the trench.

All the evidence pointed to the fact that Luke

Brimley, despite being determined to stymie Vance's operation, had, in sinking the *Hedgehog*, unwittingly led us right to the U-564. Did Brimley and Lord know that? It was a pretty good assumption that they did. That was why they'd reported that the barge had disappeared. Any salvage effort to bring up the *Hedgehog* would also have uncovered Hess's downed U-boat.

When I saw both the attack periscope and the sky periscope protruding up into the black-green water, I knew where the hatch was located. I doubted that entry was going to be any kind of a problem. In all probability, the hatch, like the snorkel tube forward of the con tower, had been left open to facilitate the flooding. Nor was there much doubt in my mind that I would find the same with both the fore and aft torpedo tubes—they would be wide open. The thoroughness of Hess's journal indicated he wasn't the kind that left much to chance.

It was a tight squeeze wearing the dive pack, but I entered through the hatch in the conning tower, worked my way down the ladder into the periscope area, disturbed a couple of crystal fish, and finally descended still another level into the sub's control room.

The U-564 was intact. Even with fifty years of swarm quakes, the damage was minimal.

In one sense, Ambrose Vance was right. The U-564 had been stripped to the bare bones. Any resemblance to the fighting machine that had at one time been the scourge of Allied shipping in the Atlantic was incidental.

The night Vance had signed me on, he'd handed me the drawings for a type VII-C. "If I were you, I'd know these inside and out," he had warned me. I had done my homework, and now it was coiming in handy.

That study, coupled with Daddy Wages's long-remembered admonition stressing the value of homework, had prepared me for just such an eventuality. One night poring over the ship's blueprints had convinced me that the only place Hess could have stored the bullion was in those areas where the batteries had been located in battery rooms 1 and 2, and where the U-boat's fourteen torpedoes were formerly stored. That included both the fore and aft sections.

Logic also told me that since the fighting days of the war were over when this scenario was unfolding, Hess didn't need the batteries. He wasn't going to go any deeper than a shallow subsurface run—and at that level the snorkel supplied air to run the diesels.

By the same token, he didn't need the torpedoes either. Therefore, disposing of the torpedoes and freeing up that space also seemed logical. Out of all of this came the realization that in the end, Hess was sounding a whole lot more like a predictable mercenary than a devoted officer of the Third Reich.

By the time I got to the U-564 control room,

my E-time indicator was reading 0:41:28—
which meant that I had just under thirty-five
minutes of dive time left. There wasn't much
time left for exploration. I started aft, got
through the cramped crew mess, and looked for
a spot where I could pry up the steel-grid flooring that separated the crew's mess from the aft
battery storage area. I rummaged around in the
engine control room until I found a rusting
screwdriver, pried up the grid, and opened the
area leading to the aft battery compartment.

I wasn't prepared for what happened next.

When I pulled back the sheet-metal grease
pan that kept debris from running down into
the battery area, the skeletal remains of what
had once been a uniform-clad German submariner undulated in unseen eddies and currents.
After fifty years it was still standing guard over
what Albrecht Hess had kept of the national
Spanish treasury of Francisco Franco. The right
hand of the remains still clutched a rusting automatic.

The rest of what I saw in that hold area defied
description. How does a man go about explaining what it is like to be in a room filled with
over a hundred million dollars in gold bullion?
I tried counting, lost count, and decided instead
to do a couple of fast calculations.

According to Hess's and Vance's estimate, the
commander of the U-564 had been able to get
away with "more than half" of the bullion
aboard the *Wilhelm Leichter*—and while

Vance's earlier recovery had been sizeable, estimates were based on the gold being valued somewhere in the neighborhood of $42.00 an ounce, the 1976 standard.

Now, over twenty years later, the gold could be worth incalculable amounts.

I took out the Pentax and began squeezing off a roll of film, taking pictures of the hoard as fast as the camera would forward the film. At the same time I was counting again. The loaf-shaped bars, each the result of over a million kilograms of ore processing, filled the entire room.

I was still documenting my find when I felt the U-564 begin to shudder and vibrate. The room began to shift, and tilted further to port. The water was suddenly clouded with silt and debris. Finally, I lost my balance.

By the time I regained it, my concern centered, not on whether or not there was any way to get the gold to the surface—but whether or not there was any way to get Elliott to the surface.

It was still a world bordering on chaos when I heard Packy's voice. Her "swarm quake" warning came a little late. I shoved the Pentax into my game bag along with a couple of other pieces of suddenly not-so-important pieces of diving paraphernalia, and started to claw my way out of the battery area.

The U-564 was being subjected to another round of violent shakes and I was on my way up when the nozzle on my air tank caught in the mesh of the steel-grid flooring. When that happened, I knew it would be impossible to get out wearing the BCD, the regulator, and both tanks. I unbuckled my gear, wiggled free, held my breath, disconnected the main tank, and activated the pony. I checked my chrono, pressed the E-time indicator, saw the 0:15:00 flash twice, and started up through the grid. After that, I knew I would have to clear the mess area, work my way into the control room, and then up into the conning tower.

It was a good plan, but it had one very big flaw. The ladder leading up to the periscope area had dislodged and was wedged into the hatch. I could get up—but there was no way to get out. I started back down to the control area and began working my way back to the fantail.

The submarine lurched again, this time more violently than either of the two earlier occasions. I reeled, slammed into the bulkhead, and felt myself careen into the engine room.

When that happened, the area suddenly went from being partially illuminated to being plunged into an eerie kind of sobering darkness. I reached down and felt the jagged edges of the broken acrylic lens on my halogen.

All of a sudden, the situation had gotten a whole lot worse. Now, Mama Wages's bouncing baby son was completely dependent on remembering the sequence of compartments in the aft section of Hess's U-boat. I wasn't at all sure my memory was that good.

I started ticking the sections off in my head. Just aft of the main diesels was the torpedo loading hatch; beyond that was the maze of engine room controls—on both sides of the passageway. In the darkness, I groped along, using the piping and wires until I located the open end of the three aft torpedo tubes. I took off my gloves, stuck my hand into the firing tube, and prayed that I was going to be able to detect some sort of movement or flow in the water. When I did, I took off my BCD for the second time, shoved the pony tank and regulator into the tube in front of me, kept the mouthpiece in place, and crawled into the tube. There was just enough clearance to wedge my arms against the walls of the firing cylinder and work my way forward.

The business end of the tube cleared just above the twin rudders. I crawled out and used the hydroplanes, which were located just aft of the props, as a place where I could get back into my diving gear and strap on my BCD. The halo light on the DC indicated my E-time on the pony tank had just passed the six-minute mark. Even with Wages's luck factored in, getting back to the *Barbella* on nine minutes of air was going to be a virtual impossibility.

I connected the regulator, made certain the O-rings were seated, checked my valves a second time, kicked off, and started up and out of

R. Karl Largent

the trench. There was no way I could have been prepared for what happened.

I had just reached over the gunnel on the deck of the *Hedgehog* when I saw the diver coming straight at me. The diver was one surprise, because at first I figured it was Packy. But as it turned out, the shark knife was an even bigger surprise.

The knife, all twelve inches of nasty-looking steel, came up, caught the backpack harness strap, sliced through, and suddenly the tangle of tank, hoses, weights, and gear pulled me off balance. The pony tank peeled around in front of me and the mouthpiece was jerked out of my mouth.

I didn't need Daddy Wages to tell me that the situation was headed in the wrong direction. But this time it was Elliott who got lucky. Admittedly, most of what happened was reflex action. I grabbed the pony tank with both hands and when my assailant made the second pass, he got the full silver bullet shot square in the face—valve end first. His mask shattered, the mouthpiece twisted out of his mouth, I saw the startled look on his face rapidly turn to panic, and the water suddenly got a whole lot cloudier. Only this time it wasn't the bottom sediment deposited by half a century of swarm quakes that was being agitated.

This time it was a whole lot of blood and tissue and the stuff that holds a face together.

This time there wasn't any doubt about the

318

eventual outcome. Even so, the intruder still had a few histrionics to work through. He tried a couple of sweeping slashes with his oversized piece of cutlery; missed, flailed, gestured—and then started acting like a man who knew he was in a whole lot of trouble.

By then it was too late. All I had to do was wait.

The final bit of posturing would have been comical—if the man hadn't been dying.

I backed off. Under the circumstances, it was all I could do. Over the years I've seen more than one man die—and I've developed a theory or two about how these things happen. First of all, it never happens quite the way you think it's going to happen. Secondly, the victim never does quite what you think the victim is going to do under the circumstances. Once again, my theory held up.

For all the bravado, posturing, and violence demonstrated in the initial attack, the guy died like a milksop. He went quietly and without a helluva lot of dignity.

It was my turn to hold on. I say that because most of us can exhibit some pretty basic survival instincts when it comes to saving our earthly ass . . . and old Elliott is no exception.

I snatched his dive light away from him, kicked the knife away, unbuckled his diving gear, and struggled into his BCD. His gauges indicated he had a helluva lot more time left on his tank than I did on mine. It was a tricky maneuver, and I've since likened it to a buddy system with a dead man, but it was no time to get squeamish.

I gulped in some air and felt an obtuse slam in my brain, the quick kick in the lungs, and the taste of bile in my mouth as my system tried to adjust to its newfound luxuries. The deprivation period had lasted far too long to foster good health.

It took several seconds to get everything regulated, but when I did, I reached down and pulled away the remnants of my attacker's mask.

I knew no one was going to believe me—but I wasn't all that surprised when I saw who it was. The only question I had was, how had Luke Brimley pulled it off the day we thought he'd died? The realization that it was Brimley allowed another piece of the puzzle to tumble into place.

I probably would have taken time to congratulate myself, but the mere fact I was still ninety feet down in the shark-infested waters of the Sargasso tempered my inclination to celebrate.

It did not, however, temper my inclination to add a bit of Wages flair to the situation. I dug the transponder out of my game bag, activated it, reached down, and tucked it in Brimley's weight belt. If anyone did come to check on him, they would discover they had been getting the wrong signal. It was my little joke—but I was enjoying it.

When I looked up again, I saw Packy swimming toward me.

There are times when communication isn't necessary, at least not communication the way we humans are prone to think of it. She swam past me, around the prone figure of Brimley, and when her eyes finally searched out mine, I knew she knew.

Still, her fingers coiled into the "are you okay?" signal, and I nodded. I thumped my chest with the right hand to indicate I was working on borrowed air. Packy Darnell nodded her understanding.

I could see the red light on her comsys, and I could tell that she was trying to communicate. But we were no longer connected. Luke Brimley had tried to kill me—but the irony of it was, thanks to him, I was alive. I had his tank, his regulator, and a new lease on life. I say "irony" because in all probability, if Brimley had left me to my own devices, I would have run out of air long before I got to the surface.

I gave Packy the "you lead, I'll follow," signal and pointed to the surface. She took another look at Brimley, circled the body, and started up.

There were pastel remnants of pink and purple low on the horizon when Packy and I finally surfaced. Maydee, Chuco, and the Boots girl had been joined in their vigil by Shula Carson and Fritze Ritter.

Word had circulated that we were making one last attempt to retrieve the auxiliary generator from the *Hedgehog*. But when Packy informed them that we were a day late and a dollar short as far as the generator was concerned, the last bit of hope seemed to go out of them.

"Then we're stuck here," the Boots girl muttered. Chuco's response was to stare absently out at the water.

Carson sighed and reported on their progress with the *Barbella*'s diesel. "We got her back together, but we can't get her to fire."

"Injectors?"

"We'll have to jump-start the old son of a bitch," Ritter complained.

"Suppose we get her to fire," I said. "Think you can keep her running?"

Carson laughed. "Who the hell knows. All I know about diesels you can put in the corner of your eye. She'll do one of two things. Either she'll hump along and get us back to civilization or she'll blow higher than a fuckin' kite."

"So how do we kick-start her?"

While I peeled out of my diving gear, Carson explained how he would preheat the coils, disconnect the generator from the refrigeration and running lights for a second time, prime the fuel pump, apply the spark, and hope for the best. While Ritter and Carson explained the firing sequence step by step, I handed my dive gear to Chuco and Mookie. The fact that it wasn't *Barbella* gear escaped them.

"Where's the generator now?" I asked.

Ritter scratched at his four-day growth of beard. "We've got it sitting on the B deck, about halfway between the two points. I think we've got enough line to stretch down to the engine room."

"And if we don't?"

"We can always move her," Hew grunted.

I was helping Mookie and Packy stow the dive gear, when Shula approached. He took me aside. "I need to talk to you," he said. He kept his voice low so that the others couldn't hear him.

I nodded and looked at Ritter. "When will you be ready to give her a try?"

"I still need a couple of hours," he said. He looked at his watch and admitted his uncertainty about the outcome.

"Best-case scenario?" I asked.

"Early hours of the morning," Carson estimated.

"Worst case?"

"Tomorrow morning . . . after sunrise?"

"Or," Ritter added, "maybe nothing."

After that, Shula Carson had me follow him down to the B deck and forward to the freezer department. "What's up?" I asked.

"I think you better see this," he cautioned. "After we stretched the lines back up here to the cooler this afternoon and fired up the generator,

I decided to make certain the refrigeration units were working. And while I was at it, I figured, what the hell, with the refrigeration unit shut off most of the day, no one had the opportunity to inventory and check what we had in storage."

I followed Carson into the cooler. There were two sections. The first was where the *Barbella*'s provisions were stored. The second section was the one that had been converted into a temporary morgue. I opened the door and stepped back. China Porter's body was stretched out on the cooler's meat table. He was still wearing the soiled T-shirt and the blue trousers. His skin color was pasty white and his extremities were swollen.

I took a deep breath and waited until I had regained my equilibrium.

There were two other bodies, those of Bench and Kritzmer. Both had been discreetly wrapped in cotton sheets. I peeled back the cover on the first. It was Kit Bench. The ravages of the cyanide was inside. With the exception of dull but still-open eyes and the curious shape of his mouth, Kit Bench looked like a man who might have died of natural causes.

"The other one is the Kraut," Carson said.

I nodded, dropped the sheet, took Carson by the arm, and steered the *Barbella*'s first officer back out into the passageway. "One question," I said. "Do you trust me?"

Carson wasn't pulling any punches. "At this point I don't trust my own mother—and I sure as hell wouldn't trust you or your girlfriend."

"Good," I said. "For the time being, listen. Draw conclusions later. Less than two hours ago, Luke Brimley attacked me on the deck of the *Hedgehog*."

Carson looked at me like I was crazy. "That's impossible," he snorted, "Brimley's been dead for—"

I shook my head. "No, we thought he was dead; which is exactly what we were supposed to think."

"But how the hell did—"

"I don't know," I admitted, "but there's got to be a logical answer, an answer that doesn't have anything to do with this being the Sargasso or the damn Bermuda Triangle or any of that hocus-pocus stuff."

"But . . ."

"Think back," I said. "What do you remember about yesterday morning?"

Carson's face was a craggy frown. He looked back at the door of the cooler, and finally at me. "Well"—he hesitated—"I remember the fog, and the fact that . . ."

"And . . . something else . . ."

"What the hell are you getting at, Wages?"

"When I got to the bridge, you were staring off into the fog and you said . . ."

"I said I thought I saw something out there . . ."

"Not some damn monster . . . or some figment of a Bermuda Triangle legend; you saw a . . ."

"Another ship?" Carson finally allowed himself to say aloud.

"Exactly." I grinned.

"But no one is supposed to know where we are. Vance and Porter took every possible precaution to make certain no one knew where we were; salvage divers are taught from the outset that . . ."

"Exactly," I repeated. "You just put your finger on it. Who was the third person who had to know our position in order to prepare the salvage charts?"

"Brimley," Carson said. His voice was flat. "But he's . . . we never recovered the body."

"We didn't recover the body because there wasn't any body. What's the one modification Brimley insisted on in all of the MD-SH-3 sleds?"

Carson thought for a moment. "Brimley had us disconnect the onboard LS system and the divers went with a dive pack on their backs. He said it was so they could work independent of the sleds."

"The perfect cover," I said.

I closed the door to the coolers, I took Shula Carson up to the B-deck and Brimley's cabin. I opened Brimley's locker and showed him the empty cartons that had contained A-44JT Random Impulse Transponders. "One of these," I explained, "was attached to the hull of the

Hedgehog. Five will get you ten that the other one is attached somewhere to the *Barbella.*"

"But why would . . ."

"I can't prove a thing at this point, it's all conjecture," I cautioned, "and it will be until I find that second transponder."

"I still don't get it. How did Brimley know you were down there?"

I was still putting the pieces together, and until I actually heard my theory out loud, articulated in some way, treated in some fashion other than letting it rattle around in my brain without definitive shape or texture, it was going to continue to be amorphous.

"Start," I said, "by asking yourself what Brimley knew. Well, for one thing, he knew that he had put a transponder on the hull of the *Hedgehog,* and that the little jewel was working—because he had been monitoring it."

I had Carson's attention.

"Then . . . all of a sudden he loses his signal. That signal is important. Why? Because it indicates where the *Hedgehog* is. And the reason the location of the *Hedgehog* is important is because it marks the spot where Hess's downed U-564 rests."

"Then he knew where the sub was all along?"

"He knew—and my guess is that Bench and Lord knew as well. But they sure as hell didn't want Porter, or anyone else for that matter, to know that they had located it."

"If you're sucking all of this out of your

thumb, Wages, I gotta give you an A for imagination."

I was on a roll. "Suddenly the transponder isn't working and our boy Brimley, who's been monitoring the situation from the comfort of that ship you thought you saw yesterday morning, gets a little nervous. So what does he do? He puts on his diving gear and heads down to the *Hedgehog* to have a look around."

"Keep going," Carson urged.

"He gets there, checks on the transponder, discovers that it's missing, and just about then, yours truly blunders out of the U-564 and runs smack into him. He did his damnedest to carve me up with his shark sticker, but this time it was my turn to get lucky."

"There's a big hole in your theory, Wages. How the hell did Brimley put the cyanide in the duct system, cut Kritzmer's throat, and put a bullet in Porter from a damn ship that you theorize is anchored at least two or three kilometers from here? Then when you answer that one, how the hell did he sabotage the *Barbella*'s diesels and set the fire that burned out the Com Cen?"

"He had help," I said matter-of-factly.

Carson started to laugh, then checked it. "Come on, Wages, who, that skinny Boots kid?"

"She's Porter's daughter," I informed him. He looked at me, astonished "No, not her. That kid is terrified."

"Well, to hear you tell it, it ain't you—and it

damn sure ain't me. So who is it?" Carson began to tick off the names. "Chuco, Fritze, the Darnell dame, Jewel Simon? The Darnell woman came aboard with you, and everyone knows Jewel Simon stepped out of a goddamn comic strip with all that talk about giant sea creatures and monsters."

At that juncture, I didn't see any point in telling Shula Carson that in some ways, Jewel Simon was right; the massive six-giller I had encountered—not once, but twice—and the king-sized mantas Fredrich had viewed from his observation port in the bow of the Barbella were real. Doing so would probably have taken us even further from determining who Brimley's cohort actually was.

Carson was still ticking off names. "That leaves Hew, and Marion Fredrich." He paused for a moment. "It's Fredrich, isn't it?"

I had no intention of telling Shula Carson who I thought Brimley's accomplice was until I could prove it, but I was eliminating candidates fast. Hew was a crochety old bastard, but that sure didn't make him a murderer. Ritter was no more a candidate than Hew . . . and Marion Fredrich and Chuco seemed less probable than the other two.

"I've still got some homework to do," I admitted.

Carson cocked his head to one side.

"It's like putting a puzzle together," I said. "Piece by piece. Even though it seems logical that Brimley had an accomplice somewhere aboard the *Barbella*, we can't rule out the fact that Brimley did his own dirty work."

"But how?" Carson challenged.

"What's to have stopped Brimley from coming aboard—"

"No way," Carson said, cutting me off. "I was on watch when both Kritzmer and Porter were killed. I sure as hell would have heard something if anybody tried to board the *Barbella*."

"Heard something? Maybe. Saw something? I doubt it. There was a wall of fog out there."

Carson stared back at me. Finally he said, "Okay, I'm buyin' it. I'm with you. What's our next move?"

"It's my hunch that if Brimley did have an accomplice, that accomplice is starting to get pretty nervous along about now. Brimley is dead, we know that for a fact . . . Lord probably is . . . and Bench is wrapped up in that cooler . . ."

When Carson started toward the door, I stopped him. "There's something else I want you to see," I said. I opened the door to Brimley's wall locker and took out the torn picture. "Have you ever seen this before?"

Carson looked at it for a moment and said, "Sure. Hell, every salvage diver up and down the east coast of Florida was there. That was Bill Lord's retirement party. They tell me Ringer Blanchard throws one hell of a party." One by one he began pointing them out. "That's Brimley, that's Lord, that's Bench . . . ," Then he stopped. "Where's the rest of it?"

"That's the way I found it," I said.

"I saw the same picture in Lord's cabin one night when me and him was tryin' to obliterate the world's Scotch supply," Carson said.

The *Barbella*'s second officer walked across the hall, opened the door to what had once been Gabe Lord's cabin, and pointed to the desk. "Right there," he said, then stopped. "Damn, it's gone."

It was nearly 22:30 by the time I opened the door to my cabin, dropped the personal effects of the three *Barbella* divers in a pile on the floor, sat down on my bunk, and wondered what I had overlooked.

Twice during the previous hour Ritter, Carson, and Hew had managed to get the *Barbella*'s diesel to turn over, but neither time were they able to keep it running. Each time the lights flickered momentarily and died. On each occasion I had gone down to the engine room to offer encouragement. The second time I was greeted by Ritter, who informed me that in all probability it had been our last hurrah. "I think we fried them damned injectors again."

When a low-hanging cloud deck moved in, it was pointless to keep the signal going. I helped the crew dredge up more rystmus weed and sargassum for the next day's fire, then called off the smoke signal brigade for the night. Both

Jewel and her accomplice looked like they needed a break.

After that, I made certain everyone was paired off and that I knew where each of them was spending the night. If everyone was cooperative . . . it was because everyone was more than just a little bit scared.

The three women readily agreed to keep an eye on each other; Ritter and Hew advised me they planned to spend the night in the engine room, and Chuco, Fredrich, and Carson offered to maintain the watch.

Still the most suspicious, Maydee Hew was the only one to protest the fact that I was the one person who didn't have someone monitoring my comings and goings.

"If anyone wants me, I'll be in my cabin. I'll be going through the personal effects of the three divers, to see if I can learn anything."

Then I offered Maydee the opportunity to sift their effects with me. He declined.

It was somewhere around midnight by the time I finished sifting through Bench's effects and turned my attention to Gabe Lord's papers. Unlike his colleagues', the senior diver's papers were neatly organized in one of those ebony black, portable plastic file folders they sell in discount houses.

The life story of Gabe Lord was all wrapped up and cataloged in the space of eight by twelve inches. There were medical papers relative to his most recent dive physical, a copy of his salvage recertification, a copy of his mother's death certificate, a letter from a young woman who said how sorry she was that she had to leave before she could "explain," and the one thing that I was looking for, a copy of the group photograph taken at Bill Lord's retirement party.

The only difference between the copy of the photo in Gabe Lord's plastic file folder and the one I had taken out of Luke Brimley's cabin was that Lord's photograph was intact. None of it was missing.

Now I knew why the effort had been made to conceal who was at that party. And now I knew who the third man in the picture was, the one that had the "where the hell have I seen him before" face.

The exhilaration that accompanies discovery isn't always a good thing. Get a little elated and it's easy to get a little careless. I got careless.

While I was applauding myself on my investigative prowess, the door to my cabin was opening. When I realized what was happening, I was staring down the gun-metal-gray, ominous-looking barrel of a .38 automatic.

Incident:

There were tears in her eyes and her hand was shaking, not enough to make me think I might be able to get the weapon away from her—but enough that if she decided to pull the trigger, the bullet could have taken me out anywhere between the stomach and the throat.

"I didn't want it to come to this," Packy said. "From the very beginning this is the one thing I didn't want to happen. I didn't want you to get hurt."

"When you play these kind of games," I said, "someone always gets hurt."

"You had it pretty well figured out, didn't you?"

"Not all of it," I admitted. "The hardest part was trying to figure out how you got involved."

Packy Darnell wanted to talk . . . wanted to explain. "After Randy was . . . killed," she began, ". . . it got pretty tough. I . . . I . . . had a hard . . . hard time putting things back together. And then, when things looked the worst, along came Peter. He took care of me, Elliott; Peter Cannon took care of me."

"And your money," I reminded her.

"Have you ever lost everything, Elliott? Have you ever been so terribly alone that you sit in a room and hear your own heart beat? That's how alone I was, Elliott. I sat in that damned apartment in Pensacola after Randy died and I was so alone I could hear my own heart beat." There were tears in her eyes.

"Cannon roped you into this, didn't he?"

"You're sweet, Elliott," she said, "but no, Peter didn't rope me into this. I came of my own free will. I knew what I was getting into."

At that point there didn't seem to be a whole lot more to say. I had questions, lots of questions, but knowing the answers now wasn't going to change things.

"How did you know this was where we were going to end up?" I pushed.

"Oh, what a web we weave, when first we practice to deceive," Packy recited. "Remember that one? That was back in the days when we used to read quotations to each other and try to figure out what they really meant."

I nodded.

Packy's face sobered. "It wasn't hard. Ambrose Vance went to Chester Blanchard for help in staffing the search for the U-564. Old Man Blanchard unwittingly turned to his son, Ringer, who turned to Brimley, and the plot was hatched. From the outset, Brimley planned to get rid of Bench and Lord, because he knew he couldn't count on them if the going got tough. It was a simple plan, find the U-564, then sabotage the *Barbella* search to the point that it couldn't continue. Then, when the Vance expedition returned home with its tail between its legs, Brimley and the Cannons moved in and became very wealthy. See? Simple?"

To this day, I don't know how I intended to respond to Packy Darnell . . . because the words never made it out.

It happened so fast that any recounting of the sequence of events probably leaves something out. Packy was lifted up, and out of where she stood, her body hurtled across my cabin like some kind of disconnected, rag mannequin.

I heard her head hit the bulkhead. It made the kind of sickening sound you think an overripe melon might make if it was thrown against the same heavy steel barrier.

I didn't fare a whole lot better, I was rocketed backward, picked up and slapped by some giant hand . . . then just as quickly discarded. The difference was, I had been thrown up against my bunk; there were sheets and pillows and a mattress to cushion the impact . . . there weren't any such things to cushion Packy's impact.

The door was ripped off of its hinges and there was the instantaneous acrid smell of fire.

I didn't have to be told that explosion had occurred in the engine room. The ball of fire had rampaged down the passageway; a rogue, deadly, death-dealing, life-quenching force, ricocheting from cabin to cabin, creating an instant inferno, squeezing the oxygen out of the air, and sucking the life out of its victims.

I was dazed and hurt. Yet somehow I managed to claw my way into a kneeling position. My cabin, smoke-filled, was awash in a surreal pallet of reds, oranges, purples, and things charred and torn apart. I could see Packy Darnell. The fire was everywhere.

What was left of Peter Cannon's accomplice was propped up in a grotesque kind of challenging posture across from me. I know it had to be Packy, because she was the only person in the room with me when the explosion occurred. If I had stumbled upon the carnage after the fact, there would have been no way of knowing.

A human being without a face is a curious and grotesque thing. The cosmetic balance between the montage of facial features and the network of muscles, subcutaneous tissue, and bone that gives the human form individuality is disrupted and the viewer has no reference point.

Once lively and lovely, Packy Darnell had

been transformed into something so macabre it defied description. I crawled over to her, checked her pulse, realized the futility of my gesture, and tried to stand up. The *Barbella* was undulating in the water like a drunken dancer.

I don't know how long it actually took me, but I somehow managed to get through the choking smoke to the door of the cabin and out into the companionway. I was disoriented, uncertain of my surroundings and unsure about what I should do next. Frantic, half-formed questions were flashing through my brain—when a ship catches fire, what is there to burn? After all, it's steel—and steel defies even the violent and destructive forces of nature. But a ship like the *Barbella* is more than steel. There is paint, and varnish, and teak, and plastic, and wiring, and fuel oil, and in this case, flesh. There was the sickening stench of burnt flesh.

By the time I managed to reel my way to the aft hold and the engine room where Hew, Chuco, and Ritter had been working on the *Barbella*'s engines, I knew the extent of the explosion. The *Barbella* had a gaping hole in her lower deck near the stern. She was taking on water and the charred bodies of the three men, blackened by burning diesel fuel, gave mute testimony to the violence of the explosion.

The cable from the winch was hanging down into the aft hold area, and I looped it back over one of the cargo cleats to create a ladder. The water was beginning to swirl around my ankles and I crawled up on some crates, grabbed hold of the cable, and pulled myself over the hatch seal onto the main deck. The *Barbella*'s fire was lighting up the Sargasso sky.

I used the overhang on the roof of the dive locker to pull myself up on the main deck behind the smokestacks. From there I could see two people on the bridge. There was another body in the passageway outside of the burned-out Com Cen.

I jumped down, pinned my back up against the wall, and inched my way past what had been Porter's stateroom, the galley, and finally, the lab. The searing, thundering wall of flame had roared through the A deck like a runaway commuter train. The roof had been blown away and Mookie Boots had never had a chance.

At that point the smoke had become so thick and acrid that I could feel it clawing its way down my throat and into my lungs. I managed to get past the body of the Boots girl to the ladder. And I figured I might have a chance if I could get up the ladder and onto the bridge. At that point I would be on the main deck near the wheelhouse.

From the bridge I could see both Jewel Simon and Shula Carson. They were forward of the bridge, struggling to launch the port lifeboat.

The flames had already started eating through the roof of the Com Cen. There was smoke, and chaos, and turmoil. I tried shouting at the pair, but my voice was drowned out in what seemed like an unending series of explosions.

Then I heard him. It was Marion Fredrich. His face was bloodied and he was standing on the bridge, screaming, gesturing, pointing at Carson and the Simon woman. "You must stop them, Wages," he shouted, "Carson—Carson is the one. He's the one—and that woman is helping him."

I started for the railing around the bridge, but as I did, I saw the German kneel down, steady a revolver on the steel rail, and squeeze off two rounds. The shots went astray, but Carson stumbled sideways, caught himself, and somehow managed to find a hiding place. The Simon woman dropped at the first shot. At first I couldn't tell whether Fredrich had hit her or if Jewel Simon's survival instincts had taken over.

"Put the damn gun down," I shouted.

When Fredrich turned toward me, I saw how badly he was hurt. There was a gaping hole in his midsection where the blast had caught him. In the surreal yellow-orange world of the burning *Barbella*, he looked like some kind of grotesque fugitive from a Grade-B movie.

Fredrich was gesturing with the gun. "I caught them, Wages, I caught Carson and that woman stowing supplies in the lifeboat. When I tried to stop them, they hit me—" Fredrich's ranting and raving was turning to racking sobs.

"Give me the gun," I said. I was doing my best to sound collected and rational.

Fredrich hesitated for a moment. He was getting weak. Finally he laid the revolver on the deck and shoved it toward me.

"Now," I said, "kick your legs over the edge, drop down to the A deck, and start working your way to that lifeboat."

Fredrich hesitated.

"Damn it, Marion, move. That lifeboat is the only chance we've got."

The *Barbella* had become an inferno. I grabbed Fredrich and started dragging him toward the lifeboat. At first he struggled; then all of a sudden, he quit. I was pulling dead weight. At first I read the look in his eyes as one of terror. Then I realized it was the glazed stare of death.

At about the same time, Jewel Simon began working her way toward me. She got to me at just about the time I saw the first indication of the approaching lights.

"Oh, thank God," Jewel whimpered.

I knew that if I survived this one, there would be a day when I looked back and realized how many times I had fallen asleep at the switch during the unfolding of the Sargasso incident. I wasn't about to let it happen again.

"Get back to the damned lifeboat," I shouted. "Tell Shula to get it launched . . . now."

The face I should have recognized in the picture taken at Bill Lord's retirement party was none other than the man Packy Darnell had convinced me she was trying to get away from.

It was a helluva time to finally figure out where the final piece of the puzzle fit. From the bridge of the approaching boat, Cannon opened fire. Considering where he was firing from, he was one helluva marksman. The first slug buried itself somewhere in the meaty part of my right thigh, and the second found a home dangerously close to where I kept the family jewels. I went down like the proverbial ton of bricks. My arms and legs went numb, my eyes glazed over, and despite efforts to the contrary, I had started down the checkout lane.

While I remember hearing a lot of things at that particular moment, the thing I remembered most was hearing Peter Cannon, the man I had encountered only once previously, scream that he couldn't see Packy anywhere on deck. There was shouting and profanity, and then the voices were drowned out by the sounds of the burning *Barbella*.

"What do we do with them?" I heard one voice shout.

"Leave 'em right where they are," Peter Cannon ordered. "The way that old tub is burning, that fire will take care of every last trace of . . ."

I still couldn't get the old dependable Wages parts to do what I wanted them to do. And there wasn't a helluva lot I could do when I heard Peter tell the other man to "get the hell out of there."

I heard the sound of fire, and the roar of Cannon's engines as he pulled away into the night—and then, with nothing to hang on to, I spiraled down into the comatose world of the uncaring. I had given Ambrose Vance my very best shot. He owed me.

Awareness is often ill-timed. Looking back, I realize there was no reason to feel good about the fact that I was slowly becoming cognizant of my surroundings. My mood at the time could best be described as tentative and apprehensive. Above me there was an orange glow. Beyond that there was a depressing blackness . . . the kind of blackness that comes about when nothing, not even stars, is visible.

I could hear voices. They were muted, and nothing I could do seemed to make them comprehensible. I strained, turned my head to one side, and tried to get a look at my surroundings. When I couldn't see anything but half-formed images, I tried to listen.

"See if he can understand you," one voice said.

The other repeated my name. "Elliott," she said. The voice was soft and musical. For a moment I thought it might be an angel. If it was, the angel smelled like soot and smoke.

My eyes were still closed. They wouldn't open, so I tried a grunt. It seemed to work. The angel bent over and put her ear close to my mouth. "Who's out there?" I asked.

"Ask him if he can sit up," the other voice said.

When she did, I tried . . . but things hurt. My leg thing, my crotch thing, the base-of-my-skull thing. The parts that weren't hurting, were spinning. I forced my eyes open and tried to focus on the orange and red and yellow monster enveloped in flames no more than two or three hundred yards from where I was viewing the proceedings.

The *Barbella* was dying a horrible death and Ambrose Vance wasn't there to hear Jewel Simon mutter the last rites.

"Jesus," she said, and closed her eyes. We all did . . . and because we did, we missed that part where the Barbella took her final breath and slipped beneath the surface.

The oil slick on the surface of the water continued to burn.

It took some time . . . and some doing, but I finally managed to get my brain and mouth synchronized to the point that I could ask some questions. The first one was the obvious one. "Where the hell am I?"

Jewel Simon seemed almost amused. "You are in what might laughingly be called a lifeboat. I say 'laughingly' because it's damn well likely that we're going to die in this stinking lifeboat."

Then Shula Carson bent over me. I could see

just enough of his face in the orange glow to recognize him.

"Whoever the hell they were, they made a couple of passes, shot up things, apparently didn't find what they were looking for, and roared off into the night. They didn't even say good-bye."

"They probably think we went down with the ship," Jewel said. Then she added, "Maybe we would have been better off if we had. We don't have much drinking water, few provisions; and not much to protect us from the sun."

"Did you see who else was on that damn ship?" I finally asked.

Carson nodded. "I recognized him. Ringer Blanchard. That little son of a bitch; I knew his daddy."

In the Sargasso, you don't do much drifting. I nodded off a couple of times during the next few hours, and when I awoke, I saw a few stars twinkling low on the horizon. If the skies were clearing, it was a mixed blessing. There was no way we were going to be spotted with a low-hanging cloud deck. On the other hand, we had minimum shelter from a hammering Sargasso sun. Our only hope was that someone had seen the fire and that with the first light of day, the air, sea, and rescue boys would be out in force.

Jewel and Shula were both asleep. In the darkness I pulled myself up into a sitting position, took inventory of precious Wages body parts, and tried to think back through what had happened.

Seeing Peter Cannon had cleared up the matter of the radiogram that each of the divers had received. The "Penguin" referred to in the mysterious message was obviously the ship that not only Cannon and Blanchard, but the supposedly dead Luke Brimley, had been operating from after I accepted Ambrose Vance's offer. As for the code name, pussy cat, if I hadn't been chasing my own tail so vigorously, I might have recognized the fact that the phonetic code for salvage divers usually incorporates the individual's initials. Hence, P. C., pussy cat, or Peter Cannon; take your pick. I could truthfully say that I had met Peter Cannon twice—and that I didn't much care for the man no matter what he called himself.

I was still sifting through the mental flotsam of a venture gone bad when I peered over the gunnel of the life boat and saw the first orange-red strips of light on the eastern horizon. It had the effect of jarring me awake again, and my thoughts returned to what had transpired aboard the *Barbella*.

I remembered the night that Kit Bench had died and how I had so readily dismissed the fact that the vents in Packy's stateroom had been closed when the cyanide was placed in the *Barbella*'s ventilation system. It was supposed to look like an attempt on Packy Darnell's life; an attempt that had gone wrong and killed a veteran salvage diver.

When I wasn't berating myself for missing that one, I was chastising Mother Wages's son, Elliott, for refusing to see other things . . . the significance of the fire in the Com Cen, and the sequence of events that led to China Porter's death.

Why hadn't I paid more attention, for example, to the fact that at the time of Kritzmer's death, the only two men on board who were capable of hefting the man's considerable bulk were with me, conducting a cabin-by-cabin search for something that had never been there in the first place.

Now, in the light of the emerging dawn, I realized that Brimley had moved about in the fog like some sort of ghostly specter. They had come damn close to pulling it off.

How easy we all made it for them. Now, when it was too late, the pieces were all falling into place.

Packy, dispatched by Porter to retrieve Brimley's body, returned to the ship, reported that she hadn't found anything . . . not because she couldn't find him, but because she knew he was already safely aboard the boat with Cannon.

The pieces were still coming together.

The mastermind was obviously Ringer Blanchard. Young Blanchard had very likely learned about Ambrose Vance's mission from his father. The senior Blanchard, CEO of the Lauderdale Salvage Company, was the man Vance had turned to when it came time to staff the search for Hess's downed U-boat. Young Blanchard recognized Vance's operation for what it was, an opportunity to get very wealthy, very fast.

All he had to do was arrange an elaborate double cross by persuading Luke Brimley, Gabe Lord, and Kit Bench to go along with his plan—a not-too-difficult task considering the fact that Ringer Blanchard was in a position to promise them a far bigger share of a pie that didn't have to be split so many different ways.

On the surface, at least, that was probably the plan. But there is no honor among thieves, and now it was apparent that Ringer Blanchard had a far more Machiavellian scheme up his sleeve.

When Vance decided his mission needed help, he turned to Cosmo Leach. Leach, in turn, recommended yours truly, and when young Ringer learned that new blood was about to be pumped into Vance's search for the U-564, he seized the opportunity to make certain Brimley had help. Bench and Lord may not have been the type who had trouble switching allegiance, but they may have been the type who had trouble with the concept of murder.

Solution: To get the job done, inject one Peter Cannon and his new wife, the former Packy Darnell, into the equation. The game goes by another name as well; it's called, play Wages for the sucker.

There were still parts of the sordid little scenario that hadn't come together. I still hadn't figured out what had happened to the girl I once knew as Packy Darnell. Or what makes a sweet young thing turn into someone willing to kill for her greed? Was she always like that and I didn't see it? At the moment I was allowing myself to feel pretty stupid.

The sun was still emerging from haze on the horizon when Jewel Simon stirred and looked around the boat. Her face was soot-covered and swollen; her eyes were hollow and tired. She looked at me, then the still-sleeping Shula, and I could tell she was trying to get her bearings.

Each of the *Barbella*'s lifeboats had been outfitted with polyethylene sealed "contingency" packs that contained a variety of emergency rations and drinking water. Jewel, who had feared the worst, rummaged around until she found the bottle of water, took several swallows, and handed it to me. I hadn't realized how thirsty I was.

She stared off at the sunrise for several minutes before she spoke. "Well, so much for my one-half-of-one-percent dream," she said.

I tried to work up a smile in response. I knew what she meant.

"Are you surprised about your little playmate?" Jewel asked.

"We don't see what we don't want to see," I admitted.

"When did you put it all together?"

"Parts of it are still missing. I still haven't figured out how Brimley pulled off that little trick the day he disappeared."

Jewel Simon laid her head back against the gunnel and closed her eyes. "When they finally got you to the surface, Porter sent your friend Packy down to look for Brimley. No one was quite certain what had happened to him. We knew that the dive crew had been hit by the swarm quakes, and we knew you were in trouble—because we were recording everything on the mission tapes."

I waited while Jewel took another sip of water and pushed her hair back out of her eyes.

"That's the night we had the fire, lost power," I said.

"The rest is, as they say, 'history,'" Jewel observed with a sigh.

I nodded.

"If Brimley and the rest of the divers were behind all of this, what happened to Bench and Lord?" she asked.

"Somehow, someday, I'll have to give Ambrose Vance a full report of what went on out here. And unless someone conducts a full-scale, exhaustive investigation, we may never know for certain."

"So," Jewel said, "I'm interested in theory. You can consider this a dry run in preparation for your meeting with Vance."

"Try this one on for size," I began. "Vance's first salvage expedition, by all standards except perhaps Mel Fisher's, was pretty damn successful. The old boy not only retrieved a helluva lot of money, he got a lot of notoriety in the process.

"So, when he was able to verify that Hess's journal was authentic, he had a pretty good idea where he could locate the rest of the Francisco Franco treasury. Up until that time, there had been lots of rumors about a sunken U-boat full of bullion at the bottom of the Sargasso, but no proof. Now, all of a sudden, Vance had that proof.

"The next question you have to ask yourself is, why Blanchard? Obvious answer; Ambrose Vance is an entrepreneur, not a salvage expert. He turns to his old friend, Chester Blanchard, who runs Lauderdale Salvage. Blanchard makes all the arrangements; commissions a salvage barge, outfits the *Barbella*, and tells his son, Ringer, to find Vance a crew of qualified salvage divers. Follow me so far?"

Jewell nodded.

"But—there's one flaw in all of this. Young Blanchard is not the honorable businessman his father is. He rounds up some qualified divers, all right, but he also hires a man by the name of . . ."

"Let me finish," Jewel said. "Luke Brimley."

"Exactly. He tells Brimley about his little plan. The plan is a simple one. He hires a captain with a past, one who he knows has the credentials but one who he also knows won't give him a lot of grief as long as there is plenty of coke to keep the captain from having to face reality. Brimley has a mission. As soon as the U-564 is located, he puts it in motion. The *Hedgehog* is the first victim. Key personnel are lost and vital equipment is no longer available."

"But what about . . . ?"

I nodded. "Here's where I figure their plan started to come apart at the seams. Brimley still needs to find the U-boat, and he has lost two divers on the *Hedgehog*. He tells Porter he needs more divers . . . and Porter reports to Vance. He tells him accidents happen, and he reminds Vance that salvage operations can be risky business."

"That still doesn't . . ."

". . . doesn't explain how I got involved?" I finished. "Well, I figure Vance got hold of his old friend, Cosmo Leach, told him he needed someone out there that he knew he could trust, and Cosmo gave him my name. Vance told Old Man Blanchard. Old Man Blanchard told his son . . . and young Ringer Blanchard goes in search of someone to neutralize my impact on the situation. He gets in touch with Peter Cannon, a longtime member of the diving fraternity, who in turns tells him he has recently married a woman who was 'involved' with yours truly sometime in the past."

Jewell managed a smile. "They're right," she said. "Nice guys do finish last."

I shook my head. "We haven't played the last

chapter of this one," I insisted. "The game's not over."

Her laugh was tinny, but at least she laughed. "I don't know. Those guys are on that boat that pulled alongside of us last night. They've probably got food and water . . . and to hear you tell it, they know where Hess's U-boat is located. The way I look at it, they're doing better than we are."

I shifted my weight to take some of the pressure off the hole in my thigh and continued. "It was either Ringer's plan to begin with, or Luke Brimley's little innovation, but someone decided it would be a whole lot cleaner if there wasn't anyone around to tell authorities what had happened. With the U-564 located, Brimley figured it was safe to get rid of his diving buddies because the fewer people that knew about the plan, the better, and fewer people meant fewer splits on the bullion. Then he started on the rest of the crew. I'm certain he started the fire in the engine room and the Com Cen in the hope that it would spread out of control."

Jewel was listening intently.

"He probably would have pulled it off if I hadn't discovered the U-564 when I went down to investigate the wreck of the *Hedgehog*."

"Then you know where the U-564 is located?"

"Correction, I knew where the *Hedgehog* was located. I'm the one who removed the transponder."

"But what about the charts?" she protested.

"Those were history when the *Barbella* went down."

Jewel's shoulders sagged. "Damnnnn," she muttered. "Then this is all for nothing?"

It was almost sunset when an ancient Gruman SA-16B Albatross found enough weed-free space to chance putting down for us. The sixty-one-foot-long, twin-engined godsend with a crew of four took us aboard at 19:47 hours and informed us that the worst was over.

Jewel was still muttering a string of barely audible thank-yous when the flight nurse stuck a needle in her arm to balance her electrolytes and keep her from further dehydrating. She checked out shortly after that.

Shula Carson wasn't much better off, but someone on the crew saw fit to give him a cigarette—and for the time being, Shula was happy. He curled up in a corner, rubbed some salve on his blistered face, finished his cigarette, and like Jewel, fell asleep.

The captain, a pretty little vixen with an Oklahoma accent, turned the controls over to her copilot, came back, sat down, and started asking questions. For a change they were the kind of questions I could answer.

"Are you the one in charge of this floating disaster circus?" she asked. She had beautiful teeth, a symmetrical face, and close-cropped black hair that augmented a Bermuda tan. Her name was stenciled on her flight uniform; C.

Ballinger. She let me guess what the C stood for;
Connie, Carol, Cynthia, or something more exotic. I never did find out.

"No one's 'in charge,' but I'll try to answer
your questions."

"Let me answer one for you first," she said.
"You're probably wondering how we found
you."

I nodded.

"Well, at 05:10 hours this morning, we started
receiving a distress call from a privately owned
yacht called the *Penguin*. In three different SOS
transmissions, she gave us three different sets
of coordinates."

"The *Penguin*?" I repeated.

C. Ballinger nodded. "If you can believe it, the
Penguin claimed she was under attack, suffer-
ing severe damage, and sinking hard by the
stern."

"Attack from what?" I muttered.

C. Ballinger shrugged her shoulders. "We
never did find out; they just kept saying they
were being 'attacked.' So you can thank whoever was making those distress calls. We were
getting low on fuel and had decided to pack it
in for the day. We were heading back to our
base in Bermuda when our spotter caught sight
of you."

"Any word on the *Penguin*?"

C. Ballinger shook her head. "Nope."

Incident:

Single Note Sal's Bar on Front near Water Street on Marathon is where I go to heal. The *Perpetual Motion* is tied up in a slip about a half a block down the street, and for the next couple of months at least, it would take an army to take me away from here.

On Sundays, Sal fixes her regulars, among whom I have the pleasure of numbering myself when I'm on Marathon, an exotic mocha cream espresso that goes well with catching up on the news. Sal doesn't allow television—just radio. So on Sunday mornings, Sal's regulars get a steady dose of whatever fare NPR is serving up

357

and a big fat copy of every Sunday newspaper in the area.

For the most part, I am content—and I am healing.

The superficial bullet wounds I collected my last night on the *Barbella* are now nothing more than two-inch-long streaks of pinkish proud flesh that validate my claim to adventure. They'll be pink for a long time; they're located where the sun isn't going to get to them.

That's the physical side of it.

The emotions, on the other hand, are still a little battered. I spent a few sleepless nights thinking about Packy. The worst part of it is, I only had to go back a few years to remember the day when I considered her to be one of the treasures in my life.

It has been eight weeks since Lieutenant Crista Ballinger of the 477 Air Sea and Rescue Squadron, 47th Recovery Wing, deposited Jewel Simon, Shula Carson, and yours truly on the moon-bathed runway in front of the Operations Building of the 2-211 Bermuda Recovery Station. After that, the Navy medics spent a couple of days poking us with needles and probing us with questions before turning us loose.

I caught a flight to Miami, was picked up at the airport by Cosmo and Honey Bear, and ultimately plunked down in front of Ambrose Vance to tell him the whole story.

Which I did.

In the process, however, I must have left

something out. Ambrose Vance called it "important details."

The day I unfolded the saga for the old boy, Vance sat looking at me the way a lizard eyes a fly, as if he wanted to reach out at any minute and choke the life out of me. Why? Because I couldn't tell him where he could find the U-564.

"And you say have no idea how to find the area where the U-564 is located, Mr. Wages?" he asked. It was the third time he'd asked me the same question. He hadn't even bothered to put a different twist on it.

I shook my head.

Vance looked around his office. He had an expression of complete and total exasperation. "Why is it," he said in his unpleasant, raspy, doomsday voice, "that I am convinced you will walk out of here, summon your equally nefarious colleagues, and go back to the Sargasso to claim Hess's cache for yourself?"

"That, Mr. Vance," I said with a sigh, "is the farthest thing from my mind."

Vance eyed me, then steered his wheelchair across the room to a position in front of the window. From there he could look down on a carefully manicured private garden protected by a flagstone wall. "See that man standing by the gate, Mr. Wages?"

"Yes, sir," I said. The man would have been hard to miss. He was big enough to eat Wheaties without taking them out of the box.

"His name is Robert. Just Robert. His last

name is unimportant. Do you know how many Roberts I have working for me, Mr. Wages?"

I shrugged. Any number would have been impressive. Guys like Robert cost a lot of money.

"I have no doubt that you are a great deal more clever than any of the Roberts I employ, Mr. Wages. And I do not doubt your ability to elude them when you so desire. But when you do, I will simply send another Robert to find you, and then another, and then another . . . and at some point in time, you will begin to comprehend the futility in trying to escape the ongoing surveillance."

"And all this because you think I intend to return to the site of the U-564?"

Ambrose Vance turned away from the window and looked at me. "That is exactly what I think, Mr. Wages, and I believe it is only a matter of time."

I laughed. Vance didn't know it yet, but Robert wasn't going to have a hell of a lot to report.

Still, just so I could say I had cooperated, I reiterated the sequence of events leading up the demise of the *Barbella*, and for good measure, threw in my theory on how his trusted colleague's son, Ringer Blanchard, had, with the help of one Luke Brimley and a Mr. and Mrs. Peter Cannon, almost pulled off the heist of the century.

Then I left. Broke, tired, and a little worse for the wear.

I did spend a few days with Honey Bear and

Cosmo, licked my wounds, drank a little of
Cosmo's private stock of Scotch, and when I
was certain I had quit bleeding, headed down
in the Keys to retrieve the *Perpetual Motion* and
start another book. I needed the money. One
percent of nothing is nothing.

All of which is backdrop on this second Sunday in September. I call it backdrop because, as
I turn my attention to the second section of the
paper, an article catches my eye:

BERMUDA TRIANGLE CLAIMS ANOTHER VICTIM

Hamilton, Bermuda Island.
*Bermuda-based authorities today reported
finding the wreckage of a 65-foot Miami-
based vessel. The* Penguin, *62-4571, is registered to a local businessman, Mr. Ringer
Blanchard of Bay Reef Beach Marina in
South Miami.*

Sources claim the Penguin *was last seen
in the vicinity of Bell Donna Island east and
slightly south of Bermuda the morning of
July 20. The* Penguin *did not file an itinerary
with Bermuda port authorities prior to its
departure.*

*Authorities who discovered the wreckage
of the* Penguin *in 80 feet of water reported
that the luxurious pleasure cruiser was se-
verely damaged. "The fantail had been inex-
plicably ripped out," one spokesman said,
"almost as if the ship had been attacked by*

*some large creature. No trace of the crew was
found.*

I folded up the paper, laid it aside, and leaned
my head back. The sun felt good.

RED SKIES
KARL LARGENT
"A writer to watch!" —*Publishers Weekly*

The cutting-edge Russian SU-39-Covert stealth bomber, with fighter capabilities years beyond anything the U.S. can produce, has vanished while on a test run over the Gobi Desert. But it is no accident—the super weapon was plucked from the skies by Russian military leaders with their own private agenda—global power.

Half a world away, a dissident faction of the Chinese Red Army engineers the brutal abduction of a top scientist visiting Washington from under the noses of his U.S. guardians. And with him goes the secrets of his most recent triumph—the development of the SU-39.

Commander T.C. Bogner has his orders: Retrieve the fighter and its designer within seventy-two hours, or the die will be cast for a high-tech war, the likes of which the world has never known.

_4117-0 $6.99 US/$7.99 CAN

THE PHALANX DRAGON

TIMOTHY RIZZI

"Rizzi's credible scenario and action-filled pace once again carry the day!" —*Publishers Weekly*

After Revolutionary Guard soldiers salvage a U.S. cruise missile that veered off course during the Gulf War, Iran's intelligence bureau assigns a team of experts to decipher the weapon's state-of-the-art computer chips. But fundamentalist leaders in Tehran plan to use the stolen technology to upgrade their defense systems. With improved military forces, they'll have the power to seize the Persian Gulf and cut off worldwide access to Middle-eastern oil fields.

Sent to stop the Iranians, General Duke James has at his command the best pilots in the world and the best aircraft in the skies: A-6 Intruders, F-16s, MH-53J Pave Lows, EF-111As. But he's up against the most advanced antiaircraft machinery known to man—machinery stamped MADE IN THE USA.

_3885-4 $6.99 US/$8.99 CAN

A KILLING PACE
Les Whitten

"Gritty, realistic, and tough!"
—*Philadelphia Inquirer*

For George Fraser, dealing and double-dealing is a way of life. But with the body count around him rising higher, he decides he wants out of the espionage business. As a favor for an old friend, Fraser agrees to take on one last job: just running some automatic weapons—no big deal. Then the assignment falls apart, and Fraser is caught in the sights of terrorists determined to see him dead. Suddenly, Fraser is on a harrowing chase that takes him from the mean streets of Philadelphia to the treacherous canals of Venice. He is just one man against a vicious cartel—a man who can stop countless deaths and mass destruction if he can keep up a killing pace.

_4017-4 $4.99 US/$6.99 CAN